4

COOPER'S CORNER

Get Set for Christmas

Sleigh bells ringing, church bells singing, snowflakes falling on the village green... Christmas is coming to Cooper's Corner, and the town's getting all decked out for the ninth annual Christmas Festival. Organizer Grace Penrose promises the festival will be the best one yet. A Christmas play written and starring our own local celebrity Rowena Dahl is one of the highlights this year, along with a snow-sculpting contest, horse-drawn sleigh rides and the annual parade down Main Street.

Cooper's Corner itself is wrapped up like a Christmas gift with holiday glitter. Local high school students have decorated the store windows, Christmas banners wave over Main Street and houses are bedecked with pine wreaths and colorful lights. At Tubb's Café, hot chocolate and brown sugar shortbread are now a daily special, and Clint Cooper is baking the Cooper family's traditional fruitcake for afternoon tea at Twin Oaks Bed and Breakfast.

We managed to catch up with Grace Penrose, clipboard in hand, as she raced around town making sure everything is on schedule for the festival. "We're right on track," Grace assured us breathlessly. "Now, if only the weather will cooperate and bring us a fresh blanket of snow...."

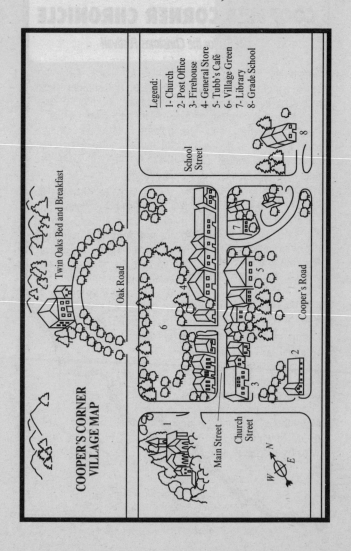

COOPER'S CORNER VILLAGE MAP

Twin Oaks Bed and Breakfast

Oak Road

Main Street

Church Street

Cooper's Road

School Street

Legend:
1- Church
2- Post Office
3- Firehouse
4- General Store
5- Tubb's Café
6- Village Green
7- Library
8- Grade School

W N E S

COOPER'S CORNER

KATE HOFFMANN

My Christmas Cowboy

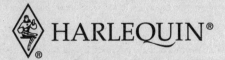

HARLEQUIN®

TORONTO • NEW YORK • LONDON
AMSTERDAM • PARIS • SYDNEY • HAMBURG
STOCKHOLM • ATHENS • TOKYO • MILAN • MADRID
PRAGUE • WARSAW • BUDAPEST • AUCKLAND

To my editor, Marsha Zinberg
For her patience, encouragement and enthusiasm

HARLEQUIN BOOKS
225 Duncan Mill Road, Don Mills,
Ontario, Canada M3B 3K9

ISBN-13: 978-0-373-61255-0
ISBN-10:   0-373-61255-9

MY CHRISTMAS COWBOY

Kate Hoffmann is acknowledged as the author of this work.

Copyright © 2002 by Harlequin Books S.A.

Visit us at www.eHarlequin.com

Printed in U.S.A.

Dear Reader,

Christmas is one of my favorite times of year! I love to shop for gifts and decorate the tree and plan a huge Christmas Day dinner. And then there's the fun and anticipation of opening gifts on Christmas Eve. But Christmas wasn't always such fun, especially when I worked in retail. During December, Christmas became a job.

Grace Penrose, my heroine in *My Christmas Cowboy*, feels the same way. Her job is to provide the entire town of Cooper's Corner, and a bunch of tourists, with a picture-postcard Christmas. She spends so much time giving, she doesn't allow herself a chance to receive—until cowboy Tucker McCabe turns up in town. Tuck has never put much stock in Christmas, but Grace is determined to change his mind.

After writing this story, I got to thinking. Maybe next Christmas I should forget about asking for practical gifts—the kitchen gadgets, the books and CDs, the decorator items. I'm going to ask for my own Christmas cowboy. I'll have just one problem— how am I going to fit him under the tree?

Best,

Kate Hoffmann

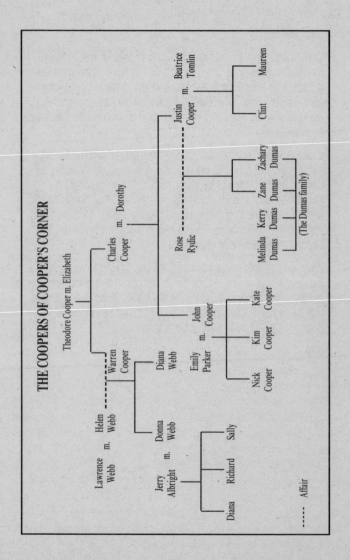

THE COOPERS OF COOPER'S CORNER

Theodore Cooper m. Elizabeth

Charles Cooper m. Dorothy

Warren Cooper

Justin Cooper m. Beatrice Tomlin

Lawrence Webb m. Helen Webb

Diana Webb

Donna Webb

Rose Rydic

John Cooper

Clint

Maureen

Jerry Albright m.

Emily Parker m.

Melinda Dumas Kerry Dumas Zane Dumas Zachary Dumas

(The Dumas family)

Diana Richard Sally

Nick Cooper Kim Cooper Kate Cooper

------ Affair

CHAPTER ONE

GRACE PENROSE PEERED through the window of Tubb's Café, squinting behind her horn-rimmed glasses to see the patrons who had packed the place for breakfast that morning. Spying the subject of her frantic search, she shoved her glasses up the bridge of her nose and sighed in relief. Thank goodness Enos Harrington, the oldest resident of Cooper's Corner, was a creature of habit. Most mornings he could be found either chewing the fat with Philo Cooper over at the general store or sharing a cup of coffee with Felix Dorn, a retired doctor—a man Enos referred to as a young whippersnapper, even through Dr. Dorn was eighty-four years old.

The door opened and Grace waited while Clint Cooper stepped out, his morning latte clutched in his hand. "Hello, Gracie," he said with a smile. "How are the plans for the festival coming along?"

That was the question everyone asked over and over again until she was tempted to tear her hair out and run screaming down the street. It would serve them all right. They just assumed that planning the town's annual Christmas Festival was easy, that after eight successful festivals, the endlessly energetic and compulsively cheerful Grace Penrose could plan the Macy's Thanksgiving Day Parade with one clipboard tied behind her back. Little did they know how close her carefully maintained competent facade had come to cracking over the past week.

It wasn't that she *couldn't* be organized. She just never seemed to have the time. Some disaster always came along and threw her personal or professional life into utter chaos, and she usually managed to extricate herself just as another disaster was looming on the horizon. First there'd been the moth-eaten elf costumes that would take hours of mending before the parade. Then came the gallons of free cider that had turned to vinegar last week. And snow that refused to appear on schedule.

Grace returned his greeting with a tight smile of her own. "Everything's right on schedule," she lied.

Clint stared up at the sky, a brilliant blue, not a cloud in sight. "Sure wish it would snow. I can't imagine a Christmas Festival without snow."

Up until a few weeks ago, Grace might have stood on the steps of the café and chatted with Clint. After all, he was one of the town's most eligible bachelors, handsome, sophisticated, the co-owner of Twin Oaks Bed and Breakfast with his sister, Maureen. And Grace hadn't had more than a handful of dates since her husband had walked out on her seven years ago. She and Clint had plenty in common—they were both single parents, and his son, Keegan, and her son, Bryan, were great friends.

But Clint was not the kind of man who'd be attracted to a perpetually disheveled single mother like Grace Penrose. She glanced down at her feet to make sure her shoes matched today, then sighed inwardly. She was thirty-six years old and her first priority was her children. Her second was her job. Her social life—and men—came in somewhere around tenth or eleventh on the list, behind a pint of premium ice cream and an Audrey Hepburn video. Even if she had time to think about dating, she certainly couldn't spare a few moments to flirt with Clint Cooper. Right now, she had business to discuss with Enos Harrington.

"There'll be snow," she reassured him, smoothing her tangled hair. "There always is."

She went inside and made a beeline to the empty stool at the counter beside Enos, her steps short and purposeful. She slid her ever-present clipboard onto the counter then nodded to Lori Tubb, co-owner and chief waitress at the café, who poured Grace's usual large coffee in a to-go cup.

"So?" Grace said, leaning over to gaze at Enos. "How's your bursitis today?"

Enos's bursitis had long been known as the finest indicator of meteorological events in this northwest corner of Massachusetts, better than Doppler radar or weather satellites or even the Weather Channel. Enos could tell just by the ache in his joints whether there would be rain on the fourth of July or sleet on Easter morning. Farmers depended on him for the proper planting time and he was a favorite of the local gardeners. Grace had even heard of a few June brides who had consulted with Enos on their choice of a wedding date.

But right now, Grace was interested in just one thing. Would there be snow for her Christmas Festival? Already, the weather had caused consternation for the owners of the many ski resorts that dotted the Berkshires and southern Vermont. An early snow followed by a December thaw had left the countryside gray and dreary. At least the resorts could manufacture snow. Grace didn't have that luxury. Even if she wanted to haul in one of those huge snowmaking machines, her budget could never absorb the cost.

Enos considered her question for a long moment, scratching his white beard as he worked each one of his joints then evaluated what he felt. He pointed to his left shoulder. "Temperature's going to drop," he said. "That's a good sign." He worked his right elbow. "And there's moisture movin' up from the south."

"Gosh darn it, Enos," Dr. Dorn said. "A man your age shouldn't have to put up with all those aches and pains. You can buy yourself a good anti-inflammatory at any drugstore. One or two of them first thing in the morning will take care of the pain right off."

Enos and Grace both gaped at the doctor as if he'd just suggested that Enos cut off his nose to keep it from itching.

"A man my age?" Enos repeated. "Are you callin' me old, Felix Dorn?"

"You're ninety-seven, Enos. If you got any longer in the tooth, you'd start looking like Bugs Bunny. But there are days when I figure you could run the Boston Marathon just to spite me. So I'm going to stop giving you free medical advice and finish my French toast."

"So, what about my snow?" Grace asked. "I'm looking for big snow. The festival is two weeks away and I need at least a foot for the sleigh rides. Actually, two feet would be best. Those little mounds on the sides of the streets look so pretty. A nice, white fluffy snow so that everything looks like a picture postcard. But it has to pack well, too, for the snow sculpture contest."

"Well," Enos said, "my right ankle's been a little achy. And the last time that happened and my big toe went numb was that big snow we had in '78. Now that was a big snow. We must have had three or four feet in just a few weeks. One day it would snow like crazy, then it would stop for a day and start up again." He chuckled and nodded at Grace. "I remember I had to ask your dear mother, God rest her soul, to loan me one of her sleighs so I could get the mail delivered. Silas Rawlings hitched up a pair of his Morgans and off we went."

"Silas is lending us his horses again this year for the free sleigh rides," Grace said. "The rides are a highlight of the festival. And I know you'll want your turn behind the reins, Dr. Dorn.''

Felix frowned, his fork poised over his plate. ''That's odd. I talked to Silas last week and he told me he's moving to Louisiana to live with his sister. He's supposed to leave any day now. He's already sold all his stock. The horses are going to some ranch in Montana.''

Grace gasped. ''What? He can't sell those horses. We always use his horses.''

The doctor shrugged. ''He's been planning to move since September. The cold winters are just too much for an old guy like him.'' He sent Enos a pointed glare. ''Didn't he mention this to you when you asked about using the horses?''

A warm blush crept up Grace's cheeks. She'd been so busy. Why, only yesterday she'd forgotten to pick Susan up from the library after school and she'd driven away from Bryan's basketball practice with his shoes on top of the car. As for the formal letter to Silas Rawlings, it had been pushed down her ''to do'' list until it fell right off the bottom.

''I—I just assumed it would be all right,'' she said. ''We've been using his horses for eight Christmases in a row, ever since the very first festival. His horses have been a part of the tradition.''

''Well, you better go see if you can stop your tradition from getting on a trailer and leaving for Montana,'' Felix said. ''I saw Silas walking toward the post office. I suppose if he's got business there, you might still be able to catch him.''

Grace grabbed her clipboard—it wasn't adding much to her air of competence—then took a quick sip of her coffee before she jumped off her stool, the paper cup clutched in her hand. ''Enos, I'll talk to you tomorrow morning. And

I want you to call me if that big toe stops hurting. If it's not going to snow, I might just have to bring in one of those machines.''

She hurried out of the café, calling to Lori Tubb to put the coffee on her tab. As she strode down Main Street, everyone she met asked her about the festival. But she was too preoccupied to bother with her usual cheery responses. How was the festival going? It was slowly turning into a disaster. No cider, no snow, and now, no sleigh rides.

The pressure for success had grown almost overwhelming. She'd planned the first festival as a favor—and as a volunteer. Her father-in-law, Art Penrose, had been president of the village board, and he and his fellow board members had come up with the idea to draw more tourists to the village in December. At the time, Grace thought the project would be fun, a way to fill the quiet hours after three-year-old Bryan went to bed.

Her husband had been especially busy, working late nights at the new Penrose Hardware store in nearby Pittsfield, and Grace agreed to become the festival's official volunteer coordinator. That first year, the festival wasn't much more than a small parade on Christmas Eve day, a concert of Christmas carols at the church and free evening sleigh rides. When only a few tourists showed up, she'd assumed that the event would go down in history as the *only* Annual Cooper's Corner Christmas Festival.

But the next year, the village board gave her a $200 budget and Grace surprisingly returned $556.94 in profits from a hot cider booth she'd set up on Main Street for the two-day festival. Unfortunately, her professional success was tempered with personal upheaval. A few months later, she gave birth to Susan, and when the baby was six months old, Dan Penrose decided that he couldn't do ''the family thing'' any longer. He ran off with the nuts-and-bolts salesgirl at the hardware store. Completely humiliated, Grace soon learned that all her husband's long nights of inventory were actually spent at a cheap motel.

Grace wasn't sure when the festival finally became a Cooper's Corner tradition, but the third year she put her heart and soul into planning it and the profits soared. By the fourth year, she'd been officially given the title of director of tourism for Cooper's Corner, though her only job was the festival. But with the small salary came the pressure to deliver bigger crowds and higher profits year after year. Profits that now funded everything from new books in the library to playground equipment at the grade school to pothole repair on Main Street, and crowds to patronize the growing collection of shops and cottage industries that had popped up all over town.

Picking up her pace, Grace turned onto Church Street and headed toward the post office. She caught sight of Silas Rawlings just as he stepped out the front door.

"Mr. Rawlings! Mr. Rawlings!" Grace clutched her clipboard to her chest and took off running. By the time she reached the spot where he stood, she was out of breath and could barely talk. Her glasses had slipped down her nose and she pushed them back up impatiently. "Horses," she gasped. "Sleigh rides—tourists—have to stay. Please!"

Silas frowned, then patted her on the shoulder. "Are you all right, missy?"

Grace nodded, swallowed hard, then patted her chest. "The horses. Dr. Dorn said you're moving to Louisiana and that you've sold your Morgans. Please tell me this isn't so. I need those horses for the festival's sleigh rides."

"I left a note for you months back. I slipped it in your mailbox in September. I figured that was plenty of time to line up some other horses."

"But we can't just use *any* horses," Grace said. "Your

horses are accustomed to pulling the sleighs. They're calm and dependable. Can't you just let us use the horses for the festival and then sell them?''

"They're already sold," Silas explained. "Some guy named McCabe from Montana will be here first thing tomorrow morning to pick them up. Maybe you can convince him to leave the horses here till after the festival." He gave her a sympathetic shrug. "Good luck. And if he agrees, you can keep them in my barn. The farm hasn't sold yet so the place is all yours for as long as you need it."

With that, Silas turned and ambled down the street toward his battered pickup. A tiny groan slipped from Grace's lips but she couldn't help calling out a cheery farewell. "I hope you enjoy living in Louisiana!" She slowly lowered herself onto a bench in front of the post office. Could anything else go wrong? Earthquake, tornado, landslide? Considering her luck lately, she wouldn't be surprised if a meteor dropped out of the sky right on top of Cooper's Corner the day before the Christmas Festival was due to begin.

She pushed to her feet, drew a deep breath of the crisp morning air, and forced herself to smile. This was all just a test. She'd faced adversity before. There was the year the ice carving contest ended prematurely when Harley Sawyer dropped a block of ice on Sarah Ann Perkins's foot. And the year when her Santa Claus, Charlie Parks, had a few too many hot-buttered rums at a Christmas party and fell out of the sleigh halfway through the parade.

This latest kink in her plans could easily be conquered. All she'd have to do was convince this man from Montana to delay his departure by a couple of weeks. After all, what could a rancher really need with four aging Morgans? The most it would cost her might be a round-trip plane ticket to Montana for the man, an expense that would probably wipe out most of her profits. But the festival had to go on and Grace could be very persuasive when she put her mind to it.

She'd appeal to his sense of fairness and understanding, his notions of charity. And if that didn't work, she'd beg and plead. And if that didn't work, she could always cry. But there was one thing she wouldn't do. She would never give up.

Because the ninth annual Cooper's Corner Christmas Festival was going to be the very best festival ever.

TUCKER MCCABE HAD BEEN on the road for two hours already and the sun had just peeked over the horizon. He pulled his pickup into the muddy drive of Silas Rawlings's farm, then carefully backed the trailer up to the barn. Pulling a fifteen-foot trailer all the way from Montana to New England and back might seem a little crazy, especially just to get a free herd of goats and a good deal on four Morgans. But then, Tuck had never taken the easy route when it came to living his life.

He grabbed his hat, hopped out of the truck and slammed the door, adjusting the brim of the battered black Stetson until it blocked the low glare of the rising sun. With his arms over his head, he stretched the kinks out of his body, the chill air chasing away the early-morning cobwebs from his brain. It would take him no more than an hour to load the horses. The goats were already roped off in the front section of the trailer. If he got right back on the road, he could be well into Pennsylvania by nightfall. He'd made arrangements with a local vet to board the animals overnight before he took off for another day on the road. Tuck figured it would take three and a half days to get back to Snake Creek Ranch, if the weather held. But he was in no hurry.

In truth, he had wanted to delay this trip out east until just before Christmas. He'd never been a fan of the holiday season, and hanging around the ranch thinking about his complete lack of Christmas spirit was always depressing. But one of his old professors from Tufts vet school had offered him a herd of nine goats for the ranch and then mentioned a terrific price on four harness-broke Morgans in the nearby Berkshires. An agreement was reached, and since Silas Rawlings had a timetable for his own departure, Tuck had headed east two weeks before the holiday. If the trip wasn't so hard on the animals, he might have considered taking the scenic route back to Montana—through Florida—arriving home after Christmas had passed. But there was no way to do that.

He started toward the weather-beaten farmhouse, reaching into his jacket pocket for the check Ray Ruiz had cut. Tuck had known Ray since they were kids, fourteen-year-old juvenile delinquents. They'd both ended up at Snake Creek Ranch, working for Ike Randall instead of serving time in juvie.

But unlike the other boys who'd moved on, he and Ray had never really left Snake Creek. For Ray, it had been a logical choice to accept a share in the ranch once he'd completed his degree at the University of Montana. He was great at the business end of horse and cattle breeding. When Ike offered him a third share of the ranch, he'd enthusiastically accepted.

With Tuck, it had been different. He'd never really been sure what he wanted. He'd simply taken life as it came to him. He'd worked hard in high school to prove to himself that he wasn't as stupid as his mother insisted he was. He'd gone to college because the local rancher's association had offered him a scholarship. And veterinary school had been a practical choice, once he'd seen the mounting vet bills at the ranch.

But through it all, he'd avoided any real responsibility, anything that might tie him down permanently. Ray had gotten married and had a kid. Tuck was still dating girls he met in the local bars and honky-tonks. Ray had built the ranch into a thriving business with a social conscience, providing an outlet for other juvenile delinquents. Tuck had avoided setting up a real veterinary practice, instead working "freelance" out of his rooms at the ranch when the mood suited him.

Right now, Ray was at Snake Creek, preparing for a real traditional Christmas with his wife and baby, and Tuck was here—alone—trying to figure out a way to avoid that whole happy family scene, trying to forget that he didn't have anyplace to be or anyone who cared where he was on Christmas. Actually, maybe he did have a family. Though his mother had drunk herself to death when he was sixteen, he had a father somewhere out there in the world. The guy had disappeared thirty-two years ago, right about the time Tuck was born. But if his father had fathered any other children after that, then Tuck probably had stepbrothers and stepsisters he didn't know about.

But family you didn't know wasn't real family. Ike Randall was almost like real family. The cranky old rancher had come along at a time when Tuck was standing at a crossroads. Had he turned one way, he'd probably be locked up in some prison right now, doing hard time for God knows what. But he'd turned the other way, accepting Ike's offer to work on his ranch after school and on weekends, anxious to prove that he could make something better of his life.

But was his life really better? Tuck shook his head and cursed softly. The holidays always made him feel a little cheated. But he knew exactly the cure. He'd just find himself a warm and willing woman, someone who could take his mind off life's shortcomings for a week or two. It had worked in the past. Maybe a nice Caribbean vacation. Beautiful women in skimpy clothing should do the trick. "I'll get these horses back to the ranch, then I'll find myself a woman," he muttered as he reached out to knock on the back door of the house.

"Hello! Hello, there! Excuse me, are you the man from Montana?"

Tuck turned and watched as a woman with windblown brunette hair hurried over from a nearby car. She slipped once on a muddy patch, almost sprawled face first on the ground, then righted herself and continued toward him. She wore a tidy houndstooth blazer, wool trousers and sensible shoes, and a camel-hair coat that did nothing to enhance her figure. Horn-rimmed glasses were perched precariously on an impossibly pert nose.

He'd been wishing for a woman, but this wasn't exactly the image that had been floating through his brain. At first glance, he assumed she was Silas's wife or maybe his daughter, but her attire seemed completely out of place on a working farm.

When she finally reached him, she was breathless, the color high in her cheeks. "Are you here to pick up the horses?" she asked, brushing a flyaway strand of hair back behind her ear with unadorned fingers.

Tuck nodded. "I am. I'm Tucker McCabe." He yanked off his glove, then held out his hand, the gesture automatic. She had very pretty hands, soft and delicate, so unlike his scarred and calloused fingers. It had been ages since he'd touched a woman, and the warmth of her skin sent an unbidden tingle up his arm. She, on the other hand, was oblivious to his reaction.

"It's a pleasure to meet you, Mr. McCabe," she said, grasping his hand in a firm shake. "I'm Grace Penrose."

Her voice was low and throaty, entirely too sexy for a woman in a prissy little tweed blazer, much less one with the very proper name of Grace Penrose. The strand of hair escaped once again and Tuck fought an impatient urge to push it back from her eyes himself. Instead, he cleared his throat and tried to focus on the job at hand and not her Cupid's bow mouth and perfect roses-and-cream complexion. "I've got a check here for Silas. Once he gives me a bill of sale, I can load the horses and be on my way."

Grace drew a deep breath and smiled brightly. "You can't take the horses," she said.

Tuck pushed his cowboy hat back and frowned. "Lady, Silas and I had a deal. I drove all the way from Montana. Are you telling me he's backing out?"

"Oh, no," she said. "It's just that I need those horses. I probably should have asked Silas sooner, but I just assumed it was all okay, and he said that if you agreed, you could leave the horses here until after the festival. So you can pay Silas and the horses will be yours. And then you can lend them to me. And when I'm done with them, you can take them home. I promise they won't be harmed." She paused to draw a quick breath. "Oh, and of course, if you'd like to return to Montana in the meantime, we'll purchase a roundtrip plane ticket for you. Or—or pay for gas for your truck or whatever."

Tucker paused. She'd laid out her bizarre plan with such logic and determination that he almost considered her request. But the horses were his now, and he intended to load them into the trailer and leave for Montana within the hour. "Lady, who the hell are you?"

A flush crept up her already rosy cheeks. "Oh, I'm sorry. I thought I introduced myself." She held out her hand again and Tuck cursed inwardly at the unbidden urge to touch her once more. "I'm Grace Penrose."

"I know your name."

"I'm director of tourism for Cooper's Corner," she added, as if that explained everything.

"And this job you have gives you the right to appropriate livestock whenever the whim strikes?"

Grace stared at him for a long moment, her wide eyes the color of campfire coffee. "Well, no. Not just any livestock. These horses are important. They're a Cooper's Corner tradition. And we take our traditions very seriously here in Cooper's Corner."

"Well, lady, we have a few traditions that we take seriously in Montana. And one of them is that a deal's a deal. I've got business with Silas Rawlings," Tuck muttered, turning to knock at the door again.

She hurried up the steps, stumbling on an icy plank until he was forced to reach out and grab her elbow. Once again he noticed the absence of a wedding band on her left hand, then silently chided himself for even bothering to look.

"You have to at least give me a chance to explain," she said as he pulled her up beside him. "I'm desperate. The sleigh rides are one of the most popular activities at the Christmas Festival and you can't just use any old horses to pull those sleighs. Silas's horses have been a part of our festival for eight consecutive years."

She stood so close on the cramped confines of the steps, her body brushing against his, the scent of her hair drifting through the crisp morning air. "And that makes it a tradition," he murmured.

The door swung open and an elderly man stood in the doorway, his face careworn, his beard grizzled. He hitched one suspender up over his shoulder, then smoothed his hands over his flannel workshirt. "You Tucker McCabe?"

Tuck nodded and handed him the check. In return, Silas Rawlings gave him a bill of sale for four Morgan horses. "Thanks," Tuck said. "I'll just load them up and be on my way."

Grace Penrose glanced between the two of them. "No!" she cried, stomping her foot. "Silas, tell him we need the horses."

Silas held up his hands. "They ain't my horses anymore. You work out your deal with him. Me, I'm moving to Louisiana and I'm gonna eat Cajun gumbo and spend every day fishin'." With that, he firmly closed the door, leaving the two of them standing on the top step.

Tuck carefully folded the bill of sale and slipped it into the breast pocket of his canvas jacket. "I have to hit the road," he muttered. "I've got to be in Pennsylvania by nightfall."

All hope drained from her expression and she reluctantly nodded. "I—I suppose you have a wife waiting for you at home. Big plans for the holiday."

"Nope," he replied as he jogged down the steps and headed to the barn. "No wife. But I do have plans." Plans to find himself a woman. But he couldn't say that out loud.

"Why do you even want these horses? You haven't looked at them yet."

"My friend at Tufts has and he says they're a good buy. And I've been looking for some harness-broke stock for a while."

She was beside him in an instant, her fingers clutched around his arm. He stopped and only then realized the effect of such an innocent touch. God, he really did need a woman. "Let me make you another offer I don't think you'll be able to refuse," she said.

He stared down at her. Tuck wasn't sure what it was about Grace Penrose that he found so appealing, whether it was her guileless beauty or her unabashed pluck, but he suspected once she turned those huge doe eyes on any man, he'd have a hard time refusing. Hell, why not listen to her offer? He didn't have any place to be. Pennsylvania could wait. And that warm, willing woman would be there when he needed her—she might even be here in Massachusetts. "All right," he muttered. "I guess my plans could wait. Let's hear it."

"I can offer you the picture-perfect New England holiday experience," Grace said. "You'll enjoy Christmas here, in Cooper's Corner. I'll get you a room at our very popular bed-and-breakfast, the Twin Oaks. It's a lovely place. I'll pay for the feed for your horses."

"What about my kids?" he asked.

"Kids?"

"I have nine kids in the trailer. They have to be fed, too."

Grace's eyes went wide. "You—you let children ride in a smelly old horse trailer?"

The look of sheer horror on her face was enough to make the misunderstanding worthwhile. "Yeah, come on." He took her hand and pulled her along after him. "I want to introduce you. After all, you'll be spending a lot of time together in the next few weeks. And they do love to eat."

She tagged along after him, and when they reached the trailer, he unhitched the door and swung it open. Tuck hopped inside and held out his hand. Grace reluctantly took it, then followed him into the dark interior of the trailer. When they reached the front, Tuck leaned over a rope barrier. "These are my kids," he said.

Grace pasted a smile on her face and stepped up beside him. Her smile faded. "These are goats," she said.

"Kids. Young goats are called kids."

"I—I thought you—I mean, when you said 'kids,' I assumed you meant—"

"I know what you assumed," he said. "No wife, no plans and no children, either."

She studied the goats for a long moment. "All right, nine goats and four horses. Silas has already agreed that you can keep them in his barn until the festival is over. So that solves one problem. I think I can get Dave over at the feed store to donate food for the animals. Do we have a deal?"

"Not so fast," Tuck said, enjoying the barter a little too much. "We've decided how to feed my animals. What about me?"

Grace blinked. "You?"

"Who's going to feed me? If I'm correct, a bed-and-breakfast only provides breakfast. I'll need lunch and dinner."

"Well, I suppose I could give you a small stipend for your meals. There's a nice little café in town where you could—"

"Naw. I'm not much for eating out. How are you in the kitchen?"

"What?"

"I'm pretty much a meat-and-potatoes kind of guy. Nothin' too fancy. I like my lunch at noon and dinner at five. In between, I can fend for myself."

Grace gasped. "You expect me to cook for you?"

Tuck watched the expression of horror return to her face. She was so easy to tease, and so pretty to look at. Grace Penrose probably appeared quite plain to the casual observer. But looks could be deceiving. A man had to look closer—to the perfect complexion and the full, sensual mouth. To eyes that mirrored her every emotion and to a voice that could make a man go crazy with lust just listening to it. To a body not fashionably thin, but feminine, with curves in all the right places.

Not that he was looking, Tuck told himself. Grace was definitely not the kind of woman he usually associated with—the type who wore her desire on the outside. She wasn't the kind of woman a guy just seduced, then dumped. Grace Penrose was the kind of woman that a guy—a nice guy—might marry.

Tuck swallowed hard. "And I expect some help caring for the horses and the goats. If my horses are going to appear in public, they're going to have to look good. And that takes work. Hard work."

She thought about the deal for a long moment, then nodded. "All right. It's a deal."

He smiled. Maybe this wouldn't be such a bad holiday season, after all. It would be like a little vacation, a stay in a picturesque New England town with all his needs catered to by a pretty woman. He glanced down at the hand she offered, and he took her fingers in his, wondering at the warmth that seeped up his arm at her touch. "Deal," he murmured. He let his grasp linger for a moment before he dropped her hand. "Now, why don't you and I get my goats unloaded, then we'll take my stuff over to this bed-and-breakfast place."

Grace pushed her glasses up the bridge of her nose, then nodded, watching the goats warily. "Do goats bite?"

Tuck chuckled. She was quite a woman, this Grace Penrose. And he was looking forward to knowing her a little better.

FOOTSTEPS THUDDED ON THE PORCH of Twin Oaks Bed and Breakfast. Maureen Cooper looked up from the front desk, her instincts on alert. Her hand automatically went to her side, to the spot that used to hide her service revolver. But she wasn't carrying her gun anymore, and right now that made her feel very vulnerable. This edgy nervousness was going to drive her mad. Every time she heard a strange noise or saw a strange face, her stomach lurched.

She waited for the front door to swing open, expecting to see one of the guests step inside. But when no one did, she slowly released the breath she was holding. "Calm down," she murmured to herself. "Owen Nevil isn't going to show up here in the middle of the day. Even he isn't that stupid."

No, if Owen Nevil ever found her here in Cooper's Corner, he'd bide his time, waiting for the best opportunity to carry out his plan for revenge. After all, that's what he was known for, putting a hit on a person and then making it look like an accidental death or even death by natural causes. And Maureen knew he was out to get her.

It had been Frank Quigg, her old boss at the NYPD, who had put his former detective on alert. First there had been the threatening letter addressed to Maureen. Then he'd informed her that Nevil had skipped parole and gone missing. Maureen remembered the instant feeling of dread she had, the instinct to run. Nevil wanted revenge on her, retaliation for Maureen's testimony, which had put his brother Carl away for murder. He'd stop at nothing.

How Owen Nevil had ended up on the outside was one of those mysteries of the American justice system that frustrated homicide detectives like herself. He'd been convicted of conspiracy to commit murder in a murder-for-hire plot. And he'd been suspected of several other contract murders. But he'd served his time and had fooled the parole board. Maureen had spent too many years on the force not to know the mind of a criminal like Nevil. If he really wanted her dead, he'd find a way.

Her mind flashed an image of the coat she'd loaned to

Emma Hart, a recent guest at the inn. And the bullet hole that had come with the coat when it was returned. As far as the local authorities were concerned, the shooting was an accident, an errant shot by a hunter who had probably fled in fear of prosecution.

But Maureen suspected the truth. The bullet that had flown through the coat and wounded Emma's companion and now fiancé, Blake Weston, was just another strange coincidence that Maureen couldn't ignore. First, there had been the private investigator who'd stayed at the inn. She suspected he'd been hired by Nevil to find her. And then the shooting in the woods. Would it take three strikes before she finally accepted that she was truly in danger?

The front door suddenly swung open and Maureen jumped. She pressed her palm to her chest, her heart pounding beneath her fingers. But her anxiety was instantly quelled when she saw her friend Grace Penrose step inside. She was followed by a stranger, a tall, lanky guy in a canvas jacket and cowboy hat. He smiled at Maureen when their gazes met, then tipped his hat.

Grace murmured a few words to him and he wandered over to the fireplace in the large gathering room as she approached the desk, her hair mussed by the wind, the color high in her cheeks, and her shoes and stockings muddy up to her ankles.

"What happened to you?" Maureen asked.

Her friend glanced down at her feet, then groaned softly. "I was herding some goats and they got out of control. This was my favorite pair of shoes and now they're ruined."

"Goats?"

"Yes," Grace said breathlessly. "Vicious little animals with pointy hooves and sharp teeth. They nearly stampeded me."

"Goats?" Maureen repeated.

"It was nothing," Grace said. "I need a room."

Maureen's eyebrows rose. "You need a room? Would this be overnight or just for the next few hours?"

Grace's eyes went wide. "No! I need a room for him. Not for us. Why would I need a room? I live here."

Maureen laughed softly. She and Grace had known each other years ago, when they were just kids living in Cooper's Corner. And Grace hadn't changed a bit, still bursting into rooms, her cheeks rosy, her breath coming in quick gasps, excited about some wonderful plan she had or some secret discovery she'd made. As a little girl, Maureen had enjoyed Grace's company, even though Grace was a few years older. Maureen's family had moved from Cooper's Corner when she was only seven, but when she returned, she had quickly come to the conclusion that Gracie Penrose was still the warmest and sweetest person in the whole town.

And the last person who would do something scandalous like participate in a "nooner" with a handsome cowboy. "I'm teasing," Maureen said. She nodded toward the stranger. "Who's your friend?"

"His name is Tucker McCabe. He bought Silas Rawlings's horses. The same horses I use for the sleigh rides at the festival. And if I don't find him a place to stay, he and his horses are going to leave for Montana."

Maureen stared down at her reservation book, happy to know this was one stranger she didn't have to worry about. But no matter how hard she looked, the facts didn't change. She sighed softly. She'd love nothing more than to do Grace a favor, but business was business. "We've been booked for weeks," she said. "I can put together a night here and there, but not two solid weeks."

She glanced over Grace's shoulder at Tucker McCabe. He stood at the fireplace in the huge living room that served as the common area for the bed-and-breakfast. In his faded canvas jacket, battered black Stetson and scuffed cowboy boots, he looked completely out of place, even a little dangerous among her carefully chosen New England antiques and traditional decor.

Grace drew a shaky breath and rubbed her arms. "Please, you must have something."

Maureen turned the reservation book toward Grace. "Take a look. I only have five rooms here and they've been booked since last summer. I've been referring people to some of the places in Pittsfield. There are a couple of motels that probably have a vacancy."

Grace gnawed on her bottom lip as she considered the possibility. "I promised him a room here, close to his animals. And the perfect Christmas experience. If I don't make good on that promise, he'll leave." She sighed softly. "I suppose I could ask Silas if he could stay at his place since he's moving, anyway."

"I don't think that's such a good idea." Maureen winced. "Silas isn't much of a housekeeper. I went over to his place to look at an oak secretary he wanted to sell. The place was a mess." She stared at Tucker for a long moment. "I wish I had a room. He's one guest I wouldn't mind having around." She grinned. "He's gorgeous in that rugged, Marlboro Man kind of way. The closest thing we have to cowboys in Cooper's Corner are all those city boys who come up here dressed in their Ralph Lauren." She looked back at Grace. "Why don't you invite him to stay at your house?"

"No!" Grace cried, loud enough to elicit a concerned glance from her cowboy. She brought her voice down to a whisper again. "No, I couldn't do that. It wouldn't be proper."

"Good grief," Maureen said, rolling her eyes, "this is

the twenty-first century. If you want to invite a man to stay at your house, you're allowed to do that. Besides, your house is easily as large as the bed-and-breakfast. And you've got that room on the third floor. You'll hardly know he's there."

"You don't think people will talk?"

Maureen waved her hand. "Let them talk. Besides, once it gets out that you're only letting him stay for the sake of the festival, everyone will understand the huge sacrifice you're making. Besides, they all know you, Grace. They know nothing scandalous will happen."

Grace's expression fell. "No. Of course not. I'd never do anything to harm my virtuous reputation."

Maureen looked at her for a long moment, surprised that Grace appeared insulted. "I didn't mean—"

"I know what you meant," Grace said, forcing a smile. "Of course nothing would happen. But I can't let a complete stranger stay in my house. He could be a—a psycho killer."

Maureen gave Tucker McCabe the once-over. She knew how to read people, especially the criminal type. And she'd be willing to bet her share in the inn that Tucker McCabe was a straight-up guy. Though he might have a dangerous streak beneath that rugged exterior, he obviously respected women. He'd opened the front door for Grace and rested his hand on her back as she passed through. He'd tipped his hat to Maureen. And now he stood at the fireplace, pretending that he couldn't hear every word that was being said. "He looks like a perfect gentleman."

"All right," Grace conceded. "I'll ask him to stay at my place. But I want *you* to tell him you're booked. Otherwise, it will seem like I really wanted him to stay with me all along." She swallowed hard. "Which I didn't, of course."

Without hesitation, Maureen did as she was told. When Tucker McCabe heard that he wouldn't be staying at the inn, he merely shrugged, then sent her a dazzling smile that made her heart beat just a little faster. He tipped his hat in thanks and followed Grace to the door.

"So what's the plan?" he asked as he pulled the front door open. "I'm not going to sleep in the barn with my animals. And my legs are a little long to bed down in the front seat of my truck. All I need is a soft mattress and a hot shower every night."

Grace glanced back at Maureen, smiling nervously. "Actually, I know a place that has both. I have a large house and a lovely room on the third floor, with a four-poster bed and a pretty view. I was thinking you could stay with me."

The door closed behind them both and Maureen smiled. She grabbed the reservation book and turned it back around to face her, then picked up her pen. "I wonder how long that virtuous reputation is going to protect you, Grace. Especially with a sexy cowboy like Tucker McCabe living under your roof."

CHAPTER TWO

"I WANT YOU TO BE VERY QUIET and very polite," Grace muttered, frantically putting away the groceries she'd just purchased, stuffing cans and boxes into cabinets that were so disorganized she wasn't sure what they contained.

She dreamed of the day she'd have time to clean the closets and rearrange the cabinets and clean out the junk drawer that never seemed to hold anything of importance. Bills piled up and notes from school went unread. And something as simple as trying to find a few dollars for lunch money turned into a major crisis almost every morning.

Bryan and Susan had arrived home from school just minutes after she'd walked in, throwing off their jackets and dropping their backpacks on the floor, before settling down for a late-afternoon snack of their favorite store-bought cookies. They never could keep cookies in the house more than a day or two, but Grace had decided it might be best to treat them, since she'd had to tell them all about the cowboy who would be spending Christmas with them.

"So where is he?" Bryan asked in a sullen voice.

"He had to go get food for his animals," Grace explained. "He said he'd be here before dinner."

"He's eating with us, too?" Bryan laughed derisively, a habit that was growing more common of late. "Once he gets a taste of your cooking, he'll be out the door in ten seconds flat." He methodically began to crumble a cookie in front of him, making a mess on the table. "We don't need him here. He'll just wreck our Christmas."

Though her son didn't come right out and say it, his meaning was obvious. *We don't need a man in the house. I'm the man of this house.* "He's here because I need his horses for the festival," Grace explained. "And there's no place else for him to stay. The bed-and-breakfast is booked. Besides, he won't be around much. He'll just join us for meals and he'll sleep here. You'll hardly know he's staying in our house. But when he is here, I want you both to be nice."

"Does he have a gun?" Susan asked, her eyes wide, her cheeks still rosy from the walk home.

Grace gasped. "A gun?"

"Cowboys always carry a gun," she explained. "A sick-shooter."

"That's *six*-shooter," Bryan corrected, rolling his eyes. "And that's only in the movies, dummy."

"Don't call your sister 'dummy,'" Grace chided. She set a glass of milk in front of each of them, staring down at the mismatched glasses. "I want you to treat Mr. McCabe like a guest. Be nice but don't bother him. He doesn't have children and he's probably not used to all the excitement and noise."

"Why can't we ever have brownies for our snack?" Bryan complained. "Or homemade cookies? When I have snacks over at Keegan's place they actually taste good." He shoved back from the table. "I have to go."

"Where are you going?" Grace asked.

"I'm meeting Keegan. We're going to play hoops." He headed toward the back door. "Can I eat at his house for dinner? His dad said it's all right."

"No," Grace said. "I want you back here before five. We're going to eat together tonight so you'll get a chance to meet Mr. McCabe. And I want you to change out of your school clothes before you leave.''

Bryan grabbed his jacket and raced out the door. ''I won't get dirty!'' he called.

Grace shook her head. He was growing up too quickly, and the lack of a father figure in his life was beginning to show. He rarely listened to what she said, choosing to do everything on his schedule, in his own way. He was often sulky or belligerent or simply uncommunicative, hurling subtle insults at her as if that was the only thing he knew how to do. He wanted nothing to do with his father, although Grace really didn't have to worry about that point. The most Dan Penrose could manage was an occasional card or gift on birthdays and Christmas. As for her and Susan, Bryan rarely wanted to spend time with them anymore, preferring to hang out with his school friends.

''I think the cookies taste good,'' Susan said in a chipper voice.

Grace smiled down at her, then ruffled her daughter's dark brown hair. ''Thank you, sweetie.''

She stared at her cookie pensively. ''Why can't the cowboy sleep in your room?'' Susan asked.

''What?'' Grace cried. She drew a slow breath, hoping the hysterical edge in her voice would abate. ''I told you, he's going to stay in the room on the third floor. Where Grandma used to live.''

''If he slept in your bed, then he'd be our dad,'' Susan said in a matter-of-fact tone as she munched. ''Martha's mom and dad sleep in the same bed. Annie says that's what mommies and daddies do. If you let him sleep in your bed, then he'd have to be our daddy.''

With a sigh, Grace then pulled out the chair next to Susan and sat down. Her daughter had been just a baby when Dan had walked out. Only six months old. She barely remembered him. She didn't even know what a real marriage was supposed to be like. "Martha's mom and dad are married," she explained. "So are Annie's parents. And they love each other. But Mr. McCabe is just a guest and I don't love him. Besides, he has a home of his own in Montana."

"Maybe he would want to be our dad," Susan said. "Did you ask him?"

Grace reached out and slipped her arm around Susan's shoulders and drew her into a hug. "Honey, that's not going to happen."

Susan gave a little shrug. "Can I go play with my Barbies now?"

"All right. You can do your homework after dinner." She handed Susan the plate of cookies, willing to trade treats for answers. "Here, take your snack along."

As she continued to search for room in the cabinets for her groceries, Grace's mind wandered, her thoughts returning to her conversation with Maureen Cooper. She knew she shouldn't have been insulted, but the insinuation still stung. Grace did have a certain reputation around town, and she suspected it came from the way she had handled her husband's affair and the subsequent divorce.

Throughout it all, she'd maintained her dignity, hoping that the scandal wouldn't taint her life in Cooper's Corner for long. But she'd put herself above it so well that people had begun to hold her up as some paragon of virtue, an example of proper behavior that harkened back to her great-grandmother's impeccable comportment.

And now, seven years later, that reputation still held. Of course Grace could invite Tucker McCabe to stay at her home. After all, her life was so completely bereft of passion and spontaneity that she'd never be tempted, not even by a sexy-as-sin cowboy.

Besides, even if she wanted to indulge, she wouldn't

know what to do. How did one go about having a…liaison? Her experience with the opposite sex was severely limited. There'd never been a long line of men standing on her front porch. She'd married her high school sweetheart, settled down in the town she'd grown up in, and started a family, certain that Dan was the only man for her.

But since he'd left, she'd come to realize there were certain needs she had that Dan never could have satisfied. She ached for passion and excitement in her life, dreamed of a man who might make her forget her leaky roof and her rattletrap station wagon and orthodontia bills that stretched on for years to come. She fantasized about throwing herself into a torrid love affair, tossing aside all her inhibitions and experiencing overwhelming desire and uncontrolled lust. And now she had a fantasy man to insert into her dreams—Tucker McCabe.

A shiver skittered up her spine and Grace groaned inwardly, pushing her silly fantasies to the back of her mind. Though she might dream of torrid sex, her real life was much more mundane. There were dirty dishes to wash and wrinkled laundry to fold and dinner to make.

Tucker had told her he was a basic "meat and potatoes" kind of guy. Unfortunately, Grace had never been a great cook, so she'd come to depend entirely too much on convenience foods. If it came frozen in a box with microwave directions, it became a staple around the Penrose house. She pulled a pound of hamburger out of the freezer, a bag of potatoes from the counter, then set the box of sauce mix on the counter.

"Meat and potatoes. We've got them both in one dish." At the last minute she retrieved the can of instant biscuits she'd also purchased. Cowboys ate a lot of biscuits. At least they did in the movies. "Manly food," she said, dropping the can onto the counter.

It had been a long time since she'd had a man around the house and the prospect was a little disconcerting. Not that she couldn't control her impulses. She certainly knew the difference between fantasy and reality. But Grace liked to believe she was still interested in that sort of thing. She swallowed hard. Just because she'd been celibate for seven years didn't mean she'd forgotten about sex. After all, it was like riding a bike, wasn't it?

Her mind wandered back to her previous…bike rides. She and Dan had never been very good at bicycling, always taking the same roads, never venturing into new territory. And the rides were just so short, she barely had time to appreciate the…scenery. In the end, sex had become more of a chore than an enjoyable pastime.

But somehow Grace suspected that a man like Tucker McCabe wouldn't be just an ordinary lover. "Sure, he's a little rough around the edges," she murmured. "But he's probably the kind of man who would turn lovemaking into an adventure, into something so unforgettable that just the memory of his hands on my body would—"

"Am I in the right place?"

Grace spun around, the package of frozen hamburger slipping from her hand and dropping squarely on her toe. She bit back a yelp of pain, then quickly bent to retrieve it as it slid across the floor. "You—you startled me."

He looked as handsome as he had that morning. His sun-streaked hair was windblown and the cold had made his complexion ruddy. Tucker grabbed the strap from his duffel bag and set it on the floor. "I'm sorry. I knocked, but I guess you didn't hear me. You were deep in conversation with your refrigerator." In three long strides he was beside her, squatting down to help her pick up the hamburger. His hand brushed against hers and Grace froze.

He'd touched her before, at Silas's place. But here, in

her house, the innocent contact seemed so much more intimate…more dangerous. Grace quickly snatched the hamburger from his hands and scrambled to her feet. "Dinner
will be ready in about an hour," she murmured, shoving
her glasses up her nose. "Why don't you let me show you
your room and you can get cleaned up."

"Sounds good," he said.

She set the meat on the counter, then wiped her hands
on a dish towel before brushing past him into the dining
room. He stopped for a moment and took in the beautiful
mahogany dining table and the crystal chandelier that hung
above it, all remnants from the days when her great-
grandparents had owned the house. "The house has been
in my family for four generations," Grace explained. "My
great-grandparents built it as a summer house in the early
1900s. My great-grandfather was a shipbuilder in Boston."

"It's very…elegant," Tucker said.

"We never eat in here. We used to, but—"

"We?" he asked. "You and your husband?"

His question seemed to be more than idle curiosity. He'd
assumed she was married. "No," she said. "Me and my
kids. I mean, my children. Not goats. I have two. Kids."
She forced a smile. "Two *children*. Bryan and Susan. I
don't have a husband. I thought I'd mentioned that. I did—
have a husband. But I don't anymore." When his eyebrow
arched up, Grace decided it was time to stop babbling. She
turned on her heel and started toward the stairs. "I'll just
show you your room now."

He followed her up the stairs to the third floor. The
rooms there had once been meant for the servants who had
traveled with her great-grandparents from their home in
Boston. When Grace had moved back home after the divorce, her mother had relocated on the third floor, using
the largest bedroom and the sitting area as her own space

and leaving the four bedrooms on the second floor for
Grace, the children and an office.

"The bed up here is very comfortable." She opened the
door and stepped back as Tucker entered. It was a beautiful
room with an old four-poster bed and a pretty patchwork
quilt and lace curtains.

He set his duffel down on an overstuffed chintz chair.
"This is fine," he agreed.

"There's a bathroom right through there," she said,
pointing to a door in the far wall, "but I'm afraid the
shower doesn't work. The drain leaks through the ceiling
below and I haven't had a chance to get it fixed. But you
can use the shower on the second floor."

"No problem."

He turned and fixed his gaze on her and she felt her
cheeks warm. What had ever possessed her to invite him
to stay? She could have booked a motel room for him. Or
asked Silas to let him stay in his house, mess and all. Heck,
weren't cowboys used to roughing it?

"Did you find food for your animals?" she asked, anxious to break the tension she felt.

"I did," he replied. "Your friend Dave is running a tab
for me at the mill. He said forget the freebies, he'd give
you a fifty percent discount. And horses and goats are all
settled at Rawlings's place."

"I really appreciate this," Grace said. "I can't thank you
enough."

Tucker took a step toward her and she retreated, certain
he was going to touch her again. But his gaze was fixed
off to the side, and Grace slowly turned to find Susan peeking around the edge of the doorway.

"And who is this?" he asked as he squatted down and
smiled. "You must be Susan."

Grace held out her hand and Susan hesitantly walked into

the room, clutching her Barbie. "Yes, this is my daughter, Susan," Grace said, surprised at the ease with which she made the introductions. "Susan, this is Mr. McCabe."

"Tuck," he insisted. "You can call me Tuck." He nodded at the doll she held. "And who is this?"

"Barbie," Susan said. "Ballerina Barbie. Would you like to play Barbies? I have another doll. We could play fashion show. I made a stage out of a potato chip box that Mommy gave me."

Grace knelt down beside Susan. "Honey, I don't think Mr. McCabe—"

"Tuck," he repeated.

"I don't think Tuck wants to play fashion show. He probably wants to relax. He's been working very hard today."

"And I can't think of a nicer way to relax than playing fashion show," Tuck countered. "Why don't you get everything ready downstairs, and as soon as I'm cleaned up, I'll come down. All right?"

Susan nodded and ran out of the room, leaving them alone together. Grace smiled in gratitude. "You really don't have to—"

"I want to," Tuck said. "It's been a long time since I've played fashion show. I usually travel with my own Barbie dolls, but I left them behind in Montana this trip."

Grace laughed. He really was quite charming, in a rough-hewn, rugged sort of way. If she wasn't careful, she might just fall head over heels for that charm. "All right," she said. "I'll go get dinner ready. If you need anything, extra towels, shampoo, whatever, don't hesitate to ask."

"I think I have everything I need," he murmured. "For now."

For a long moment he stared deeply into her eyes, leaving Grace to ponder whether there was another meaning to his words. The way he was looking at her, she'd almost think he needed *her*. Then she mentally gave herself a shake and hurried out of the room and down the stairs. Once she reached the second floor, she stopped and leaned back against the wall.

Her heart was pounding in her chest and Grace suddenly felt all light-headed and breathless. This was silly! She was an adult, a mother, a responsible citizen. These crazy feelings were meant for schoolgirls, not a thirty-six-year-old woman with two children.

"Get a grip," Grace muttered. "He'll be here for thirteen more days and you've got more important things to think about than passion and lust. You've got a Christmas Festival to coordinate."

TUCK SAT ON THE FLOOR of the living room, doll clothes and accessories scattered in front of him. He picked up a tiny plastic high heel and attempted to shove it onto the Barbie doll's foot, but his fingers were too large and clumsy to get it to stay. "I think she should go barefoot," he said.

"She can't go barefoot in a ball gown!" Susan scolded. "Only in a swimming suit!"

"Oh, I see," Tuck replied. He handed her the doll. "Why don't you choose shoes that match."

"That rhymes," Susan said. "Choose. Shoes."

"Snooze," Tuck added.

"Lose," Susan said.

"Gooze," Tuck continued.

"Mooze," Susan shouted, throwing herself on the floor in a fit of giggles and waving her Barbie around above her, the doll's platinum-blond hair flying wildly through the air.

Tuck laughed at her silly antics. On the ranch, he'd been surrounded by budding testosterone, not a little girl in sight. He'd learned to deal exclusively with problem teenage boys and he'd almost forgotten there was a whole world of children out there who led happy, carefree lives, who played and laughed and were well loved. And who acted silly on occasion. His own childhood had been severely lacking in silliness.

Susan was a miniature version of Grace, with her dark hair and her chocolate eyes. Even her mannerisms, so prim and proper, so feminine, were a reflection of her mother. Tuck couldn't help but wonder about the man who had fathered such a beautiful child, the man who left Grace and her children behind.

"What's going on in here?"

Tuck glanced up to find the object of his speculation standing in the doorway to the kitchen. She'd changed out of her work clothes and wore a soft sweater in a pretty shade of pale blue with a worn pair of jeans. A dish towel was tucked in the waistband, her hair was mussed and her glasses had slipped down onto the end of her pert nose. He was immediately struck by how domestic she looked—and how oddly alluring "domestic" could be on the right woman.

"Susan is giving me a badly needed education on accessorizing," Tuck joked. "I had no idea that choosing shoes was so difficult. I'm afraid I don't have your daughter's fashion sense."

"Neither do I," she said, sending him a warm smile. "I'm lucky if I get out the door in the morning with a matching pair." She paused, a blush rising in her cheeks, as if she'd revealed too much. "Dinner is ready," she added quickly, shoving her glasses up on her nose.

He stood, then grabbed Susan's hand and pulled her to her feet. "Come on, Susie Q, the fashion world will have to wait. I'm starving." He strolled into the kitchen, Susan giggling at his side. The smells of dinner drew him nearer to the table and he found it neatly set with a mishmash of dinnerware and wrinkled cloth napkins. At the ranch, they usually ate off chipped plates and used a wad of paper toweling for napkins, so this was a step up.

"You can sit next to me," Susan suggested, sliding into a chair and patting the seat next to her.

Tuck did as he was asked, then watched as Grace moved around the kitchen, bringing dishes to the table. Though the food smelled good, it didn't look very appetizing. From what he could tell there was some type of runny meat-and-potato dish. In addition, he saw a basket of scorched biscuits and a bowl of overcooked broccoli. The only thing that looked appealing was a container of macaroni salad from the grocery's deli counter.

He forced a smile. So Grace Penrose wasn't a great cook, Tuck mused. She wasn't even a good cook. "This looks interesting," he said.

"It's supposed to be a stew," Grace murmured, indicating the main dish. "I thought it sounded…hearty. But I didn't think it would turn out so soupy. I don't know what I did wrong."

"Well, I'm sure it will taste fine," Tuck replied.

Grace was just sitting down at her place when the back door swung open and a young boy raced inside, his face red from the cold, his breath coming in gasps. He looked up at the clock on the wall, then over at Grace. "I'm not late," he told her defensively as he threw his jacket to the floor. He gave Tuck the once-over. "You're in my place."

"Bryan, this is Mr. McCabe. He's our guest."

Tuck rose, leaned over the table and held out his hand to the boy. "Nice to meet you, Bryan." The gesture seemed to take the boy by surprise. He hesitantly reached out and shook Tuck's hand, then took a place next to his mother.

Dinner began in an uneasy silence, with Bryan watching

Tuck suspiciously and Grace sending him apologetic looks for her son's rude behavior. Tuck had dealt with his fair share of troubled youths. Though he'd only known Bryan a few seconds, gut instinct told him that Grace's son was more than a handful. The boy was impatient and abrupt with his sister and moody and insulting to his mother. He refused to eat what he was served, choosing instead to make himself a hot dog and baked beans.

As Tuck tried the main course, he groaned inwardly. Maybe Bryan had a point. The stew tasted as bad as it looked. The potatoes were crunchy, the thin gravy was filled with lumps of powdered sauce mix, and there were unidentifiable brown bits in the stew that he hoped might be bacon. If there was one thing he could count on at Snake Creek, it was good food. After a long day of work, he depended on a hot meal. If this was the best Grace had to offer, he'd be better off cooking for himself.

"So, Bryan," Tuck began, searching his plate for something edible. "You spent much time around horses?"

Bryan laughed dismissively, as if the question was preposterous. "No."

"That's too bad. I was hoping I might find someone who could help me get my horses ready for this Christmas Festival your mother is planning. Of course, I can understand if you wouldn't want to. Some people are a little scared around horses. They're so big and sometimes they're a little unpredictable and—"

"I'm not scared," Bryan said. "I just have stuff to do after school. My mom likes me to get my homework done early."

"I'm sure if you'd like to help Mr. McCabe, we could work on your homework after dinner instead," Grace said.

"What about me?" Susan asked. "I can help."

"You can't help with horses," Bryan muttered. "You're just a baby."

"But you're the perfect size to help with my goats," Tuck suggested. "I have nine kids and they all need special attention because they're very special goats."

Susan gazed up at him with an adoring look. She was the easy one, Tuck mused. Bryan was proving a bit more difficult, though he had to admit, the kid didn't bother hiding his hostility. The Penrose he couldn't get a handle on yet was Grace. Though he sensed there was a passionate woman beneath the prim exterior, he wasn't sure what it would take to discover that woman. All he knew was that he wasn't the man who'd be venturing into that territory.

Tuck knew enough about women—and himself—to know that Grace wasn't his type. Far from it. She was the kind of woman that a man married, the type who could make a nice home and take care of the kids. She didn't have that hard, cynical edge that he preferred in a temporary bedmate, a quality that usually kept the relationship short and simple, with no expectations and no regrets.

He'd do best to nip this attraction to Grace right in the bud. He could appreciate her from a distance, but anything more than that would be trouble. He took another bite of her stew and forced himself to swallow. Regardless of her cooking skills, the next two weeks would be an interesting challenge. He'd never really spent time around a pretty woman without trying to charm her into bed. But Tuck figured there was a first time for everything.

THE HOUSE WAS SILENT as Grace stared at her reflection in the bathroom mirror. Susan had gone to bed after playing dress-up with Tuck, draping his neck with beads and wrapping him in a feather boa. Grace wasn't sure where the man found his patience. He seemed completely charmed by her daughter and the feeling was mutual.

Unfortunately, Tuck hadn't had the same luck with Bryan. All night long, her son watched from the shadows, his expression at times suspicious, then hostile, then indifferent. When he was invited to join in the conversation, all he could manage was one-word answers. Grace made a mental note to have a long talk with him about manners and hospitality at the first available opportunity.

She smoothed her damp hair back from her face, pushed her glasses onto her nose and examined herself critically in the mirror. In an objective light, she wasn't unattractive. Good skin went a long way and her mother had taught her from an early age about the benefits of cold cream. And her eyes were nice, though they usually couldn't be seen from behind her glasses.

She took off her glasses and set them on the edge of the sink. She had contact lenses but had given up on them as too time-consuming in the morning rush. Grace opened the medicine cabinet and pulled them out. Maybe she should give them another try.

After cleaning them quickly, she drew a steadying breath and carefully put the lenses in her eyes. She blinked once, then twice, then studied at her reflection in the mirror. "Not bad," she decided. She'd wear the contacts until bedtime, then try again tomorrow.

Grace grabbed her robe from a hook on the back of the bathroom door and pulled it over her cotton camisole and pajama bottoms, not bothering with the tie. Then she slipped out of the bathroom and headed downstairs to grab her briefcase. A few hours of work would make her drowsy—and get her mind off the man who slept one floor above.

There was something very sexy about a man who was

so good with children. Why he didn't have a family of his own, Grace couldn't understand. She'd told herself all the good men were taken, a logical rationalization for her lack of a social life. But Tucker McCabe had somehow slipped through the net. That fact gave her hope—hope that maybe there was a man out there for her.

She strolled through the dark house, finding her way without the help of lights. But when she got to the kitchen, she reached over and flipped on the switch. Grace froze as she watched Tuck McCabe straighten from his spot in front of the open refrigerator. Damn, she'd meant to replace that burned-out bulb.

He gave her a sheepish smile. "You caught me."

Grace clutched at the front of her robe, suddenly aware of her state of undress—and of his. He wore only a pair of sweatpants that hung low on his hips. It had been a long time since she'd been in the presence of a half-naked man, and she hadn't remembered the experience as being quite so…breathtaking.

"Grace?"

She blinked. "I—I'm sorry. You startled me. I was just coming down to—" She drew a ragged breath. "Are you hungry?"

"Yeah," he said. "I'm used to having a bedtime snack."

"Didn't you get enough to eat for—" Grace paused, then sighed, raking her fingers through her hair. "Dinner was horrible. I know. I'm a terrible cook. I shouldn't be allowed in the kitchen. In my hands, a stove becomes a deadly weapon."

"No," Tuck said. "Dinner was fine."

"You don't have to spare my feelings," she assured him. "I'll see if I can come up with something better tomorrow night." Her hands fluttered to the front of her robe again, before she grabbed the back of a chair and held on for dear life. A long silence grew between them and Grace took a quick breath. "I—I wanted to thank you…for entertaining Susan…and for trying with Bryan."

"Trying?"

"He's been so obstinate lately. And you were very… understanding."

"He's a kid. He sees me as a threat," Tuck said. "He's used to being the man of the house and I'm trespassing on his property."

"I'm just not sure what to do with him," Grace confessed. She turned to the cupboard and tried to reach the top shelf where she'd hidden some fudge cookies inside an old fondue pot. Tuck stepped up behind her and grabbed the package, his body brushing against hers, pinning her against the counter. Though her first impulse was to slip away, Grace held her ground and slowly turned, enjoying the tremor of attraction that raced through her. "Lately, he seems to go looking for trouble," she murmured, staring up into his eyes.

"Sometimes we feel compelled to do things we know aren't very sensible," he said, his voice low. He reached over and brushed a damp strand of hair from her eyes. "And sometimes we do things that are downright dangerous." He drew his hand away, then handed her the cookies.

Grace clutched the package tightly, in part to keep her hands from trembling. "Milk," she murmured. "Would you like milk?"

Tuck nodded, then pulled a chair out from the kitchen table and sat down. "All boys go through this phase. Testing their limits."

"Philo Cooper caught him pinching a candy bar from his grocery store last month. When I asked Bryan why he did it, he wouldn't say. I give him money to buy candy. He knows that stealing is wrong."

"I did a lot of things when I was a kid," Tuck said, "gave in to a lot of bad impulses. I stole a car once and took it for a joyride. That landed me in juvenile hall. But I was lucky. I had someone to talk some sense into me."

"Your father?" Grace asked.

Tuck shook his head. "Naw. I never knew my father. And my mother pretty much drank herself to death. I was talking about Ike. He's this old rancher who taught me everything I know about horses and cattle. He's the one who convinced me I could become a vet. And when I got the grades, he helped put me through school."

"You're a veterinarian?" Grace asked.

"Yep. I don't have a traditional practice." Tuck smiled. "I kind of have an aversion to that type of commitment. But there's plenty of work at Snake Creek and the surrounding ranches to keep me busy."

"So Snake Creek is the name of your ranch?"

"It's not exactly mine. It belongs to Ike and me and another friend, Ray. And the kids who live there."

"Kids? You mean more goats?"

"No," Tuck said with a chuckle. "These kids are juvenile delinquents. Teenage boys who have gotten in trouble with the law. We give them jobs at the ranch, try to straighten them out. We've got all sorts of animals for them to work with, different breeds of horses and cattle, chickens, ducks and now goats. You'd be surprised what a little back-breaking labor and a few marketable job skills will do for a kid's self-esteem."

Grace set a glass of milk in front of him, then circled the table and sat down. "Is that why you tried to get Bryan to help you? Because he lacks self-esteem?"

He shrugged. "I don't know Bryan. I just thought he might like to get to know a little more about horses. I guess he doesn't. No big deal."

"Don't give up on him," Grace urged. "Try again. I think he'd probably love to help with the horses. He's just too cool to admit it."

"How long has it been since Bryan's dad left?" Tuck glanced down at his hands. "I mean, he did leave, right?"

"Oh, yes, he definitely left," Grace said. "One day he was here and then he was gone. And Bryan hasn't seen him since. Dan Penrose wasn't cut out to be a father. There are just too many pretty women in the world to distract him."

"We don't have to talk about this," Tuck said as he dipped a cookie into his glass of milk.

"Dan walked out when Bryan was four," Grace continued, grateful to have someone to unburden herself to. She never talked much about Dan to her girlfriends. It was easier to relive her humiliation with a total stranger who hadn't been here to witness the original event. "Susan doesn't even remember him."

"He doesn't see them?"

Grace shook her head. "He lives in California with his...current girlfriend. I lost track of her name. The names and the girls change pretty often."

"I'm sorry."

"There's no need to be. We're better off and we get along all right. And the children see his parents every Easter and for two weeks in the summer. They live in Florida since they sold the hardware stores." She paused. "I married him for all the wrong reasons. I'd known him for such a long time I never saw him in an objective light. I loved the boy and I never saw the man he'd become." She took a sip of her milk. "But I have Bryan and Susan, so any trouble I went through in the marriage was more than worth it."

"Kids are resilient," Tuck said. "Look at me. I didn't exactly have the best start in life, but I got past that. It's all about choices.'' He finished his milk, then set the glass down.

Grace quickly picked it up and moved to the refrigerator, hoping that by getting another glass for him he'd continue their conversation. She was curious about the man staying in her house, curious how such a troubled past could mold such a good man. But when she turned from the refrigerator, the jug of milk in her hand, she found him standing in front of her.

He took the glass from her hand and set it on the counter, his movement pressing her back against the open refrigerator. ''I should get to bed,'' he murmured, his gaze skimming over her face.

He was so close, Grace could feel the warmth of his body radiating to hers. She stood perfectly still, afraid to move, afraid to breathe. Somehow, she knew he wanted to kiss her, though how she knew was a complete mystery. Her experience was limited to a handful of men and she suspected that none of them possessed even half the passion that Tuck McCabe had in his little finger.

Her gaze inextricably locked with his, Grace waited for what seemed like hours. Waited for him to lean forward and brush his lips over hers, or to reach out and touch her face. Sweep her into his arms and make wild, passionate—

Her left eye began to water. At first, she thought it might be the emotion of the moment, but then she remembered the contact lenses. This was why she didn't wear lenses. They bothered her at the most inopportune times, causing her eyes to water uncontrollably.

She blinked, hoping he wouldn't notice. Just a few more seconds and she was certain he'd kiss her. But the sting of tears was unbearable, and she reached up and rubbed her eye with her fingers. ''Sorry,'' she said. ''Contact lens.''

Her words broke the spell that had descended around

them and he stepped back. "I should get to bed," he repeated, his voice cool.

She swallowed hard. "Me, too." A moment later, she realized how her words sounded. "I mean, I should go to bed, too. In my own bed, of course. Not yours." She pushed the jug of milk into his arms, then deftly slipped away from him, grabbing her briefcase as she hurried to the door. She turned, holding up the briefcase against her chest like a shield. "I'll see you tomorrow," Grace murmured.

"Bright and early," he called.

"Bright and early," she repeated. But as she hurried up to her bedroom, anxious to rid herself of the contact lenses, Grace knew that sleep would be hard to come by this night. Her mind was whirling with unbidden thoughts and her body pulsing with unfamiliar feelings. She'd had her doubts about inviting Tucker McCabe to stay at her house.

But after just one evening under the same roof, Grace wasn't sure whether the invitation she'd extended was the best idea she'd had in years—or a colossal mistake.

CHAPTER THREE

TUCK SEARCHED THE KITCHEN for a frying pan in the pre-dawn silence. He'd never known anyone quite as disorganized as Grace Penrose. She avoided organization about as much as he avoided commitment. The logical spot for pots and pans would be in the cabinet next to the stove. But when he opened the door, a clutter of plastic containers tumbled out along with a deflated football and an embroidered pillowcase.

With a soft curse, he tried to push the items back in the cupboard, then realized they weren't meant to fit. So he squatted down and carefully sorted through the mix of old margarine tubs and mismatched plastic storage containers, until everything was nestled logically by size and put back into place, the football and pillowcase on top. Then he levered himself to his feet to resume his search.

Ten minutes later, he found an old cast-iron frying pan on a shelf in the broom closet, underneath a wool sweater and a newspaper from three years ago. It took another twenty minutes to gather all the ingredients for flapjacks, including an unopened can of real Vermont maple syrup that he discovered hidden in a drawer of tools. He even found a pound of bacon in the back of the freezer, nearly embedded in ice, but salvageable.

If he wanted a decent meal, he figured he'd have to cook it himself. Breakfast would be easy. He'd just make sure he got up before everyone else did. He could always survive on sandwiches for lunch. But dinner would be another matter.

As Tuck mixed the batter, he glanced through the kitchen window to find the sun peeking over the horizon. "So much for an early start," he murmured. But then, if Grace was going to help him with the animals, they'd have to wait until her kids left for school, anyway. He sat down at the table and sipped at a mug of strong coffee and waited...and waited.

At precisely 7:15 a.m., the house suddenly came to life and Tuck turned on the stove. Footsteps pounded on the floor above his head and he heard shouting as he poured batter into the pan. Water ran and pipes clanked. Then, in one chaotic rush, Grace, Bryan and Susan hurried down the stairs, just as he turned from the stove with a plate of hot flapjacks and crispy fried bacon. They stumbled into the kitchen, stopped dead in their tracks and stared at him as if they'd suddenly come across some alien life form. Bryan and Susan were dressed, but Grace still wore her robe, her hair in complete disarray.

"Good morning," he said, holding up the plate. "I made breakfast."

"Breakfast?" Grace asked, tucking an errant strand behind her ear. A blush rose in her cheeks. "Oh, I'm sorry. I was supposed to make you breakfast, wasn't I. That was part of the deal." She stared down at the platter heaped with flapjacks, an apologetic smile quirking her lips. "Those look good. Mine always turn out a little pale."

"Sit down," Tuck insisted. "I've made breakfast for all of us. It's the least I can do." The least he could do if he didn't want to starve in the next two weeks.

Grace did as she was told, then plucked a piece of bacon from the plate Tuck set beside her. "You found bacon? I didn't realize we had any."

"It was in the back of the freezer."

"Oh. Then it's probably been there for a while. I think I bought it last summer for a potato salad I was going to make."

Susan slipped into her place at the table and stared down at her plate, her eyes wide with disbelief. "We never have pancakes for breakfast," she said. "Sometimes we have waffles from a box, but never pancakes."

"From a box?" Tuck asked as he added another flapjack to her plate.

"In the freezer," Susan said. "They go in the toaster, and when Mommy doesn't watch them they get burned."

"Well, this is a real ranch breakfast," Tuck said. "Homemade." He slathered Susan's flapjacks with a glob of butter, then drizzled syrup over the top. "There, try that. That's what cowboys eat before heading out on the range. Sometimes we even cook our flapjacks over a campfire. We'll have to try that some morning. We'll build a fire in the backyard and I'll show you how we do it."

"A campfire? Really?" Susan reached for her fork and dug in. "That would be neat," she added once her mouth was full.

Bryan wasn't as enthusiastic. "I gotta go," he muttered. "I'm gonna walk to school." He grabbed his backpack and jacket from a hook near the door, then stuffed an apple in his pocket before walking out.

Tuck stared after him, then forced a smile. "Well, more for the rest of us."

Susan looked up from her flapjacks, her gaze shifting between Tuck and her mother. "I'll eat more," she said, syrup dotting the corners of her mouth. "These are really good."

Tuck suspected that Susan would have eaten them if they'd tasted like sawdust. It was clear that he'd become the object of her adoration, and he was beginning to enjoy the lofty position. Charming a little girl was a whole lot safer than charming her mother.

He added another flapjack to Susan's pile, then poured Grace a cup of coffee and sat down beside her with his own plate of food. "I figure we'll muck out stalls and feed the animals right after breakfast. Then we're going to have to groom the horses. They're starting to get their winter coats and they're looking pretty shabby. Then we need to get a look at the sleighs and the tack. If we have to do any repairs, we need to get going on that right away. And I want to hitch the horses up and see—"

"Stop," Grace said, holding up her hand. "Please. Not until I've finished my first cup of coffee."

Susan sent him a cautionary look. "Mommy doesn't talk much until she has her coffee," she whispered.

They ate in silence, Tuck and Susan exchanging amused glances, Grace staring into her mug. When a car horn sounded outside Susan jumped up. She struggled into her coat and grabbed her backpack, then gave Grace a sticky-lipped kiss. "Bye, Mom," she said. As she passed Tuck, she grabbed him around the neck and gave him a hug. "Thanks for breakfast, Tuck. It was great."

When he turned back to the table, he found Grace watching him from over the rim of her coffee mug. She took another sip, then set it down in front of her. "This was very nice of you." she murmured.

"I was up early," Tuck said as he began to clear the table. "It gave me something to do."

"Did you sleep well last night?" she asked.

"Like a rock," Tuck lied. In truth, he'd spent the night staring at the ceiling, his thoughts occupied with the woman sleeping just one floor below, regrets mixed with relief. He'd wanted like hell to kiss her as they stood in front of the refrigerator staring into each other's eyes. It had taken every ounce of willpower to walk away, but in the end, he'd been glad that he had. Once he kissed her, there was no taking it back.

Besides, he wasn't quite sure how she'd react. Though she looked like she wanted to be kissed, Tuck wasn't used to reading the signs from a woman like Grace. The women he dated made their needs quite obvious, a sexy look here, a tantalizing touch there. By the time they got around to kissing, he already knew they'd end up in bed. Tuck couldn't remember the last time he'd kissed a woman simply to kiss her. He did know that women like Grace preferred to be wooed, to be courted and complimented. But beyond that, he hadn't a clue.

That was probably for the best. Kissing Grace Penrose wouldn't be the most sensible course of action, even if he was the kind of guy who was ready to settle down. Where would it lead? She was a mother with two children and a life in New England, he was a rancher from Montana with a life of his own. Not much common ground there.

He'd have to write off his desire as simply one of those reckless urges that came to him every now and then. He'd learned to control those impulses a long time ago, but that didn't make them any less tempting. The next time he felt the need to kiss her, he'd just remember the complications and the urge would pass. "Come on," Tuck said. "We need to get going."

Grace rubbed the sleep from her eyes. "I really need to go back to bed. I was up all last night working on the parade permits and the program notes for the play."

Tuck reached down, grabbed her hand and pulled her to her feet. "This was part of our deal," he reminded her.

She groaned softly, then looked up at him with sleep-tinged eyes, pleading silently for a reprieve. In a single, blinding instant, another impulse hit him full force and Tuck didn't even bother to acknowledge it before acting. He bent down and captured her mouth with his, seizing the moment while he had the chance. To hell with self control and complications.

He expected surprise, perhaps even indignation. And he was prepared for a slap across the face. What he didn't expect was for Grace Penrose to instantly go soft in his arms, to sigh and open her mouth beneath his until their tongues tentatively touched, to weave her fingers through the hair at the nape of his neck, drawing him nearer.

Her lips were sweet, like maple syrup, and he moved his mouth against hers, wanting more. If he hadn't known better, he might think she was waiting for this, desperate for the taste of a man. She offered no resistance. Instead, she sank into his body, her breasts pressed against his chest, and took all that he offered, as if only he could quench her thirst for passion.

When he finally drew away, Tuck was certain that she'd wanted to kiss him as much as he wanted to kiss her. He gazed down at her face, smoothing his thumb across her lower lip.

Slowly, she opened her eyes. "That wasn't part of our deal, was it?" she asked.

"Not really," Tuck said. "But we can always renegotiate."

"Okay," Grace said in a tiny voice. "That would be good."

Tuck chuckled softly, then grabbed her around the waist and turned her around. "Go get dressed. Wear something warm. And you'll need sturdy boots. We're not going to a tea party."

She shuffled out of the kitchen, and when the door swung shut behind her, Tuck leaned back against the edge of the counter. He'd worked so hard since his misspent youth to conquer his impulses, yet this was one time he was glad he'd forgotten about doing the right thing. Kissing Grace Penrose might not have been the most sensible course of action, but it had sure felt good.

GRACE STOOD IN THE DOORWAY of Silas Rawlings's barn, her nose crinkled against the odors that assaulted her. "Does it always smell this bad?" she asked.

Tuck held out a pitchfork. "That's pretty much the way horses smell," he explained. "Goats aren't much better. But you'll get used to it." She grabbed the pitchfork and he motioned her inside.

Reluctantly Grace followed him into the dark interior of the barn. She ducked her head as she walked beneath a rafter, certain there were huge spiders lurking above her, ready to drop down on top of her head. This was definitely not part of her job as director of tourism for Cooper's Corner. She had been hired to plan the festival, not shovel horse poop.

If it weren't for the deal she'd struck, right now she'd be hiding under the covers of her bed, reliving the most embarrassing moment of her life. How could she have done something so stupid? It wasn't the kiss that bothered her. After all, Tuck was a man—a strong, sexy, virile man. And like it or not, she was a moderately attractive, available woman. But did she have to enjoy it so much? Did she have to act as if she hadn't been kissed—really kissed—in seven years?

She'd dated a few men around town, men she'd known since childhood. And there had been a few chaste goodnight kisses on her porch, but nothing like the surprising intimacy that she'd shared in the middle of her kitchen with Tucker McCabe, a virtual stranger. Exactly what had prompted him to take such liberties? Had she given off some kind of signal that she was ready to be ravished? And if she had, could she do it again?

Grace watched Tuck as he showed her how to skim the pitchfork over the floor of the stall, picking up the dirty straw as he went. She tried desperately to concentrate on his patient instructions, but her mind wasn't on shoveling horse apples. Instead, she found herself completely preoccupied with a study of Tucker McCabe's features—his strong jaw and his straight nose, his expressive eyes and that finely sculpted mouth—

She swallowed hard. Resisting him was an exercise in futility. No woman could deny such a charming and handsome man. He had that whole cowboy thing going for him—the perpetually windblown hair, the complexion burnished by the sun, that lazy smile and easygoing manner. There was something so undeniably masculine about a man who worked with his body as well as his brain.

Her mind flashed back to an image of him the previous night, bare-chested, dressed in just his sweatpants. Tuck had a magnificent physique, all hard muscle and sinew, the kind of body a woman might... Grace hesitated. She had never considered herself a very sensual person, but she couldn't help thinking about what his skin might feel like beneath her palms, how her name would sound on his lips, whether the skin on the angle of his shoulder might taste as good as she thought it would.

"Grace?"

She jumped at the sound of his voice behind her. Slowly, she glanced over her shoulder, wondering whether or not she'd spoken her thoughts out loud. "Yes?"

"You can't just keep pushing it around. You've got to pick the dirty straw up with your pitchfork and toss it in the wheelbarrow."

"Right." Grace did as she was told, but halfway to the wheelbarrow, the blob of straw dropped at her feet. She tried again and this time it fell on her foot. She glanced up to find Tuck smiling at her, his hands braced on the end of his pitchfork.

"Maybe we should let you feed the animals," he said.

Grace looked at the mess around her feet, then drew a long breath, an action she was immediately sorry for. The smell made her retch. "That would probably be best," she agreed, gulping air.

"Come on." Tuck picked up a battered bucket and walked into a nearby stall. He held the gate open and she stepped inside, only to find herself surrounded by the dreaded pointy-hooved goats. "Grab a handful of meal and hold it out to them," he instructed.

She did as she was told. Immediately a small black-and-white goat began to nibble at her palm, his muzzle as soft as velvet. Grace laughed. "He's so cute," she murmured.

"That one's a she," Tuck said. "That one's a neutered he and so is that one. They're called wethers." He pointed to a pair of goats in the crowd gathered around them. "And they aren't really kids. Technically, they're yearlings." He handed her the bucket. "I need to go get some things from my truck. Give them each a few handfuls, then pour the rest in the trough."

Though Grace was a little wary of being alone with the goats, she nodded and watched Tuck stride out of the barn. She fed a handful of meal to a pretty gray goat, but the others grew impatient and started to jostle her to get closer. In a moment of panic, she backed away, but the goats kept advancing, pinning her against the gate. With a soft cry, Grace tossed the bucket over the heads of the goats. It hit the stone wall of the barn with a loud clatter, then dropped to the floor, just as she scrambled over the gate.

When she turned around, she found all nine goats collapsed in the stall in one big heap, their eyes closed, their legs sticking out. Stunned, Grace stood at the gate, unable to move. What had she done? She'd followed Tuck's directions to the letter, except for tossing the bucket away. Nothing she'd done could have remotely resulted in the instantaneous death of his goats. She might have knocked one out with the bucket, but all nine?

Tuck's footsteps echoed through the barn and Grace steeled herself to give him the bad news. But when he arrived at the stall, he stepped up on the bottom rung of the gate and casually took in the scene. "Strange, isn't it?" he commented.

"I—I'm sorry," she said. "I don't know what I did wrong. They just…keeled over and died."

"Did you make a loud noise?" Tuck asked.

"I threw the feed bucket against the wall," Grace replied. "Did the shock give them a heart attack and kill them?"

"They're not dead. They're asleep. One of my old professors at Tufts vet school was studying them. It's a genetic condition. When they hear a loud noise, they just go to sleep. Narcoleptic goats. That's why I'm taking them to the ranch. Though they're interesting to researchers, they're not much good to goat farmers. I figured the boys would enjoy working with them."

"Narcoleptic goats? Then I didn't kill them?"

Tuck shook his head, then grabbed her hand. "They'll wake up in a few seconds. You're not really big on farm life, are you."

The feel of his fingers clasping hers sent a flood of warmth through her body. "It's dirty, it smells bad, the animals scare me, and I've got a lot of work to do for the festival. Work that won't get done if I spend half my day in the barn.''

He stopped at the barn door and faced her. ''All right,'' Tuck said. ''I won't hold you to that part of our deal.''

''You're not holding me to any part of our deal,'' she said with a guilty smile. ''You made breakfast this morning, you played Barbies with Susan, you're trying hard to tolerate my rude son, and now you're going to do all this work yourself.''

''I'll ask Bryan to help again,'' he said as he pulled her along toward his pickup truck.

''Why do you try so hard with him?''

Tuck shrugged. He opened the passenger door and helped her inside. ''I've seen a lot of kids like him, standing on the fence, trying to figure out which way he's going to go.''

''You make him sound like a juvenile delinquent,'' Grace said with a laugh.

''There's a thin line between a good kid and a bad kid,'' Tuck replied, and he slammed the door and circled around the truck.

Grace watched him through the windshield. Did he really believe Bryan was a budding criminal? Sure, he might know a little about troubled teens, but he certainly didn't know her son well enough to make that judgment. ''My son is not a juvenile delinquent,'' she said as soon as he slipped behind the wheel.

''I didn't say he was.'' Tuck leaned forward and turned the ignition and the truck rumbled to life. ''But he could use a firmer hand and a little more direction in his life. He decides when he eats and what he eats and where he goes and when he'll be home.''

Grace gasped. ''Are you questioning my parenting abilities?''

"I'm just saying that maybe you don't have the... temperament to lay down the law. He could probably use a male influence in his life."

"We get along fine without a man in the house," Grace muttered, crossing her arms beneath her breasts and fixing her gaze out the passenger window. "Living without any man in the house is better than living with the wrong one."

"You don't have to be so defensive," Tuck said as he turned the truck toward town. "I'm just telling you what I know."

"And this comes from your experience as a parent?" Grace asked. She heard the hint of defensiveness in her voice but she didn't try to hide it. The longer this conversation went on, the more irritated she became. He was a guest in her house, he had no right to interfere. As they drove through town, Grace stewed, staring out the window and refusing to discuss her son with a stranger.

"I need to stop at the store," he said. "After that, maybe we can get a cup of coffee."

"I need to change," she told him. "I've got a lot to do today. Maybe you'd better drop me off at home."

"All right," he said, his voice cool and indifferent.

When he pulled to a stop in her driveway, Grace didn't waste any time jumping out of the truck. "I'm afraid you'll need to get your own lunch. I've got to take care of hanging the banners for the festival and then I have play rehearsals. I'll see you at dinner."

With that, she turned and hurried into the house. When she reached the safety of the kitchen, she paused and drew a deep breath. This was all happening too fast. Two mornings ago, she hadn't even known Tucker McCabe's name. And now he'd suddenly barged into her life, making her crave his kisses, giving her unsolicited parenting advice and wandering around her house half naked.

"You're the one who invited him," Grace muttered. "And now, either you're going to have to learn to live with him for the next two weeks or you're going to have to find a way to get rid of him and still keep his horses."

TUCK WANDERED DOWN the aisles of Cooper's Corner General Store, the town's quaint answer to a big-city supermarket. It was actually two stores in one, a grocery store and a hardware store, and stocked everything from nails to nail polish. He found a can of shaving cream and a package of razors, then decided to go for some snacks. He couldn't count on Grace's cooking so it paid to be prepared. A few packages of cookies and chips hidden under his bed would be just the thing to quell his hunger pangs late at night.

He came around the corner of the snack aisle, then stopped short. Bryan Penrose was loitering near the candy section, his gaze darting from a display of candy bars to the gentleman standing fifteen feet away at the front counter. Tuck watched silently as Grace's son casually reached out and picked up a candy bar, then slid it into his jacket pocket. He took another, then another, putting them in his pocket as well, before strolling up to the front counter with a small package of bubble gum.

"Hey there, Bryan," the grocer said as he rang up the gum.

Bryan pulled a handful of coins from his jeans pocket and paid for his purchase. "Hi, Mr. Cooper."

"Don't you have school today?" Cooper asked.

"I have a note from my mom. I've got a dentist appointment. I have to meet her in a few minutes."

"That bubble gum won't do your teeth any good," the grocer warned.

Bryan gave the man a tight smile, then walked out of the store, getting clean away with his candy bars. Cursing softly, Tuck hurried up to the counter with his own purchases, then pulled out his wallet.

"Hey there," Mr. Cooper said. "Did you find everything all right?"

Tuck nodded, tapping his foot impatiently as the grocer squinted through his reading glasses at the price on the shaving cream.

"Do you remember how much this was?" the man asked.

"Dollar twenty-nine," Tuck said.

"Are you the guy staying up at Grace Penrose's house? The cowboy who bought Silas Rawlings's horses?"

"Yep," Tuck replied. He knew small towns, and it was clear you couldn't sneeze in Cooper's Corner without half the population wondering where you caught the cold. No doubt his presence in the Penrose household had caused a good bit of gossip and speculation.

"I'm Philo Cooper. Me and the missus own this store. We've known Gracie since she was just a little baby. Her folks settled here in town a few years before she was born. But her family goes back in Cooper's Corner to the early 1900s, to her great-grandparents."

Tuck ground his teeth and continued to smile. "I'm really in a hurry, so could you tally that up for me?"

Philo's eyebrow shot up, and a few seconds later he gave Tuck the total. Tuck tossed a ten onto the counter and didn't wait for the change, leaving enough to cover the stolen candy. He grabbed up the paper bag and rushed out the door. He saw Bryan strolling down the street and he picked up his pace to catch up to him.

When he was within a few feet, Tuck spoke. "That was a pretty slick move you pulled back there."

Bryan stopped and turned around. Though his expression

was indifferent, Tuck could see the uneasiness in his eyes. "What?"

"That move. You know, the five-finger discount you took on those candy bars. I don't think that guy even suspected. Buying the gum was a nice touch. I used to use that move myself. Always diverted suspicion. And the lie about the dentist appointment. Sounded like the truth to me."

He tipped his chin up defensively. "I don't know what you're talking about. I didn't steal nothing."

"That story might fool Philo Cooper and it might fool your mother, but you're talking to a guy who didn't just fall off the turnip truck."

"What?"

"I'm not stupid," Tuck said. "If you didn't take the candy bars, then turn your jacket pockets inside out and prove it."

Bryan set his jaw stubbornly. "You're not the boss of me. You can't tell me what I can do."

"Well," Tuck said. "That's exactly what I'm going to do. First off, you're going to give me the candy bars. Since I paid for them at the store, I figure they belong to me."

He considered the order for a long moment. "What did you tell Cooper?"

Tuck shrugged. "I didn't tell him anything." He held out his hand. "Give me the candy bars."

Bryan grudgingly reached in his pocket and produced the stolen merchandise, then slapped the candy bars into Tuck's open palm. "Are you going to tell my mom?"

"Well, that's up to you. We can tell your mom and then you and she will probably have to go down to the store and admit your crime. You'll likely be grounded for the next two or three years. Or we can go another way."

"What way?"

"Well, you can work for me. Taking care of my horses and my goats every morning and evening. Your mom is pretty busy with the festival and I can't ask her to take the time. So, you have a choice. I keep my mouth shut for as long as you work for me. Or we take these candy bars back inside and explain how they got into your pocket."

"How long would I have to work for you?"

"I'm here for two weeks," Tuck said. "I figure after two weeks my memory will be pretty dim. I'll probably have forgotten everything I saw."

"Isn't this blackmail?" Bryan asked.

"I'm not the criminal here—you are."

Bryan stared down at his feet, idly kicking a small pebble with the toe of his shoe. Tuck could sense the wheels turning inside his head as he weighed his options and evaluated his opponent. "All right," he finally said. "I'll do what you want. But you can't tell my mom. And this doesn't mean I have to like you."

"Hey, that's fine with me, buddy," Tuck said. "'Cause I don't like you much, either. Now, if I were you, I'd get my butt back to school because your mom is just down the street there. And I know you don't have a dentist appointment."

Bryan glanced over his shoulder, then quickly stepped behind Tuck. After checking both ways, he ran across the street. Tuck watched him until he disappeared from sight then smiled to himself. All he really needed was a chance with the kid. He'd had far tougher cases than Bryan Penrose. Two weeks of hard work might be just about enough to turn the kid around.

He strolled down the sidewalk, his gaze fixed on Grace as she directed the hanging of a banner across Main Street. She'd changed from her jeans back into a tidy blazer and trousers. The brisk wind whipped at her hair and her cheeks were pink from the cold. Tuck stood a few feet away and watched her as she directed two men to raise and lower the banner until it was in the perfect spot.

"That looks good," she shouted. "Tie it off."

She glanced down at her clipboard and checked off something on her list, then turned to go on to her next task. When she saw him, she stopped and slowly approached.

"Hi," Tuck said.

"Hi," she murmured, clutching her clipboard to her chest.

"Listen, I'm sorry about what happened in the truck. You're right. I don't know Bryan and I had no place commenting on his behavior. I apologize."

"It's all right," Grace said. "I just get a little touchy about the kids. I guess sometimes I feel I'm not doing a good job, that I'm a bad parent. When someone confirms that fact, it's upsetting."

Tuck smiled, then reached out and grabbed her hand, lacing his fingers through hers. "Can I buy you a cup of coffee? You look cold. And your hands are freezing."

Grace nodded. "Yes, I'd like that."

Satisfied that he'd smoothed things over with her, he pulled her along toward Tubb's Café. As they walked inside, the patrons all turned to look at them, then quickly began whispering to one another in an excited buzz.

Tuck glanced over at Grace and saw the color rise in her cheeks, but she didn't pull her hand from his. Instead, she tipped her chin up and pasted a pleasant smile on her face. He knew what that decision would cost her. Within an hour, everyone in Cooper's Corner would be speculating about the cowboy from Montana and the prim-and-proper Grace Penrose. They'd all wonder just what was going on in that big house on the edge of town.

Let 'em wonder, Tuck thought to himself as he drew

Grace along to the counter. Nothing they thought of would come close to the tantalizing fantasies that had been running through his mind since he'd kissed her that morning. But Tuck had no intention of turning those fantasies into reality. Though he might kiss Grace again, he was determined that he'd go no further.

Besides, what harm could a few kisses do?

CHAPTER FOUR

GRACE STARED DOWN AT the column of figures, then tried to add them for the fifth time. After dinner, she'd spread her work out on the coffee table, sitting on the floor in front of the fireplace. But she'd been unable to concentrate on revising her budget for the festival. At first, she blamed the distraction on Tuck, who was playing a video game with Bryan in the library while Susan cheered them both on. She'd had to fight the temptation to leave her work and join the fun.

But she didn't have any distractions now. Susan had gone to bed an hour ago. Tuck had left to make one last check on the horses and goats. To her great surprise, Bryan had volunteered to go with him, though her son hadn't mustered much enthusiasm for the job. So she'd taken a hot shower, pulled on a pair of flannel pajamas and wrapped herself in a comfy chenille robe, hoping that it might calm her jumpy nerves. And still she couldn't concentrate.

With a frustrated sigh, she rubbed her eyes, then slipped her glasses back on. "You know exactly what this is about," she murmured to herself.

This was about the kiss she and Tuck had shared just that morning, that wonderful mind-numbing experience in front of the refrigerator. All day long, her heart had beat a bit faster and her breathing had come in tiny gasps when she thought about what might happen tonight. Once the house was dark. And they were alone.

Her fingertips fluttered to her lips and Grace recalled the feel of his mouth on hers, the warmth of his tongue, the waves of pleasure that raced through her body at his touch. When she'd chosen something to wear after her shower, she'd actually considered a flimsy little nightgown with a low-cut neckline and a high-cut hem. But she couldn't possibly be that brazen.

If Tuck had any intention of kissing her again, he'd have to get by a layer of flannel and chenille before the actual seduction could begin. "I'm a mother, for goodness' sake! I can't think this way." She shook her head and turned back to her budget, determined to put Tucker McCabe out of her head.

He'd slipped so easily into their lives, as if he were an old friend on a holiday visit. Only he was like no friend she'd ever known. His presence in her house made her feel…alive. She was no longer plain old Grace, overachieving mom and aspiring nun. She felt desirable and sexy and giddy with the excitement of it all.

But it wasn't just that. His presence had also become a comfort after so long without a partner to depend upon. Already he'd fixed the balky latch on the front door, put up the rest of the storm windows on the second floor and carried in nearly a half cord of wood from the pile at the back of her lot to the stack near the back porch. And she hadn't even asked him to do any of it!

Grace crossed her arms on the table and rested her head on them. Her eyes slowly closed, and when an image of Tuck drifted through her mind, she didn't push it away. Tuck standing in her kitchen, cooking pancakes at the stove. Tuck shirtless, his chest gleaming in the low light. And Tuck naked in her bed, the sheets twisted around his long limbs.

A shiver skittered down her spine. It would be so easy

to fall madly in love with him. Susan already worshipped him. And even Bryan seemed to be changing his tune. She hadn't missed the look that passed between them when Tuck announced he was going to the barn. They'd reached some type of…Grace yawned…truce.

When Grace opened her eyes again, the fire had died to glowing embers. A chill had fallen over the house. She sat up and brushed her hair back from her face, then pulled off her glasses, which hung crookedly on her nose. The column of figures still lay unadded on the coffee table, except now there was a small wet mark on the sheet of paper.

"You should go to bed."

Grace glanced up to find Tuck standing in the doorway. His flannel shirt was unbuttoned to the waist and he leaned against the doorjamb, his arms crossed over his chest. She brushed a damp spot from the corner of her mouth and forced a smile, her heart skipping a beat at the simple sight of him. "I—I just have a little more work to do," she said. Her voice was husky and she cleared her throat. "How long have you been standing there?"

"Bryan and I got home about fifteen minutes ago. How long have you been asleep?"

Grace's gaze slid along his body, from his flat belly to his narrow hips and long muscular legs. Then she quickly looked up to find a tiny smile curling the corners of his mouth. "Just a few minutes," she murmured.

Another shiver raced through her and she distractedly rubbed her arms, knowing it hadn't come from the cold. Tuck stepped over to the fire and poked at the embers. Then he tossed another log onto the grate and tended it until it crackled with flame. "It's getting colder outside. The wind has picked up."

"Did Bryan help you in the barn?"

Tuck nodded. "Yeah. He hauled some feed and cleaned

out a few stalls. He didn't do too badly. Though I think the horses kind of scare him. They're a lot bigger when you're standing right next to them.''

''What did you talk about?''

Tuck sat down beside her, resting his arm on his bent knee. ''Not much. School, sports. I think he's got a girlfriend. He mentioned Ashley a few times.''

''Really? A girlfriend?'' Grace sighed, slipping her fingers through her tangled hair. ''He doesn't tell me anything anymore. I have to pump Susan for details and she never knows much. I guess he's going through one of those phases that boys do.''

''Right,'' Tuck said.

Grace hesitated, watching him with a sideways glance. ''Exactly what kind of phase is he going through? I'm a bit in the dark here. I've been reading all these parenting books, trying to get a handle on his behavior. But it would help to talk to someone who has actually gone through puberty—as a male.'' She met his gaze. ''And you have.''

''He's going through that phase when he wants to prove that he can get along on his own. That he doesn't need anyone but himself. He's going to make a lot of stupid choices, but you have to let him make his own mistakes, the same way I did.''

''But you made some pretty big mistakes, didn't you?'' Grace asked. ''Stealing a car is serious. I don't want Bryan to do that.''

''Luckily my mistake phase didn't have any serious consequences. Once I started working at Snake Creek, life got much better.''

Sometimes it was so easy to talk to Tuck, and at other times she became a tongue-tied bag of nerves. Tonight it was easy. ''What about your girl phase?'' Grace asked. ''When did you go through that?''

Tuck grinned softly. "Oh, that started pretty early. I guess I'm still going through it now. It probably lasts a lifetime."

Grace straightened the papers in front of her, carefully considering her next question. The subject had been nagging at her mind ever since she'd caught Bryan looking at the ladies' underwear section in the Sears catalog. "So, if you don't mind me being personal, when did you actually—I mean, when should I expect—it's just that I haven't had the talk with Bryan yet."

"The talk?"

"The birds and the bees?"

Tuck laughed softly. "Ah, the stallions and the fillies."

"Right," Grace said. "The books say I should have already had the talk. I know he's ready. I've tried to approach him twice and he gets all embarrassed and runs out of the room. Short of tying him to a chair and hauling out charts and illustrations, I'm wondering if I'll ever get him to listen."

"I'd expect he already knows the basics," Tuck said. "I did at his age."

"But he's only eleven," Grace said, shocked by the notion.

"Boys do talk."

"And when did you—you know."

"See my first issue of *Playboy?*"

"No. When did you lose your—" Grace swallowed. "Virginity."

Tuck stretched his legs out in front of him and clasped his hands behind his head. "Don't you think that's an awfully personal question?"

Grace gasped. "I'm not asking you as a man! I mean, I am, but not as an attractive, single man." She stopped.

"That's not what I meant. I'm asking you as an objective, experienced member of the male species."

"That's what I am."

"Exactly my point. Maybe you could bring up the subject with him. Sometime when you're together in the barn. Man to man. It would probably be better coming from a stranger instead of his mother. Less embarrassing. And after that, he might be more willing to talk to me."

"I could do that," Tuck said.

"You could?"

Tuck nodded. "Sure."

"Just feel him out," she suggested. "See what he knows about the basics." Grace ignored the blush that warmed her cheeks. "And if he has any serious misconceptions, tell me and I'll straighten him out." She covered her face with her hands. "I can't believe we're talking about sex."

A moment later, he pried her fingers apart, forcing her to look at him. "It's not real sex," he said. "It's purely theoretical sex." His eyes met hers for a long, silent moment. "After all, we've only known each other a couple of days."

His words sent a flood of desire pulsing through her veins. Tuck leaned forward slightly and Grace's breath caught in her throat. When his eyes moved down to her mouth, she knew what was coming. He was going to kiss her again. He was going to lean over and touch his mouth to hers and every rational thought was going to dissolve in her head and she was going to be swept away in a whirlpool of pleasure and confusion.

"It's late," Tuck murmured, his focus entirely on her bottom lip.

"Yes," Grace replied.

He rose to his feet and suddenly the room went cold again. "I'll talk to Bryan and I'll let you know how it goes." He offered Grace his hand, then helped her up from the floor.

"Thanks," Grace said, freeing her fingers from his and stifling a groan. Maybe he hadn't wanted to kiss her. Maybe she was just imagining things. She watched as he walked back toward the stairs. As he did, he stopped and pulled back the lace curtain on the window, peering into the darkness.

"I thought I smelled snow," he murmured. "And look at that."

"It's snowing?" Grace hurried to his side and drew the curtain back farther, her hand brushing against his. But she barely noticed the tremor that raced through her. Under the glare of the front porch light she saw what she'd been waiting for this past month.

With a gleeful laugh, she raced to the front door and threw it open, then ran across the porch to stand on the steps. Tipping her face up to the sky, she let the snowflakes melt on her face. "It's snowing!" she cried, turning around, her arms outstretched.

Tuck stood in the doorway and watched her, his eyebrow raised, a questioning look on his face. "This is a northern climate," he said. "You have seen snow before."

"Not this snow," Grace cried. "Isn't it wonderful? It's almost a blizzard."

He sauntered down the steps, his gaze fixed on hers, and grabbed her hand, pulling her back beneath the porch roof. "It's freezing out here."

"Yes," Grace said breathlessly. She leaned into his body, nearer to his warmth. "It's finally freezing."

He stared at her, then reached out and brushed his finger along her temple. "You have snow in your hair," he murmured as his gaze skimmed her face. "And on your eyelashes.'' He traced the arch of her eyebrow with his thumb. ''Like little diamonds.''

Grace wasn't going to wait for him to make the first move. She'd tried that before. Instead, she pushed up on her toes and touched her lips to his. For a moment, he didn't return her kiss and she feared that she'd made a mistake. But then he slipped his arms around her waist and pulled her against his body, covering her mouth and teasing it open with his tongue.

Her fingers spread over his naked chest, warm and smooth and rippled with hard muscle. She could feel his heart beating beneath her palm, strong and even and so different from her racing beat. No man had ever kissed her the way Tucker McCabe was kissing her now. This was not the brief and spontaneous kiss they'd shared earlier that morning. This kiss was filled with need and passion.

A low groan rumbled in his throat as he pushed her back against the side of the house, his body pressed against hers. Tuck's fingers found their way to the neckline of her robe, and a moment later, the warm chenille was brushed aside, allowing his hands to wander freely.

A tiny voice in Grace's head told her she should put an end to this headlong rush, before they both did something they'd regret. But the waves of sensation racing through her body had numbed her common sense so thoroughly she couldn't think…couldn't speak. All she could do was feel.

When he cupped her breast in his warm palm, Grace nearly fainted. It was so much, yet it wasn't enough. She wanted his hands all over her body, and without a layer of flannel between them. Arching against him, Grace ran her fingers through the hair at his nape, unwilling to break the contact with his mouth for fear of what might come out of her own.

She should say ''no'' or ''wait.'' All she could think to

say was "more" and "yes" and "don't stop." The porch light was on and she knew that anyone passing by would see them locked in an embrace, her robe pushed off her shoulders, his shirt caught around his elbows. But that made their encounter even more dangerous and thrilling.

When he finally drew back to look down into her eyes, his expression was serious. He braced his hands on either side of her head and pressed his forehead to hers. "What was that?" he asked, his quickened breath clouding around them in the cold.

"I—I don't know what came over me," Grace explained. "I just haven't— Well, it's been a long time."

Tuck smiled. "As an objective, experienced member of the male species, I'd have to say that you know how to kiss a man."

"So do you," Grace said, her eyes wide. "I—I mean, you know how to kiss. Not a man, but me. Or maybe other women. But not—" She bit her bottom lip to keep herself from babbling on any further.

He looked away, and for a moment, Grace thought she saw regret flash in his eyes. "Maybe we'd better stop this while we can," he murmured.

She nodded, a stab of disappointment stealing her breath, then swallowed hard. "That would probably be best." Though she heard the words coming out of her mouth, she didn't believe them. The best thing for Tuck to do right now was scoop her into his arms, carry her upstairs and ravish her.

He stepped away. "Come on," he said. "Let's go inside. I wouldn't want you to catch a cold."

"Oh, I'm fine." Grace readjusted her robe, tying a tight knot at her waist as if that would put an end to the encounter. "I think I'm just going to stay out here for a few minutes longer. I'd like to watch the snow."

He gave her a puzzled look, then nodded. "I'll see you in the morning."

"In the morning," Grace repeated, forcing a smile.

With that, he disappeared inside the house, pushing the front door shut behind him. Grace closed her eyes and slowly let out a long breath. A sudden chill raced through her, and for the first time, she noticed the cold. Rubbing her arms, she stared out across the front yard, her mind jumbled with thoughts.

She didn't regret what she'd done. After all, she'd had no choice. The impulse to kiss Tuck McCabe was too overwhelming to resist. And she'd made her point—that she desired him. And that she wanted more. But the next move was his. Grace drew a deep breath and turned to the door, confident that she was proceeding in the proper manner.

"Hey there, Grace!"

The voice echoed through the cold night and Grace spun around and squinted into the dark. She could barely make out a shadow on the other side of her front gate. Enos Harrington stood there, a leash clutched in his hand, his little beagle, Spot, relieving himself where Grace usually planted her petunias.

She waved, wondering how long he'd been standing there in the dark. "Hi, Enos," she called. Had he observed the whole sexy scene? Grace cursed softly. If he had, the entire town would know about it by lunchtime tomorrow. "It's snowing," she called, for lack of anything better to say.

"Yep," Enos said with a wave. "That'll make you happy." He continued on along the street, muttering to his little dog and poking at the slick sidewalk with his cane. When he disappeared into the darkness, Grace turned and walked back inside the house.

She softly closed the door behind her, then stood, listening to the silence. How was she supposed to sleep tonight, with Tuck McCabe right above her? How was she supposed to put all thoughts of what they'd shared out of her head? She'd probably lie awake all night long, wondering when he'd decide to kiss her again.

There was only one solution to her dilemma, short of walking up two flights of stairs and crawling into bed with him. "If he doesn't kiss me again, then I'll kiss him," Grace murmured to herself.

"THIS IS TOO DAMN EARLY to get up," Bryan muttered. He slouched down in the passenger seat of Tuck's pickup and crossed his arms over his chest, his breath clouding in the chill morning air.

Tuck scratched at the frost on the windshield, then turned up the defroster, which was still blowing cold air. "Watch your mouth," he said. "There'll be no cussin' in my presence. Or around my animals."

"You gonna tell me you don't swear?" Bryan challenged.

"Only when absolutely necessary," Tuck said.

Bryan shot him a sullen expression, then turned to watch the scenery pass by in the dark. Tuck hadn't expected sparkling conversation, but after yesterday, he thought Bryan might be a little more relaxed around him. There was no predicting the moods of a kid his age. Puberty turned even the nicest kids into churlish hoodlums. Who knew how bad he'd get once the hormones really got pumping?

"Roads are a little slippery this morning," Tuck said, determined to draw the boy into conversation, even if it was over the weather.

"Maybe that's because it snowed last night?"

"Good observation," Tuck countered. "You're a pretty sharp kid."

This time, Bryan's glare was one of annoyance. "Why do you have to feed your animals so early? It's not like they can tell time."

Tuck shrugged. "I suppose I could feed them later. But then, you wouldn't be able to come along and act like a spoiled baby. And we both know why your presence is required." They were driving by the village green and he peered into the darkness. A statue of a minuteman loomed in the center of the green, standing guard over the sleepy little village. "So who's the stiff with the musket?" he asked.

"What?"

Tuck cocked his head in the direction of the statue. "Who's the stiff?"

Bryan frowned, then couldn't help but smile at the joke. "Some Cooper. He was a hero in some war. I guess the town is named after him."

"Your history teacher would be so proud of that answer."

"Well, my friend Keegan Cooper is related to him. I know that much."

Tuck took a right and headed in the direction of the Rawlings farm. The truck skidded on a curve but he pulled it back on the road. "Yep, it sure did snow last night. Your mom was happy about that."

Bryan laughed derisively. "She gets all excited about some pretty dumb things."

"You could cut her some slack every now and then," Tuck suggested, trying to keep the impatience from his voice. "You're lucky to have a mom who cares about you."

"Yeah, real lucky."

"Better than having a drunk for a mother," he said.

The boy turned and stared at Tuck, his eyes wide. "Your mom was a drunk?"

"Most of the time. When she wasn't drunk, she was just mean. She didn't care much about what I did or didn't do."

"That must have been nice," Bryan commented. "Nobody on your back, bossing you around."

"Yeah, real nice," he said in a mocking tone. "Nobody who cared if I got in trouble, nobody who cared if I came home at night. Nobody who cared if I lived or died. Be careful what you wish for, Bryan. It's no fun to be all alone in the world."

A long silence grew between them and Tuck wondered if the conversation was over. He'd done his level best to forget his past, to put all those old wounds behind him. But maybe his experiences might mean something to Bryan. Tuck wasn't sure why he cared, but he did. He liked Grace Penrose. They'd become…friends. And friends helped each other out.

Tuck hadn't been friends with many women in his life. Ray's wife, Annmarie, was the only woman who came to mind. It didn't take a shrink to tell him why—all those issues of abandonment and self-loathing. He'd analyzed his past over and over again and had come to the conclusion that he was damaged goods. The wounds ran too deep to ever heal, so he'd just have to live with them.

He'd come to accept the man he was, a man who couldn't see more than a few years into the future, a man who avoided any truly meaningful commitments. Sure, there had been college and vet school, but that was different. He'd been anonymous on campus. People hadn't known anything about his past and he enjoyed that. As far as his buddies were concerned, he was just a normal guy. And when anyone got too close, Tuck made sure to draw away, before they learned too much.

"What about your dad?"

Startled out of his thoughts, Tuck glanced over at Bryan. "I never knew him. He wasn't a part of my mom's life," he said, hoping to put an end to the conversation.

"Like my dad."

"At least you know who he is," Tuck replied. "I don't even know my dad's name."

"That's about all I know," Bryan said, a cynical tone to his voice. "He calls sometimes, but he doesn't really care about us. My mom will never say a bad word about him, but Keegan told me that he was messing around with another woman while he was married to my mom. There was a lot of gossip around town. People still talk about how he was such a slimeball."

"And that pisses you off, doesn't it."

Bryan looked away, focusing his attention on the blackness outside the truck. "I don't care. I don't need him. I'm not like him and I never will be."

"Yeah? You could have fooled me. The way you've been acting toward your mom lately, I figured you'd grow up to be a jerk like your dad."

"He's not a jerk!" Bryan cried, turning on Tuck with an angry expression.

"Of course he isn't," Tuck said. "And I think you know that as well as I do. He's just a man. And men make mistakes just like kids do. And he made a pretty big mistake leaving a woman as nice as your mom."

Bryan watched him suspiciously. "You like her, don't you."

"She's nice," Tuck admitted. "It's hard not to like her."

"She's never going to get married again," Bryan warned. "She said so. Lots of times. And she promised me and Susan that she wouldn't."

"That's too bad. Because your mom deserves to be happy."

"She is happy. With us."

"What about when you grow up and get married? You might find a nice girl. Maybe like that Ashley girl you mentioned."

"I'm never getting married," Bryan insisted.

"That's what I used to say," Tuck told him. "All the time."

But he hadn't said it lately. In fact, he hadn't even thought it since the moment he'd met Grace Penrose. She'd made him believe that the possibility wasn't completely unimaginable, even for a man like him.

Still, a committed relationship to a woman was a long way off. First, he'd have to find the right candidate—someone who was willing to live on a remote ranch in Montana, who would accept the life he'd decided to lead there. Then he'd have to convince her to accept his need for solitude, to understand that there would be times when he'd just have to escape for a while. And as far as children were concerned, that was one issue he'd refuse to consider. He didn't have it in his genes to be any child's parent.

Tuck couldn't deny that he'd worried about the legacy his parents had left him. Maybe that's why he fit in at the ranch so well. Those boys stayed for a while, then left to begin their own lives. And when they did, Tuck's responsibility was over.

Though he wasn't certain he'd ever find a woman to fit his requirements, he knew that Grace would find a man sooner or later—regardless of Bryan's claims. He'd never met a woman more in need of a man than Grace Penrose. Never mind that her house was falling to ruin around her. Or that when she kissed him, he tasted her need, felt it in the way her body molded to his, the way her hands fluttered over his skin. No doubt about it, she needed a man.

Just not him. Had she been any other woman, he might have taken advantage of the situation. But Grace was different. A guy could lose himself in those eyes, in that face, in the feel of her body against his. He could forget everything he knew to be true. She was the kind of woman who could break a guy's heart long before he had a chance to break hers.

Besides, with Grace came her two children. And though Tuck might want her beautiful body in his bed, he wasn't ready for a wife, much less a ready-made family. For the next couple weeks, he'd do what he could for Grace and for her children. He'd help Bryan find his way as best as he could. And then he'd go back to Montana and live the life that he'd always planned to live—alone.

He swung the truck into the driveway of Silas Rawlings's farm and turned off the ignition. Tuck glanced over at Bryan. "You ready for some hard work?"

Bryan groaned, then pushed the door open.

"Hard work," Tuck said as the kid slammed the door. "That will make you forget all your problems."

THE LOW WINTER SUN FILTERED through the dust-covered windows of the coach house. Grace shoved the door all the way open to let in the maximum amount of light. As she and Tuck stepped inside, dust motes swirled in the air. The coach house hadn't been opened since last winter, yet the hulking shapes of the sleighs, covered by tattered canvases, looked as familiar as if she'd seen them just yesterday.

"I can't believe it's been a whole year since I've been in here."

Tuck slowly examined his surroundings, from the old harnesses hanging from the rafters to the coach lanterns dangling from hooks on the wall. "It's like going back in time."

Grace felt the same way every time she stepped inside. "My great-grandfather used to love his horses. At least that's what my grandmother used to tell me. He hated the automobile. Horses were more noble. Even after autos were all over the road, he insisted on driving out from Boston for the summer with his finest team and newest carriage. The trip took much longer, but that's the way he preferred to travel. In a civilized fashion."

She reached for the corner of a canvas and slowly pulled it off, kicking up a plume of dust as the canvas dropped to the brick floor. The cutter was dusty and rust tinged its steel runners, but the leather upholstery shone softly in the light from the door. "I really should do more to preserve these," Grace murmured.

"Yes, you should," Tuck said. He reached inside the boot and pulled out a tangle of harnesses and reins.

"It's kind of low on the list of priorities," she told him. "Harness oiling comes right after silver polishing and dusting the dining room chandelier."

"These cutters are beautiful," Tuck said as Grace pulled the canvas from the second sleigh.

"You should see the carriages in the back." Her voice caught in her throat and she realized how nervous she really was. Like a silly schoolgirl, she was almost afraid to be alone with Tuck McCabe. Afraid of what ridiculous impulse might overcome her. Who knew when she might feel compelled to throw her arms around his neck and kiss him again?

"I'll take a look at them later," he said, smoothing his hands along the arm of the front seat. "I'm going to need some oil for this tack. And do you have tools to do repairs?"

"I think there are tools in the back. Silas always took care of seeing to the tack. I don't know much about it."

"Bryan can help me out," Tuck said. "It'll keep him out of trouble."

"Did you have a chance to talk to him? About what we talked about?"

"Sex?" Tuck asked offhandedly.

It wasn't necessary for him to say the word out loud. It sounded so…provocative, coming from his lips. And it certainly didn't make her think about the birds and the bees. Instead she thought about naked bodies, tangled sheets, soft, low moans and exquisite waves of plea— Grace cursed silently. "Yes, sex," she snapped. She turned away from him and rummaged in the back of the sleigh for the thick lap robes, which would need to be aired out.

"We had a nice little talk. I cleared up a lot of confusion on a few issues. He had some pretty bizarre ideas about where babies come from. But once we got that straight, he was fine with it."

"Good," Grace said. She drew a shaky breath. "Thanks. I appreciate your help in this. Maybe I'll have my talk with him this evening."

Tuck shook the tangles out of a pair of worn leather traces. "We also talked about you. And his dad. He told me what happened."

Grace blinked in surprise. Her son barely gave her the time of day. Now he was talking to a complete stranger about his parents' problems. "The divorce?"

"The affair."

She gasped. "He knows about the nuts-and-bolts girl? But how could he? I've never said anything about—"

"This is a small town," Tuck said. "People talk."

"I know they talk," she said, pacing to the door and back again. "Believe me, my ears were burning for three years after my husband walked out.'' Grace shook her head, then sighed. ''What else did Bryan say?''

''That he's never going to get married.''

Grace bit at her bottom lip, a surge of emotion almost choking off her voice. ''I didn't want this to happen. I've tried to show him that not all marriages end up like his parents' did. But I've probably scarred him for life.''

''You didn't do anything,'' Tuck said. ''It wasn't your fault.''

''I could have done something,'' Grace countered, leaning against the cutter. ''There must have been something that girl had that I didn't. If I knew what it was, maybe I could have changed.''

Tuck reached out and took her hand, forcing her to stand squarely in front of him. ''It doesn't work that way, Grace. A man who'd cheat on his wife doesn't cheat because of something lacking in his wife. He cheats because of something lacking in himself.''

Grace smiled tremulously. ''I try to tell myself that. But I still feel like a failure.''

''Well, don't. Any man who would walk away from you has got to be a first-class fool.''

''Really?''

''Really.'' Tuck gave her hand a squeeze.

Grace took a shaky breath and nodded. Then, without a single thought, she threw her arms around Tuck's neck and hugged him fiercely. When she drew back, his gaze caught hers, but this time she fought the impulse to kiss him. A warm blush crept up her cheeks. ''I should really stop doing that,'' she said with a soft laugh.

Tuck bent and touched his forehead to hers, then drew away. ''You probably should.'' He paused and frowned.

''Why?'' she asked.

''Because,'' Tuck replied.

"That's not a reason," she chided lightly. "Even though my children use it all the time."

"It's the only reason I can give you."

His expression suddenly turned serious, as if he really needed to hear a convincing argument *against* kissing her. What was this game he was playing? What she thought was teasing wasn't that at all. Grace cleared her throat and tried to sound nonchalant. "Well I can give you a reason why I shouldn't. Because you're only going to be here until Christmas. Because I'm afraid of liking you too much. Because my kids are the most important thing in my life."

Tuck stepped back, giving her shoulders a soft squeeze. "Three reasons," he said, nodding.

"I—I'm sorry." Grace drew a shaky breath. She'd made a fool of herself, but maybe he hadn't noticed yet. If she played it cool, she might be able to escape with her dignity. "It's just so easy to depend on you. Maybe because you're so dependable. And I don't want to put either of us in that position."

"What position is that?"

"Where I'm standing at the front door watching you drive away forever. I can't go through that again. You're right, we should try to keep things strictly…platonic."

Tuck drew a deep breath, then let it out slowly. "Right. Platonic." He caught her gaze. "I just have one thing to say and then we'll leave it at that. Besides being a first-class fool, your ex was a jackass, too." He smoothed his palm over her cheek. "He made you feel this way. Scared and uncertain. You're a beautiful woman, Grace, and you should have a good man to love you. Maybe I can't be that man, but don't close yourself off to the possibility that there's someone out there for you."

Grace nodded. "I won't. Now, maybe we should concentrate on the job at hand. I'm going to go in the back and see if I can find some oil for those harnesses."

She was glad for the chance to escape. When she reached the rear of the coach house, she closed the door behind her, then leaned back against it. How had this happened? All she'd wanted was four horses to pull her sleighs for the festival. And instead, she'd managed to get a sexy cowboy along with the deal. None of this would have happened if Silas Rawlings hadn't preferred the climate in Louisiana. Or if Maureen Cooper had had an extra room at the B and B. Or if she hadn't kissed him that first time in front of the refrigerator.

Now that it *had* happened, Grace wasn't really sure she wanted these crazy feelings to stop. A more sophisticated, worldly woman would be able to handle this, to brush Tuck off as if he didn't matter at all. But she was Grace Penrose. Good old dependable Grace. Quiet, conservative Grace. Grace who hadn't had much experience with men.

Forgetting what she'd shared with Tuck, no matter how brief or insignificant, would be impossible as long as he lived in her house. But she couldn't get him out of her house without losing his horses for the festival.

"Well, Gracie, it seems you're stuck between a rock and a hard...muscular...cowboy," she muttered. "And now you're going to have to find a way out."

CHAPTER FIVE

"WHAT DO YOU MEAN you need four dozen Christmas cookies by tomorrow morning?" Grace glared at her son, her fists hitched on her hips, her eyes crackling with anger.

Tuck leaned against the kitchen counter and sipped at a steaming mug of coffee, watching the disaster unfold in front of him. Grace had been on edge all day long. Though the snow had been falling at a furious pace since last night, the bad weather didn't seem to brighten her spirits. He suspected their discussion in the coach house was the source of her upset, but he had no proof.

On the surface, she had moved from worrying about the weather to obsessing over the play that she was staging for the festival. Something about a change in the cast and the programs already at the printers. When he'd suggested she call the printer and explain her dilemma, he got a look that could suck the masculinity out of Arnold Schwarzenegger.

Though Tuck hadn't lived in the Penrose house for long, he'd learned one lesson—when to avoid Grace. When all her attention was focused on the festival, she got just a little bit crazy.

"How am I supposed to make four dozen cookies?" Grace demanded. "I've got play rehearsal in an hour, I haven't started dinner yet, and I have three pages of lighting instructions to type for the scenes we're rehearsing tonight!" She pressed the heels of her hands to her temples. "Why would you do this to me?"

"I gave you the note two weeks ago," Bryan said. He shoved back from the table, where he'd been doing his homework, and strode to the refrigerator, then snatched a bright red flyer from beneath a ladybug magnet. "See? Soccer Team Cookie Exchange. Saturday morning. Four dozen cookies. Proceeds to benefit the Uniform Fund."

Grace grabbed the paper from Bryan's fingers and stared at it in silence. At first, Tuck thought she was planning to continue her tirade. Then her lower lip began to tremble and her eyes grew moist with tears. He decided it was time to step into the fray.

"Bryan, go get changed. We need to see to the animals. And we're going to take Susan with us, so make sure she's dressed warm." Bryan opened his mouth to protest, but Tuck held out his hand in silent warning. "Just go." Grumbling, Bryan grabbed his sister's hand and pulled her out of the kitchen, leaving Tuck to deal with his mother's slowly crumbling emotions.

When they were the only two left in the room, Grace slowly sat down at the table and buried her face in her hands. "I'm a horrible mother," she said in a tiny voice.

"You are not."

She pulled her hands away, then stood up. In a long, silent moment, she attempted to regain control of her emotions. "I *am*. I'm neglecting my children and my responsibilities at their school. I almost accused my son of lying to me. And if this festival isn't a complete disaster, it's not for lack of me trying." A tear dribbled down her cheek and she angrily brushed it away. "I—I'm so tired, I can barely stand. I've got forty-eight hours of work to do in the next eight hours. My children are going to need therapy and it's all my fault."

Tuck stepped over to the table, then turned her to face him. "You're not a horrible mother." Her lip began to tremble again and he did the only thing he could do—beyond stilling it with a long, deep, hot kiss. He gathered her in his arms and gave her a hug. "You're just a little busy right now. And a little disorganized."

Grace nuzzled her face into his chest and sobbed. "Don't tell anyone. Everybody in town thinks I know what I'm doing. If they find out I'm faking it, they'll fire me."

"They won't," Tuck said, smoothing her hair and inhaling the sweet scent. He'd never seen Grace quite so vulnerable. She'd managed to convince him that she could do anything she set her mind to, that she was tough and resilient, that she didn't need anyone, especially not him. He'd never guessed that she didn't believe it herself. "Why don't you go finish your work? I'm going to take the kids over to the Rawlings place and we'll feed the animals. Then I'll get them supper and we'll spend the evening baking cookies."

A tiny giggle slipped from her. "You? Bake cookies?"

He scoffed at her dubious expression. "I'm an intelligent man with a postgraduate degree. I can read a recipe. I'm sure I can get the job done."

Grace wiped her watery eyes as she looked up at him. "No," she said. "I can't ask you to do that. I'll bake the cookies when I get home. It's only four dozen. That will only take a few hours."

Tuck shrugged. "All right. But I'm still going to take the kids over to the farm."

She pushed up on her toes and gave him a quick kiss on the cheek and a grateful smile. "Thank you." With that, she turned and hurried out of the kitchen. Tuck had to fight the impulse to go after her, to grab her hand and draw her back into his arms. He hadn't kissed her in nearly two whole days, although he'd been thinking about nothing else. Reaching up, he touched the place that she'd kissed, finding it still damp from her lips.

He groaned, then cursed softly. She was just a woman. He'd done without women before—and for a lot longer than two days. Tuck had always been a pretty determined guy. When he decided to do something, there was no stopping him. But this attempt to maintain a distance between him and Grace was different. He couldn't convince himself that friendship was really what he wanted—or what she wanted.

"Cookies," he muttered. "Right now you have to bake Christmas cookies. You can think about kissing Grace later." He glanced around, wondering if he'd bitten off a bit more than he could chew. Though he was a damn good campfire cook, he'd never baked a cookie in his life. As far as he was concerned, a man only needed one kind of cookie—Oreos—and they came out of a package from the supermarket.

He searched the kitchen for a cookbook and was frustrated at every turn. Then he realized that nothing was where it was supposed to be in Grace's house. "Where's the last place I'd look for a cookbook?" he muttered. "That's probably where it would be. The bathroom?" That's where they kept the reading material at the ranch.

"Mommy keeps her cookbooks in her bedroom," Susan said.

Tuck turned to find the little girl standing in the doorway, bundled in her coat, one mitten off and one on, her scarf dragging behind her. "In her bedroom?"

"I think she reads them at night to help her sleep," she said. "Sometimes she uses them to keep the windows open in the summer."

For a brief moment, Tuck considered fetching the cookbooks himself. But venturing into Grace's bedroom would be tempting fate, especially when she was still home. If he found her there, he wasn't sure what might happen.

"All right, Susie Q," he said. "I want you to run upstairs and bring me one that has pictures of cookies in it. But don't let your mother see. We'll take it along when we go to the grocery store."

"We're making cookies?" Susan asked.

"We are. For Bryan's cookie exchange." He paused. "But it's a surprise for your mom. Have you ever made cookies before?"

She nodded and grinned. "Me and my friend Martha make cookies all the time."

"Good. Maybe this won't be a complete disaster. What kind?"

"Mud," she said. "Sometimes sand, but they aren't as good. Mud with grass is really good. And then we put gravel stones in them for chocolate chips."

Tuck chuckled, his hopes for perfect cookies quickly dashed. "I can see you're going to be a big help. Go get that cookbook and tell your brother to shake a leg."

Susan did as she was told, giving him a sweet smile before she scampered off. Tuck shook his head. Maybe this was the kind of thing that a father would do, but so what? Just because he was willing to bake a few cookies didn't make him a perfect candidate. He bent down and looked inside the oven, only to find a can of peaches and one of Susan's Barbie dolls. Fatherhood was more than changing diapers and coaching Little League and finding stray peaches. Those were the easy parts.

The hard part was knowing that he'd be there for the long haul. Knowing that no matter what problems came up, he wouldn't be scared away. How could he love a family if he wasn't even sure he could love a woman? And even if he did love someone like Grace, how could he be sure it would last?

FAT SNOWFLAKES DRIFTED DOWN through the still December night, falling silently onto the sidewalk at Grace's feet. She hurried along, worried that she'd be late for play rehearsal. The old church in Cooper's Corner was lit up like a beacon in the storm. Floodlights bathed the front facade in a soft glow all the way up to the top of the steeple.

The church dated from the previous century and was built with the same solid New England craftsmanship and simplicity that marked many of the other old buildings in town. White clapboards and pointed gothic-style stained-glass windows gave it the look of a pretty picture postcard.

Inside, the old-fashioned lighting and hand-hewn pews were enough to make a visitor feel as if they'd stepped back in time. It was the perfect place to stage the first production of *The Christmas Wish,* an original play by one of Cooper's Corner's most illustrious residents.

Rowena Dahl, the town barber, had written the play especially for the festival. She was the only resident who had actual show business experience. She'd once been a famous soap opera star in New York. Grace had been thrilled when she volunteered her services as playwright, and ecstatic when she saw the first draft of the play. It was a retelling of the classic O. Henry tale, set in western Massachusetts during the American Revolution. Rowena also agreed to star in the play, portraying a woman living in the wilderness of the Berkshires, raising her children while her husband was away fighting the war.

The play was funny and tender and sad, and every time they rehearsed the last scene, tears swam in Grace's eyes. The performance would be the highlight of the festival, and with an increase in last year's ticket prices, Grace was sure there would be more profits to present to the village board.

She pulled open the front door of the church and stepped inside, brushing the snowflakes from her hair and shoulders. The vestibule was empty and Grace checked her watch, wondering if she could possibly be running early. Then she shrugged out of her coat, tossed her scarf and gloves aside and stepped through the doors leading to the sanctuary of the church.

The lights were turned down low and she found Rowena sitting in a pew in the very last row. She was still as glamorous as she was when she starred on television, her long blond hair perfectly styled, her makeup flawlessly applied.

Grace hurried over to the pew and slipped in beside her. "Sorry I'm late."

Rowena turned and smiled warmly. "Hi, Grace. Still snowing outside?"

Grace nodded. "Where is everyone?"

"Burt Tubb and Philo Cooper are in the fellowship hall, working on the scenery with Father Tom. Howard and Gina took the kids to the Sunday school room to run through their lines. And I'm just sitting here trying to finish my Christmas lists. I haven't even started shopping yet. Do you know if I can buy Godiva chocolates anywhere in the county?"

Grace shook her head. "Did Maureen call you about Daryl?" she asked.

"He's spending Christmas in the Caymans."

"I don't know how he could agree to play the husband and then just change his mind. It's so—so unprofessional!"

Rowena turned to Grace, surprised by her outburst. Then the absurdity of Grace's words hit them both and they began to laugh. "I guess Daryl hasn't read the Actor's Guild handbook," Rowena cried. "Maybe if we were paying scale he might have stayed. Still, the show must go on, even if one of the stars is lying on a beach in the Caribbean, working on his tan.''

Just then, the doors burst open and Maureen Cooper walked in, covered with snow, her scarf wrapped around her face and a baseball cap pulled low over her eyes. She yanked off the scarf to reveal a wide smile. ''I've solved all our problems!'' she said. ''I've found a new Benjamin. And he's absolutely perfect for the role and I've already altered the costume.''

''Who?'' Grace and Rowena said in tandem.

Maureen's grin widened even further. ''My brother. Clint has agreed to play the part. I told him there weren't very many lines to learn and he'd just have to come in during the last scene. I also told him we were desperate and we didn't have anyone else to turn to. And I appealed to his aesthetic nature. In other words, I gave him no choice. He either played the part or I wasn't going to approve the kitchen renovation he has planned for the B and B.''

''I'm going to kiss Clint in the last scene?'' Rowena asked.

''Well, yeah,'' Maureen said. ''That's the way you wrote the play. And I told him he had to kiss you. He was a little concerned about that, but I think it'll be all right.''

Rowena groaned. ''This is great. The only way I can get a handsome man to kiss me anymore is to write it into a script. And then no one wants to play the part! I'm a pitiful shadow of my former self.''

''It's not just you,'' Maureen said, patting Rowena on the shoulder. ''I haven't had a date since—well, since I can't remember when.''

''Cooper's Corner has never had an overabundance of eligible single men,'' Grace added. ''There's just Clint.''

"And Alex McAlester, the veterinarian," Maureen said. "He's pretty cute."

Rowena nodded. "And Seth Castleman."

The trio sat silently for a long moment, then shared a joint sigh. "There are probably plenty of handsome single men in Cooper's Corner," Rowena said. "But they've been ignoring us."

"Grace! You're here."

The trio looked up to see the minister of the church, Tom Christen, striding down the aisle. He wore a denim shirt and faded jeans, no clerical collar in sight. His blond hair was rumpled, as if he'd combed it with his fingers, and his pale blue eyes sparkled with good humor.

"I'm sorry," Grace said. "I've been running late all day. I've got the lighting instructions right here." She pulled a sheaf of papers from her folder and handed them to Tom.

"I have the stage ready," he said as he scanned the notes. "Some of the men in the congregation volunteered to help me this afternoon. I have to tell you, a few of my more conservative board members aren't happy that we're putting on a secular play instead of the usual sacred program in the church."

A surge of concern brought a frown to Grace's face. "There isn't a problem, is there?"

Tom shook his head. "No problem. They've been out-voted. Besides, we need to shake things up a bit this year. If we want to draw a big audience, we have to offer something for everyone, don't you agree?"

"I do," Grace said.

"Good. Now, I'm going to go get the sound system ready. We should be able to start in about ten minutes." He winked at Rowena. "By then, the Winicks should have your children whipped into shape."

Tom disappeared through the sanctuary doors and Grace

heard his footsteps as he climbed the narrow stairway to the organ loft.

"He's single," Rowena whispered. "And he's a hottie."

"Gorgeous," Maureen agreed.

"Shhh! He'll hear you," Grace said.

"Just because he's a minister doesn't automatically make him omniscient," Maureen said.

"I suspect he's hiding a passionate streak behind that cool exterior," Rowena added. "I'd love to be there when he lets loose in bed."

"Stop!" Grace said, laughing. "I'm not going to be able to look at him without thinking of him naked. Isn't that sacrilegious?"

"Curiosity isn't a sin," Maureen said. "Just an interesting way to pass the time. Besides, I heard that Father Tom got sent here because he liked to rock the boat at the home office."

Rowena nodded. "I certainly held out a little hope when I heard that. Any new single man in town is worth a look. Not that Father Ude wasn't a catch, but he was ninety-six years old. The last time he let loose was during the Roaring Twenties."

"You two are terrible!" Grace objected.

"Well, if you don't want us to talk about Tom Christen," Maureen said, "then let's talk about another gorgeous single man."

"Fine," Grace said.

"That hunky cowboy you have living at your house," Maureen elaborated. "Now, there's a man who wears his sex appeal on the outside. How is everything going?"

Grace had done her best to put Tuck out of her mind. But now that Maureen had mentioned his name, all her good intentions dissolved immediately. "Fine," she repeated in a tone that she hoped would put an end to the conversation before it began. "He's very…nice."

"Nice?" Rowena laughed. "When Philo told me you had a cowboy from Montana living in your house, I actually decided to start listening to the gossip at the barber shop."

"And I heard Enos Harrington talking at the diner yesterday," Maureen added. "He was saying how he thought he'd seen you kissing a man on your porch in the middle of a snowstorm. But then he blinked and you were there alone in your bathrobe. Dr. Dorn told him he needed to get his eyes checked."

"Is *everyone* talking about me?"

"Pretty much," Maureen replied. "You're the most interesting topic since Bonnie Cooper's wedding."

"Well, there's nothing to talk about," Grace said. "Absolutely nothing has happened." The lie was necessary, but she wished she hadn't had to tell it. She wanted to talk to someone about Tuck, to describe how her pulse raced when he touched her and how her mind spun when he kissed her.

"Since Maureen and I are going to have to live vicariously through you, then I guess we're going to have to do something about that," Rowena teased.

"I don't need any help. I'm not looking for a romance right now."

Maureen sighed. "Gracie, be practical. We're three single women living in Cooper's Corner. When one of us has a chance to have a torrid love affair with an attractive single man, we owe it to the others to take advantage of that chance. How do you know when the next eligible guy is going to come along? And how do you know this isn't the man for you?"

Grace gazed down at her hands, folded in her lap. Everything that Maureen had said was true. But how did one go about having an affair? She'd only loved one man in her life and that had turned into a disaster. She didn't want to think about what would happen if she allowed herself to love another.

"You should understand how it is, Maureen. Having kids and trying to have a life? When I get involved with a man, so do they. If it was only me taking the risk, it would be all right, but it's Bryan and Susan, too."

"We're talking about a little romance, not a lifelong commitment," Rowena said.

"And everyone in town is already talking," Maureen reasoned. "Maybe you should give them something real to talk about."

A slow smile curved Grace's lips. That's exactly what she'd love to do—banish her prissy reputation and give the gossips something to whisper about. Toss aside common sense and fall into Tuck McCabe's arms. "Maybe I will," she murmured, sending Rowena and Maureen a sideways glance. "I could use a little adventure in my life."

"You will?" Rowena asked, startled.

"Maybe. Or maybe not." Grace shrugged. "But if I do, I promise you two will be the first to get all the details." She stood up and smoothed her sweater over her hips. "It looks like Tom is ready. Let's get to work."

As she walked down the aisle, Grace's grin grew wider. Maybe it wasn't proper to think about things like sex and seduction in church. But she'd made a decision and she wasn't ashamed of it. If the opportunity presented itself, especially in the form of a sexy cowboy, she was going to take advantage. And if it didn't, then she'd have to figure out a way to make it happen.

GRACE DIDN'T HAVE MUCH TIME to think about adventure that evening, though thoughts of Tuck were never far from her mind. Images of him flitted through her head at the oddest times and she found herself anxious to finish rehearsal, get back home and put her plan into action.

"All right, everyone," she called. "We're through for the night. Very nice work and I'll see some of you tomorrow night."

Rowena stood on the makeshift stage, wearing a long apron and holding an old broom. "But we still have ten minutes," she said. "You never let us—" She paused and then smiled, as if she knew exactly what was on Grace's mind.

As everyone gathered their things and prepared to leave, Grace tipped her head from side to side, trying to stretch a kink out of her neck. Overall, rehearsal hadn't gone too badly. The lighting looked good, the scenery was coming along, and surprisingly, the actors knew all of their lines by heart. There were no major disasters looming on the horizon, so for the first time in a long time, she felt as if she might get some sleep that night.

"Rowena and I will go over everything with Clint," Maureen said as she pulled on her coat. "We can run through the last scene at the next rehearsal. And I should have all the costumes by then. Mrs. Wilson is finishing up the last of the kids' wardrobe, and Mrs. Theobald has to fit Rowena's costume tomorrow morning. She's also mended all the moth holes on the elf costumes for the parade."

"And if Clint has any problems with any of the—you know, lines," Rowena said, "I can just do a little rewriting."

Grace hid a smile, amused that Rowena seemed to be so nervous about kissing Clint Cooper. "Good. And thank you both. This is going to be the best part of the festival. I'm not sure how we're going to top ourselves next year."

They all walked to the front doors of the church. A swirl of snow blew in as they pushed them open, and for a moment Grace couldn't see. But then a little girl materialized out of the snow—a girl with her daughter's voice and her bright pink snowsuit.

"Mommy!"

Susan ran up the front steps of the church. She grabbed Grace's hand and pulled her toward the street.

"What are you doing here?" Grace asked, brushing snow from her daughter's hair and jacket and attempting to retie her hood.

"Tuck brought us. It's a surprise." She tugged on Grace's hand a little harder. "Come on. It's a surprise."

"What's a surprise?"

Just then the snow cleared for a moment and, as if by magic, a horse-drawn sleigh appeared in the winter landscape. It almost didn't look real, more like an object in a pretty snow globe. But then Tuck waved at her from behind the reins and she hesitantly waved back.

"Oh, my God," Maureen murmured. "Have you ever seen anything so romantic?"

"He's gorgeous," Rowena added, rubbing her arms.

Grace slowly walked down the steps, her gaze fixed on Tuck's. He *was* gorgeous, his hair windblown, his face ruddy from the cold. She shivered, but she wasn't cold. The moment she saw him, her blood had warmed and her pulse had begun to race. People gathered around the sleigh and Grace was surprised to see Bryan standing in front of the horses, his hand tight on the halter. He looked a bit uneasy, yet seemed to be focused on the important job Tuck had given him.

"Do you like our surprise, Mommy?"

Grace smiled down at her daughter. "Of course I do. What better way to get home in a snowstorm? I thought I'd have to walk!"

"There's a surprise at home, too." Susan glanced at

Tuck and leaned closer to her mother and mouthed the word "cookies" before she scampered into the sleigh.

Tuck jumped out, and when Grace reached his side, he grabbed her around the waist and easily swung her up into the sleigh. Grace's hands rested on his shoulders and she looked down at him, wondering how she ever thought she'd be able to resist him. The moment she touched him, every ounce of resolve seemed to disappear.

He made her feel pretty and desirable, things she hadn't felt in a long time. And when he looked at her, he saw only her. He barely even gave Maureen and Rowena a second look, even when they'd joined the crowd standing around her great-grandfather's cutter.

She sat down and slid over, pulling the old lap robe around her legs. Then Tuck settled himself beside her. "Ready?" he asked. When Grace nodded, he called to Bryan and her son let go of the horses and joined his sister in the back seat.

After a cluck of his tongue and a soft slap of the reins, the horses jumped into motion, easily pulling the sleigh across the snow. The snow was falling so hard that the old carriage lights did little to show the way. The streetlamps glowed like silver moons and they followed them, one after the other, until they reached the edge of town. Then Tuck slowed the horses to a walk as they turned into the driveway of Grace's house.

Somehow, the space between them on the seat had vanished and she was now leaning into his body. Grace knew it wasn't simply to keep warm. Whenever he was close, she couldn't quell the urge to touch him. It had been ages since she'd taken any pleasure in a man's body, and Tuck had a wonderful body, so solid and masculine.

Grace bit back a smile at the direction her thoughts were taking. She'd never been a very sexual person. When it came to those matters, she'd always been so nervous worrying about what she was doing that she couldn't appreciate the other half of the equation. Her ex had made her feel as if her inexperience hindered their intimacy. He wanted her to be something—or someone—else.

But Tuck liked her exactly the way she was. He teased her out of her bad moods and laughed at her attempts at humor and told her she was pretty when she knew she looked like a wreck. Grace knew, in her heart, that if they ever found themselves in the same bed together, he'd be an incredible lover.

So why not take the risk? Cast aside her apprehension and throw caution to the wind. If she felt herself getting in too deep, she could always put a stop to it, couldn't she? She wouldn't risk her heart unless she allowed herself to fall in love.

"This is nice," Tuck murmured, the lights of town fading behind them as her front porch light glowed through the swirl of snow. He pulled the reins to the right and the horses smartly made the wide curve in the driveway, the jingle bells echoing in the crisp night air. "Makes me glad I bought harness-broke horses. I think I'm going to have to find myself a sleigh for our Montana winters."

Grace forced a smile and looked away, certain her expression telegraphed her feelings. Just the mention of Montana was enough to darken her good mood and cause a sharp ache in the vicinity of her heart. Why did she insist on ignoring the fact that he had a life—on a ranch half a country away? If she was going to do this, she'd have to come to grips with the fact that the affair would be temporary.

"It is nice," she said.

When they reached the house, Tuck pulled the horses to a stop. They huffed and snorted, their warm breath clouding around their heads. Bryan hopped out of the sleigh and hurried to take his place, as he had outside the church. Tuck nodded at him with approval and Grace saw a slight smile twitch at her son's lips.

Once Tuck had helped both Susan and Grace out of the sleigh, he tied off the reins and motioned for Bryan to join him. They shared a few words next to the sleigh and a wide smile broke across Bryan's expression. He nodded, then raced up to Grace and Susan.

"Tuck says I can drive the sleigh back to the Rawlings place," he said, barely able to contain his excitement.

"Alone?" Grace asked.

"I'm going with him," Tuck said, coming up behind Grace. "Don't worry, he'll be all right. I think he has a bit of his great-grandfather in him."

Tuck's hand rested in the small of Grace's back as they walked up the front steps. He stepped around her to open the front door, and when she walked inside, the smell of fresh baking filled the air. Susan grabbed her hand and dragged her back toward the kitchen, then pointed to the counters.

"Look, Mommy. Cookies!"

Grace didn't have to feign a look of surprise or amazement. The counters were lined with pretty little thumbprint cookies, covered with toasted coconut and filled with red jam. "Wow. Look at this." She glanced over at Bryan, who hung in the shadows. He shrugged and sent his mother a reluctant smile. She hadn't seen him smile this much in months.

Susan dragged a kitchen chair over to the counter and crawled up on it to get a better view. "We all mixed the dough and then Bryan rolled them in slimy eggs and that white stuff, and I squished them with the end of this thing and Tuck stuck the jelly in the middle and then we put them in the oven and then they were done." She grabbed one and held it out to Grace. "Here. Taste it."

Tuck grabbed Susan by the waist and swung her back down to the floor. "Let your mom take her coat off and relax. She's had a long day."

"We've all had a long day," Grace said, glancing up at the clock. "Susie, why don't you and Bryan take some cookies and milk into the library."

Susan grabbed a handful of cookies and put them in a bowl while Bryan filled two glasses with milk. Bryan did as he was told and Susan ran after him, but at the last minute, she stopped, turned around and ran back to Tuck.

"I had a really good time tonight," she said, holding her arms out to him.

Tuck glanced over at Grace, as if to ask for approval. Grace gave him a quick nod and he bent down and drew Susan into his arms. "I had a very nice time, too. Thanks for helping me with the cookies."

She kissed him on the cheek. "And thanks for taking me in the sleigh."

A few moments later, she was gone. Grace drew a slow breath. "She's completely in love with you."

"The feeling is mutual," Tuck said.

Grace glanced around the kitchen. "I don't know what to say. Thank you for taking care of them tonight. And for the cookies and the sleigh ride and—" She felt a blush creep up her cheeks. "I seem to be thanking you a lot lately."

"You could always try Susan's approach," Tuck murmured.

Grace's breath caught in her throat the moment his meaning sunk in. But her mind spun with confusion. She knew he had to return to Montana, yet she didn't want that to make a difference. She wanted to step into his arms, turn her face up to his and lose herself in a long, deep kiss. After all, when would she have another chance like this?

But now that she'd decided to move forward with Tuck, she felt frozen in place, overwhelmed by insecurities and doubts. It sounded so easy, but would it be? Would she be able to make love to him and then forget him and go on with her life? Somehow, Grace didn't believe that would be possible. A woman just didn't forget a man like Tuck McCabe.

She opened her mouth, hoping that something would come to her before she had to close it again, something clever and funny. "I—I—well, these cookies are very…nice." She turned to the counter, hoping to hide the embarrassment that she was sure was evident on her face. He had to know what she was thinking. He must know what she had planned. With her fingertip, she distractedly pushed the cookies into neat little rows.

After an excruciatingly long silence, Tuck finally spoke. "I have to go. I've got to get the horses back to the barn."

"Right," Grace said, glancing over her shoulder, her courage slowly dissolving. "And I should really get Susan to bed. And then get to bed myself. After all, it's been a long—" She paused, swallowing hard, then slowly turned back to him. "Unless you want me to wait up for you."

"No," Tuck said. "Not if you're tired."

"I'm not that tired. So I could—I mean, if—"

Tuck's jaw went tight and he cursed softly. "Aw, hell. This is ridiculous." He crossed the kitchen in three long strides, grabbed her around the waist and yanked her against him. Before she could even draw a breath, he brought his mouth down on hers and kissed her, deeply and thoroughly. The taste of him was like fine brandy, setting her blood on fire and making her limbs go limp.

He kissed her for a long time, so long that Grace began

to wonder if he'd ever stop. Then he drew back, his gaze skimming her face and coming to rest on her mouth. "There. That's better."

"Better?"

"All the dancing around we've been doing. From now on, when I want to kiss you, I'm going to damn well do it. And if you don't like it, then just stay out of my way."

"But—but this is my house," Grace said. "I live here."

"And until Christmas, so do I," Tuck said with a tight smile. "Besides, it's a big house. I guess you'll have to learn to move fast." He set her away from him, then his eyes raked the length of her body and back again. "And don't wear that sweater again. It makes me crazy."

Grace stared down at the sweater she'd chosen, smoothing her hands over the front. "You don't like my sweater?"

"I like the sweater. And the body in it. But if you don't want me touching that body, then don't wear the sweater." He stalked across the kitchen and into the dining room. "Bryan!" he called. "Let's go!"

The front door slammed once, then again a few minutes later. Grace stood silently for a long time before she remembered to breathe. Then she gulped in a breath and pressed her hand to her chest. Glancing down at the sweater she wore, she smoothed her hand along the front. A giggle slipped from her lips. "He likes my sweater," she murmured. "I guess that's a start."

A start. That's all she needed. That and a closetful of tight sweaters.

CHAPTER SIX

TUCK WANDERED DOWN the stairs, raking his hands through his rumpled hair. Saturday morning meant no school for the kids, so rather than force Bryan out of bed at daybreak, he decided to cut the kid a little slack. After the strides he'd made the night before, he didn't want to push his luck.

Bryan had been so excited to drive the sleigh, so proud of himself when they reached the Rawlings place. He'd helped to unhitch the horses and bed them down, before they pulled the sleigh into a nearby shed. All the while he questioned Tuck about the ranch and the horses and the boys who lived there.

Tuck had answered every query, but his mind hadn't been on horses or Snake Creek. Instead, he had counted the minutes until he got back to Grace's house, wondering if she'd be waiting. And if she was, what might happen between them that night. But by the time he'd returned, the house was silent.

He'd been forced to lie in his bed on the third floor and review each kiss they'd shared since that very first one. It was strange to be living in her house, in such close proximity that he merely had to walk down a flight of stairs to touch her feminine shape again or taste her soft, pliant mouth. He'd tried to resist her, but the effort was getting more difficult with each day he spent near her.

Why was his desire for Grace Penrose so damn hard to deny? It hadn't been that long since he'd been with a woman. Tuck stopped on the stairs and thought back to the last time, determined to bring up every detail. But he couldn't bring either the woman or the experience into sharp focus. Grace had completely overtaken his thoughts.

How long had it been? Months. Almost a year. That wasn't typical. It wasn't as if he'd lost his desire for the opposite sex, he'd just transferred it from willing bar girls to a single mom in Massachusetts.

And though he fought it at every turn, his desire for Grace seemed so easy…so natural…so right.

He followed the scent of coffee to the kitchen and found a pot already made, proof that Grace hadn't lingered in bed that morning. He poured himself a cup then leaned back against the edge of the counter and sipped at the strong brew.

Until now, he had been satisfied with his life, happy to accept a future alone in order to deal with his past. He'd never had a stable relationship in his life, not even an example of a successful marriage to look to, so how could he ever expect to make it happen for himself? And always present in his mind was the knowledge that if he found love, he'd find a way to mess up. Maybe it was better to just avoid inevitable disaster than take the risk that disaster could be averted.

Life had been tough enough already. And nothing, not even romance, came with a lifetime guarantee. Yet here he was, ready to jeopardize everything for the chance to touch her and hold her and kiss her. It was so easy to need her, to want to protect her. He thought about Grace night and day, running their conversations over in his head, interpreting her expressions in a million different ways. But until now, he'd written off his obsession as mere proximity. She was a woman and she was close by.

He couldn't avoid the truth any longer. When he had

kissed Grace last night, he'd kissed *her*. He wanted to feel *her* in his arms—sweet, reluctant, passionate Grace, with her horn-rimmed glasses and her tousled hair and her Cupid's bow mouth. He couldn't imagine wanting another woman the way he wanted her.

So what was he going to do about it? A sensible man might pack his bags and find himself a nice motel room in the next town. But Tuck didn't feel like being sensible. He felt a little bit like a tumbleweed, willing to let the wind take him where it may. If something happened between him and Grace, he wasn't going to stop it. And he wasn't going to regret it. He was just going to take it as it came.

Tuck refilled his coffee mug, then wandered back toward the stairs. He'd thought he was alone in the house until he heard a shout from the library.

"Die, you sucker, die! Bryan Penrose, king of the world. Keegan Cooper, loooo-ser."

Hopeful that Bryan might know the whereabouts of his mother, Tuck started toward the library. He found Bryan and his friend Keegan slouched on the sofa, their backs to Tuck. Their attention was focused on a video game they were both playing. Tuck opened his mouth to ask Bryan if he was ready to head down to the barn.

"I think she's a babe," Keegan said as he maneuvered his tank around the screen. "She could be on *Baywatch*. Once, when she was cutting my hair, she bent over and I think I saw her bra. And it was black."

Tuck had to bite his lip to keep from laughing. Still, he couldn't help being curious as to who they were discussing.

"Do you really want a new mom?" Bryan asked, punching at the Nintendo controls with a vengeance while maintaining an air of boredom.

"Yeah," Keegan replied. "Why not? Don't you want a new dad?"

"No way," Bryan said. "I hope my mom never gets married again. That would wreck everything."

The vehemence of his words shocked Tuck, and for a moment, he didn't breathe. He knew that Dan Penrose's abandonment and the divorce had hurt Bryan badly, but the boy sounded so cold, so bitter for such a young kid.

"Even if it was that cowboy?"

"McCabe? Especially him," Bryan said, his voice dripping with disdain. "He thinks he can push me around and tell me what to do. He's not my father and he never could be."

"He seems like a pretty nice guy."

"That's all an act so my mom will like him more. You should see the two of them, staring at each other. It's enough to make you barf." The sound of video game ammunition filled the room and then there was silence. Bryan was proclaimed the winner with an electronic fanfare. "If he stayed here, I'd make his life a living hell."

Keegan laughed. "Yeah, I bet you would. Hey, you know my dad has to kiss Rowena Dahl for the Christmas play? I bet once he kisses her, he'll fall madly in love with her. Then they'll get married and have a baby and I'll have a brother."

"Or a *sister,*" Bryan said.

"Yeah, maybe. But Susan's not that bad. Besides, I'm used to girls with Randi and Robin around."

"They're your cousins. Sisters are a big pain in the butt. You want a sister, you can have Susan."

Tuck backed away from the door and cursed beneath his breath. "So much for progress," he muttered to himself. He'd actually thought that he was making a difference with Bryan, that he'd managed to knock that big chip off the kid's shoulder. In truth, Bryan was simply playing him, biding his time until Tuck went back to Montana. Just one more reason that he and Grace could never be—her son hated him.

Still, Tuck was a pretty good judge of troubled boys, and instinct told him that Bryan's comments were probably more of an attempt to impress his friend with his bad attitude than the truth. That didn't make it any easier to hear. He walked back down the hall, but just as he turned to go upstairs, he heard the kitchen door open. Susan ran in, chattering all the way, and Grace was right behind her. Instead of heading for his room, he turned for the kitchen, and when he got there, he found Grace tugging at her jacket, her cheeks rosy from the cold, her hair tangled by the wind.

She stamped her feet and brushed the snow from the tops of her boots. When she looked up at him through steamy glasses, her gaze met Tuck's and she smiled. Lord, she was pretty, Tuck mused. He could spend a whole day looking at her. ''Morning,'' he said.

''Hi. I was wondering when you were going to get up.''

''I decided to sleep in,'' Tuck told her.

''I was just delivering your cookies to the school for the soccer team exchange. They went over very well. Everyone was impressed. Of course, I told everyone that I baked them,'' she teased.

''Good.''

Grace rubbed her hands together to warm them, then grabbed her coffee cup from the sink. ''It's stopped snowing. I think we've had about nine inches. And we're supposed to get more on Monday. I don't think I have to worry about the sleigh rides anymore. In fact, I've decided to take the whole day off from worrying. At least, until this afternoon when I have play practice.''

''Where's Bryan?'' Susan asked.

''He's with his friend in the library,'' Tuck replied, ruffling her hair as she walked by.

Susan sent him a wide smile. "I'm having a sleepover tonight," she said. "It's my first sleepover. I'm going to sleep at my friend's house all night long. Her name is Martha." Once Susan had imparted her big news, she skipped out of the room, humming a little tune.

"Martha's mother saw us at school this morning and invited her. I was going to say no, but then I thought that it's about time to let her go." Grace poured a mug of coffee, then wrapped her fingers around the warmth. "Except for when she visits her grandparents, she's never spent a night away from me. I know that sounds silly, but she's my baby. It's hard to cut those apron strings."

"Believe me," Tuck said. "She'll be back. She doesn't have enough money in her piggy bank to head to the Caribbean, and she can't reach the accelerator on the car yet."

Grace laughed. "You have a real knack for putting my life in perspective. I'll make a note to start worrying when she gets taller and richer."

Tuck slowly crossed the room and slipped his arm around her waist. He brushed his lips against hers and smiled. "Good morning," he murmured, nuzzling her ear.

Grace wriggled out of his reach. "What are you doing?"

"I told you, from now on I'm going to kiss you whenever I feel like it. And you are wearing a sweater."

"What is that supposed to mean?" she teased. "If I want you to stop kissing me, I should wear a blazer?"

"No, that wouldn't work. I'd still kiss you." He bent to kiss her again, but when the sound of running footsteps came toward the kitchen, he drew back. An instant later, Bryan appeared with his friend Keegan.

A blush pinkened Grace's cheeks and she frantically ran her hands through her hair. Bryan watched her suspiciously, as if he knew exactly what had been going on. "I'm going," he said to Grace. "Pick me up tomorrow morning."

"Wait!" Grace cried. "Tomorrow morning? You are not staying out all night, young man!"

"I'm staying at Keegan's. Remember? You said it would be all right."

"I did? When did I say that?" Grace asked.

"I heard you say that," Keegan said. "And it's all right with my dad. You can call him."

Grace rubbed her forehead in confusion. "Go," she said. "I'll pick you up before church tomorrow morning. Be ready by quarter to nine." Bryan nodded, then raced out of the house. "I don't understand him. One minute he's happy, the next he's…" Her voice drifted off and she stared at the door for a long time in complete silence.

"You have play practice this afternoon?" Tuck asked.

Grace nodded, still distracted. "From two until six."

"Be ready at seven," Tuck said, grabbing his coffee mug and heading out of the kitchen.

"For what?" she asked, following Tuck out of the kitchen.

"It's Saturday night. I'm taking you out tonight. On a date."

This time, Tuck used Bryan's technique, making a quick escape before she could protest. He took the stairs two at a time, and when he reached the third floor, he closed his bedroom door behind him and crossed to the mirror above the dresser.

"All right," Tuck said. "You've done it now. And there's no going back."

GRACE STOOD IN FRONT of the mirror in her bedroom and smoothed her hands over the simple black jersey dress she wore. The last time she wore it was to a cocktail reception, but she'd gone through everything else in her closet and this choice made her look the skinniest. And it was the only thing she had with a neckline that dipped more than a few inches below her chin.

"I have nothing to wear," she complained. "If I'd known I was going to have a date in this decade, I would have gone out and bought something." She glanced at her watch. Ten after seven. He'd been waiting downstairs for ten minutes already.

"I should just cancel," she said to her reflection. "I can't do this. I'm so nervous I'm going to throw up."

A soft knock sounded on her bedroom door and she jumped, then pressed her hand to her chest. Her heart slammed against her palm and she couldn't catch her breath. "Who is it?" she called.

As if she didn't know! They were the only two people in the house, a fact that had been weighing on her mind all afternoon. There were no children to pose as chaperones tonight, no excuse not to— Grace swallowed hard. Act like adults. "Oh, God."

"Gracie?"

"Yes?" she replied, her voice rising at least an octave or two.

"Are going to come out anytime soon?"

"No."

"Why not?"

"I'm not sure."

Tuck slowly opened the door and poked his head inside. He stared at her for a long moment, a slow smile curling his lips. "You look beautiful," he said.

"I don't," Grace replied, nervously fidgeting with her dress. "I can't remember the last time I had a date. Actually, I *can* remember. I just don't *want* to. Harvey Winslow. He took me ice fishing. Do we really have to do this?"

Pushing the door open, Tuck stepped inside. He was dressed in casual clothes—a denim shirt, khakis and a leather jacket. But the slight change in his wardrobe made him look completely different. Like one of those sophisticated yet rugged guys who graced the pages of the men's magazines.

He sat down on the edge of her bed and crooked his finger in her direction. "Come here," he said, patting the space beside him.

She approached slowly, wondering if she had mascara on her cheek or toilet paper in her hair. But when she reached him, he slipped his arm around her waist and pulled her down.

"Why don't we just get this out of the way now and then we can have some fun tonight." He gently touched his lips to hers. At first, the kiss was simple, an easy meeting of mouths. Grace felt the tension recede. This was the man she knew, the man who cared about her, who had the ability to make her forget who and what she was. When she was with Tuck, she was a beautiful, exciting woman, not a working mother with a mousy wardrobe and a hairstyle she'd worn since high school.

Grace wrapped her arms around his neck and he slowly pushed her back on the bed, his body heavy on hers, his tongue exploring and invading. She'd nearly convinced herself that she wasn't going to throw up. But then the phone rang and she rolled out of his embrace, as if the caller had crawled through the line and stepped into the room and seen everything that had passed between them. "The phone," she said, standing up beside the bed and pointing to the offending appliance.

"Yes, it's the phone," Tuck replied.

"Maybe it's one of the children. I have to answer it."

Reluctantly he nodded his head. "All right."

She reached for the phone on the beside table, picking it up in mid-jangle. But it wasn't one of the children. The strange voice on the other end of the line asked for Tucker McCabe. Grace frowned, then handed him the receiver before she stepped out of his reach again.

Tuck didn't say much, just "yep" and "nope." A few seconds later, he stretched across her bed and replaced the phone in the cradle. "Sorry. That was Ray Ruiz, my partner at the ranch. He got a call about a feed delivery that I'd arranged and forgotten to tell him about."

"Saved by the bell," Grace said with a tiny laugh. She twisted her fingers together in front of her. "I—I guess I forgot."

Tuck rested his head on his hand as he watched her from the bed. "Forgot what?"

"That you have another life, other people depending on you, a home of your own with people who care about you."

He flopped back onto the bed and ran his fingers through his hair. "That life seems like hundreds of miles away."

"It is," Grace said. "Hundreds of miles." She'd been pushing that notion out of her head since the very first time he'd kissed her. But now the realization came into sharp focus yet again. In a very short time, Tuck would walk out of her life and back into his own. And that caused a stab of sadness that nearly took her breath way. She forced a light smile. "Let's not think about that right now. I—I think we should go. I'm famished." She hurried to the bedroom door, not trusting herself or Tuck to keep from throwing caution to the wind and falling into bed again.

Tuck caught up with her in the living room and helped her slip into her coat. "Let's go," he said. Then he pulled the front door open and followed her out. They stood on the porch for a moment and watched snowflakes drift down lazily in the still night. The light from the house gave the snow a pretty glitter, as if it had been sprinkled with diamonds.

"It's a nice night. We could walk," Grace suggested, hoping that the cold air would clear her head and the exercise would give her something to focus on. She started down the steps, and when Tuck joined her, he grabbed her hand and placed it in the crook of his arm.

"I wouldn't want you to slip and hurt yourself," he said with a grin.

They set off toward town, walking slowly on the slippery sidewalk, neither of them speaking. "So, where are we going?" Grace finally asked after they'd walked for a few minutes.

"I'm not sure," Tuck said. He stopped and looked around. "I was following you. So where does one go on a date in Cooper's Corner?"

Grace laughed. "Usually one goes to Pittsfield. There isn't much to do here."

"Dinner sounds good," Tuck said. "I like the food at Tubb's."

When they reached the café, Tuck reached out and gallantly opened the door for her. Grace braced herself for a round of curious stares, but Tubb's was nearly empty. Most of the regulars had probably already eaten. Seven-thirty was a little late for dinner in Cooper's Corner.

They found a table in a pleasant spot next to the windows and Tuck pulled out Grace's chair before he sat down next to her. She handed him a menu and then pretended to study her own. Instead, she watched him surreptitiously. He looked so handsome, his hair combed properly, rather than arranged by his fingers. She fought the urge to reach out and smooth a lock from his temple back into its rightful place.

"Does this feel as strange to you as it does to me?" Tuck asked, glancing over his shoulder at Burt and Lori

Tubb, who watched them from a spot near the cash register. He turned back to Grace. "They're staring at us."

Grace nodded. "We may have trouble making conversation, but the rest of the town is going to be talking about this date tomorrow. I'm going to have to remember to ask at the post office if I had a good time or not."

"Really? People are going to talk about this?"

"Gossiping is better entertainment than cable. And I'm Grace Penrose," she said. "Grace Penrose on a date happens about as often as a lunar eclipse."

Lori Tubb approached the table with her order pad. She glanced at them both, then smiled. "What can I get you folks tonight?" she asked.

Tuck took another look at his menu, then closed it and slapped it down on the table. "What's fast?" he asked.

"Fast?"

"Yeah. What can you cook fast? We want a couple of dinners to go. The faster the better."

"I suppose the meat loaf would be fast," Lori said, clearly confused.

"Two meat loafs?" Tuck said, turning to Grace for her approval.

Grace nodded, as confused as Lori was. "Meat loaf," she said.

"Mashed potatoes, gravy, some vegetables. Maybe a little coleslaw or a salad. Throw in a couple of chocolate malts and some cherry pie." Lori scribbled as Tuck ordered. When he was done, she waited. "That's all," Tuck said.

She hurried off, disappearing into the kitchen behind Burt. Grace giggled. "I wonder what's going through her mind?"

"She's probably wondering why we want to get home so fast," Tuck said.

Grace met his gaze, sending him a grateful smile. "Maybe they won't think of me the way they used to. Maybe now I'll have a reputation."

"I like fast women," Tuck teased.

Their food arrived in less than five minutes. Tuck handed Lori enough money to cover the tab and a tip, then helped Grace with her coat. They walked to the door and stepped back out into the cold night air.

When they reached the warmth of Grace's kitchen, she slipped out of her coat and began to gather plates and utensils for their meal. Tuck leaned against the edge of the counter, watching her, his arms crossed over his chest, his denim shirt pulled taut against the muscles of his arms.

Though Grace was grateful to get out from beneath Burt and Lori's watchful eyes, she didn't feel any calmer now that they'd returned home. The only place she really felt at ease was outside in the cold, when they were both bundled up and walking briskly, when they could make idle conversation about the weather or the scenery or her children. Whenever she stopped moving she realized she was just a heartbeat away from being kissed by Tuck McCabe.

Drawing a shaky breath, Grace methodically arranged the food on plates, taking extra time to make an attractive presentation, hoping to calm her persistent case of nerves. Then she dumped the malts into a pair of glasses and set them next to the plates. Why was he watching her so closely? And what was he thinking? Was he considering how long he should wait until he kissed her? Or was he wondering if the meat loaf tasted as good as it smelled?

Grace pulled out a chair. "There," she said. "Time to eat."

"You know, I'm really not hungry," Tuck said, shoving away from the counter and taking a step toward her.

"But—but we have meat loaf."

He took another step, his gaze fixed on hers.

"I could make you a burger," she suggested, knowing full well he had an appetite for something else. She could see it in the way he approached, like a mountain cat circling his prey. He slowly reached out and slipped his arm around her waist, pulling her body against his. He lifted her up onto the edge of the table and stepped between her legs. Taking her face between his hands, he kissed her gently.

"Wh-what are you doing?" she asked, leaning back.

"If you have to ask, then I guess I'm not doing it very well." He kissed her again, pushing her back. She braced her hands behind her and stuck her palm squarely into a plate of food, coming away with a fistful of mashed potatoes. Tuck took her fingers and slowly licked them off.

"Not bad," he teased.

Grace tugged her fingers away. "Wait," she said. "Wait. Before we do this, we have to get something straight. If we're going to do this—whatever it is that we're going to do—we can't let my children find out. As long as they're around, we're just friends."

Tuck stared down at her, then wove his fingers through hers. "All right," he murmured.

"And this is just a short-term thing. You have your life and I have mine. No strings."

He smoothed his palm along her cheek. "Are those all the ground rules or is there something else?"

Grace nodded. "I think that covers it."

"Can I kiss you now?"

"No," she said.

"No?"

She jumped off the table, then turned her back to him. If she was going to do this, she was going to do it all the way, no reservations or inhibitions. And no food getting in the way. With one sweep of her arm, she cleared the surface. Meat loaf dinners went flying, gravy and mashed potatoes splashed onto the floor, malts spilled and plates broke and silverware skittered across the linoleum.

"I saw that in a movie once," she said with a soft laugh, staring at the mess she'd made. Then she turned, grabbed him by the lapels of his jacket and pulled him down onto the table with her, until they were both lying across the scarred oak surface. Grace's breath caught in her throat and she winced as her hip came in contact with a puddle of coleslaw. "Now you can kiss me."

"Have you ever been seduced on a kitchen table?" Tuck murmured, his breath warm on her lips.

Grace wrinkled her nose, then nodded. Her wedding night. After that, everything had gone downhill. "Yes."

A vivid curse slipped from Tuck's lips. He grabbed her arm, rolled her over and they tumbled to the floor in a tangle of limbs. "Have you ever been seduced on the kitchen floor?" he asked.

Grace shook her head. "Nope. I can't say that I have."

"Good," he replied. "Because you're about to be."

His mouth came down on hers and Grace's pulse leapt, beating so fast she could hear it in her head. Sensations, wild and wonderful, raced through her body. How had she ever lived without these feelings? Until he'd touched her, she hadn't really been alive. She'd had a life, but any passion she'd possessed had been locked away. Now Tuck McCabe had come into her life and he'd handed her a key.

He slowly skimmed her dress off her shoulders, baring her skin to his touch. His mouth followed his fingers, tracing a line of damp kisses all the way to the soft spot between her breasts. Grace closed her eyes and lost herself in a wave of desire. She wanted this, to cast aside her inhibitions and become the kind of woman who could give a man like Tuck the ultimate pleasure.

She reached out and smoothed her palms over his chest, then hesitantly moved to the top button of his shirt. Her fingers fumbled at it, but she finally got it open, a sigh of relief slipping from her lips. Gathering her resolve, she tried the next button and then the next. And before she knew it, his shirt was completely open. He yanked it off, twisting to pull it from beneath him, then tossed it aside.

Grace ran her hands along his collarbone, the contact with his skin causing her fingers to tingle and her heart to race. She couldn't remember ever feeling this way about a man, aching to touch him, to taste him. She'd always thought she was lacking when it came to sex, that her husband was justified in having an affair. But now she realized it wasn't her, it was him. She'd simply needed to find the right man.

Tuck spanned her waist with his hands and pulled her on top of him, settling Grace's thighs on either side of his hips. Grace watched as his hands slid up beneath her dress, bunching the soft fabric as he moved. He was hard and the feel of his erection between her legs, with just his trousers and her panties as a barrier between them, felt naughty and dangerous.

Just the thought of slowly undressing him, of undressing *for* him, caused her to tremble in anticipation. "I've never done this before," she confessed. "I mean, not on the first date. And not on the kitchen floor. And there's only been one man. And that wasn't even that—"

"None of that makes a difference, Gracie," Tuck said, pressing his finger to her lips. "I want you just the way you are."

A slow smile touched Grace's lips. Why had she never known how it was supposed to be between a man and a woman? She had settled for something less than true passion and wasted so many years with a man who wasn't capable of making her happy. She still might be with him…settling for less… "Thank God for the nuts-and-bolts girl," she murmured.

Grace reached back for the zipper of her dress. Tuck sat up and watched her, bracing his arms behind him. And when her dress fell loose around her arms, he pulled her back down onto the floor and kissed the soft swell of her breasts. "You're the most beautiful woman I've ever seen," he said. "Since the first night I spent in your house, I wondered if this would happen."

"I did, too," Grace admitted.

He took her wrist and placed her hand on his chest. Grace could feel his heart beating beneath her fingertips. "Kiss me," Tuck said. "And touch me."

Without hesitation she bent nearer and brushed her mouth against his. At first he didn't respond, he simply watched, challenging her to take the lead. She kissed him again, but this time she ran her tongue along his lower lip before she drew away. This was nice, taking control, daring him to kiss her back.

A soft moan slipped from his throat and Grace's heart fluttered. She felt powerful. Any woman who could make a man like Tuck moan had to at least be a little bit good at sex. She drew away, but this time, he reached out and wove his fingers through the hair at her nape, pulling her back into the kiss.

His tongue teased at hers, deepening the kiss with every heartbeat. And when she thought there was nothing more exciting than kissing Tuck, he touched her. He skimmed her dress down along her arms and worked at the clasp between her breasts.

Time seemed to slow to an exquisite pace. A jangling sound in her head intruded on the whirl of pleasure as he cupped her naked breast in his hand. He teased her nipple to a peak, then covered it with his mouth, his warm tongue sending spasms of pleasure racing through her. She waited for angels to begin singing now that bells were ringing. But reality intruded when she recognized the sound of the telephone. She arched back, but Tuck stubbornly refused to let her go.

"Let it ring," he murmured, his breath warm against her skin, his lips slowly moving to her other breast.

"What if it's the ranch?" Grace said. She swallowed hard. Who cared if it was the ranch? The ranch was hundreds of miles away.

"I don't want to talk to them," Tuck said.

He made sense, but she couldn't overcome her motherly habits. She gave him one more long, deep kiss, then scrambled off him and crawled through the spilled meat loaf and gravy to the phone on the wall. One tug of the cord brought the phone down on the floor. "Hello?" Grace said in a breathy voice.

"Grace? It's Ellen Reed, Martha's mom. I just wanted to check if you were home."

Grace's instincts immediately went on alert. She brushed her hair out of her eyes and sat up straight, clutching at the front of her dress. "Is everything all right?"

"It's Susan. She's a little homesick. I tried to convince her to stay, but she wants to come home. I think she's more worried about you sleeping alone than she is about sleeping here at our house."

"Oh," Grace said, her heart twisting. "That's…sweet. Actually, she needn't have worried." In truth, Grace hadn't had any intention of sleeping alone.

"I'm just getting her packed up right now. We'll be over to your house in a few minutes."

"Oh, no, no," Grace said. "Are you sure she doesn't want to stay?"

"Quite sure," Ellen said. "Your daughter is very certain of what she wants and she wants to come home. I'll see you in a few minutes."

The line went dead, leaving Grace's protests unheard. She turned to Tuck, her mouth still slightly open. "Susan is on her way home."

Tuck slowly sat up, his brow quirked in question. He raked his hand through his hair, coming away with a bit of gravy. "Sorry?"

"Oh, my God," Grace said, scrambling to her feet. She pushed down her skirt and tugged up the neckline of her dress, forgetting about her bra. "She can't see this. There's food all over the floor."

"And in your hair," Tuck said, chuckling. "Not to mention that nice blob of mashed potatoes on your backside."

Grace craned her neck to see, then frantically brushed at the potatoes. "You have to get out of here."

"Where am I supposed to go?"

"Anywhere but here. You can't be here when Susan walks in. She's going to wonder what happened."

Tuck rose to his feet, then plucked his shirt from the floor, where it had come to rest in a pile of green beans. "I'm going to go take a shower." As he walked past her, he slipped his arm around her waist and yanked her against his naked chest. Then he stole a quick but deep kiss. "We'll have to have dinner again, sometime soon. I promise."

Grace watched him walk out of the kitchen, despondent, as if she were watching her last chance at passion ride out of town. "Oh, damn it," she muttered. With another vivid curse, she snatched a dishrag from the sink and bent down to wipe up the mess from the floor.

Minutes later she was still on her hands and knees, when Susan bounded in the door. Her daughter stopped dead when she saw the mess on the kitchen floor, her brown eyes wide with astonishment.

"Mommy, what happened?"

"Oh, nothing, honey," Grace told her with a weak smile. "That's the problem. Nothing happened at all."

CHAPTER SEVEN

BY THE TIME TUCK DECIDED to go inside, he'd nearly worn a hole in the snow outside Grace's front door. He wasn't quite sure what to expect when he saw her for the first time after…well, after last night's adventure in fine dining.

Hell, he hadn't wanted this to happen, but when she had pulled him down on the kitchen table, he didn't have much choice. He was lost. She was so beautiful, a tantalizing mix of naive schoolgirl and sexy siren. Maybe that's what made her so desirable, that strange contrast that kept him guessing. That, and the addictive taste of her mouth.

He should have seen this coming. Though he was usually out of bed and to work by six on the ranch, here he waited until he was certain Grace was up and moving about so she'd be the first thing he'd see in the morning. There were times the last few days when he'd find himself making up excuses to go back to the house, just to see if she was home—a glass of water, a snack, a phone call he had to make. Anything that would put him in the same room as her. And at night, he'd linger in the kitchen, chatting with her while he helped her clean up.

But he'd missed her this morning. She was up and gone by the time he'd crawled out of bed at eight. He'd waited around for a while, nursing three mugs of strong coffee, then left for the Rawlings place to tend to his horses and goats. When he came back from lunch, she was gone again, a note of explanation taped to the refrigerator. So Tuck had headed to the coach house and spent the early afternoon oiling harnesses and listening to the Patriots' game on an old radio he'd found.

The mundane work gave him a chance to consider his next move. There was no doubt in his mind anymore that Grace had as much trouble resisting him as he did her. But without warning, her indecision would take over and she'd retreat beneath a veil of insecurity. Tuck wanted to believe that her hesitation was a temporary "phase," like one of Bryan's phases.

But he was forced to believe it might really be a warning, a message to him that making love to her would mean something more than just a physical release. She'd said it herself—what they'd done last night was totally new to her. Maybe there was a reason for that. Grace Penrose didn't surrender her heart or her body unless there was a promise of a future.

Tuck cursed softly. He was finding it harder and harder to stay in the same house as Grace, sleeping one floor above her and spending his nights wondering what it would be like to tiptoe down those stairs and share her bed. There was only one way to keep himself from wanting her and that was to put some distance between them.

He could sleep in the barn with his horses, or in his truck. Or he could find a motel close by. Then, if Grace came to him, he'd know it was because she wanted him and not because he wanted her.

Reaching up, he took off his Stetson and ran his fingers through his hair. Well, he wouldn't answer any of his questions or solve any of their problems standing outside in the snow. He took the front steps two at a time and pushed open the door.

But it wouldn't open all the way. He gave it a shove, then stepped inside, only to find what was blocking his entrance. Grace teetered on a ladder behind the door, her hand clutching a pine garland. The ladder shifted as she tried to regain her balance. In one long stride, Tuck was below her, just in time to catch her as she fell.

With a tiny scream, she dropped neatly into his arms. They both looked at each other in shock, then turned to find Bryan and Susan staring at them with the same emotion. "Put me down," Grace said beneath her breath.

Slowly, he let her feet drop to the floor. The contact with her body was electric, causing a flood of heat to rush to his groin. Tuck cleared his throat, then shoved his hands back into his jacket pockets. "I just came in to get something to drink," he said. "I can see you're busy. And I've got work to do in the carriage house. I'll just be—"

"No," Grace said. "Why don't you stay? We're going to decorate the tree next and I could use some help wrestling it into the stand."

"I always do that," Bryan said, giving Tuck a hostile look.

"I'm sure your mother could use your help," Tuck countered in an attempt to keep the peace. "Why don't I help Susan." He shrugged out of his jacket and tossed it on the back of the sofa, then squatted down beside Grace's daughter. "What are you doing, Susie Q?"

"Stringing popcorn and cranberries," Susan said.

Tuck glanced around her spot on the floor. She'd only managed to string five or six pieces of popcorn and two cranberries. But scattered around her was nearly a half a bowl of broken kernels and a handful of squashed cranberries.

"First, you do this," she said, placing a kernel of popcorn on a small cutting board. "Then you do this," she said, stabbing at it with her needle. It shattered and she popped it into her mouth. She grinned. "Then you eat it."

Susan handed him another needle and thread and they set to work. Meanwhile, Grace and Bryan headed out to the backyard to deal with the tree. Susan seemed oblivious to the bickering that filtered in from outside. Instead, she chatted about her recent letter to Santa Claus.

"And then I put it in an envelope and me and Mommy took it to the post office and mailed it. And when you mail a letter to Santa you don't have to buy a stamp. It's for free."

Tuck smiled. "And what did you ask for in your letter?"

"A new daddy," she said, as if asking for that were no more important than asking for a new Barbie doll.

He coughed softly, trying to hide his surprise. "A—a new daddy?"

"Yeah," Susan said. She gave him a sideways glance. "I thought you could be my new daddy, but then my mom said no."

"She did," Tuck commented in a neutral tone.

"I think you'd be a really good daddy," Susan said, reaching out to pat his hand reassuringly. "You do all the stuff right."

"What stuff is that?"

"You make cookies and play Barbies and call me 'Susie Q,'" she said. "And you make Bryan behave when he's acting like a butthead. And you're nice to my mom." She paused. "And I don't think you'd run away, like my real daddy did."

"No," Tuck said softly. "If I was your daddy, I would never run away."

She stared at him for a long moment, her brown eyes wide. Then she nodded. "I asked for Shrinky Dinks, too. And a car for my Barbie dolls."

The subject of a father was quickly forgotten as Susan

launched into a story about how her friend Martha sneezed in church that morning. But Tuck was stuck on the topic.

He'd had his own doubts about his ability to be a father, but the thought that Grace shared those doubts stung. He'd been good with the kids. He was interested in what they had to say, he helped them out when they needed help, and he played the disciplinarian only when it was necessary. In fact, he'd started to wonder if his own doubts might be—

Hell, what difference did it make? She was quite clear about what she wanted. A quick affair with no strings. The exact same thing he should have wanted. But at the same time, he was beginning to wonder if he might share more with Grace, if there was some chance at a future for them. Because if there was a chance, then maybe he ought to take it.

He didn't have time to contemplate the notion further. The back door slammed shut and a few moments later Bryan and Grace appeared, dragging a Christmas tree and knocking down everything in their path. He fought the urge to get up and help them, but thought it best not to intrude on Bryan's territory.

The two of them stumbled and argued and made a general commotion until they'd managed to get the tree upright, only to find that it listed at a rather remarkable angle. Bryan crawled underneath while Grace tried to straighten the tree, but after several failed attempts, she grabbed a stack of newspapers and shoved it under one of the legs of the stand. Then she stepped back. "There," she said with a bright smile. "That looks good."

"It looks like it's going to fall down," Tuck and Bryan said in unison. They turned to each other. Bryan scowled and Tuck smiled.

"Why don't you let us fix it right," Tuck suggested, getting up. He told Bryan to hold the tree straight, then stretched out on the floor and fiddled with the stand until the tree was secure. "That look all right, Bryan?"

Grace's son muttered his assent, then let go of the tree and went back to his job of untangling a wad of Christmas tree lights. But Tuck could tell that the kid took a certain satisfaction in the men in the house getting it right.

Grace picked up a box and crossed the room to sit down next to Susan. She put the box on the table and carefully pulled off the cover. Susan's eyes brightened and she scrambled up on her knees. "Our ornaments!" she cried. She pulled one from the box and dangled it under Tuck's nose. "This is mine from when I was one," she explained.

"It's a pair of shoes," Grace said. "That's for the year that Susan learned to walk."

They pulled out each ornament in turn, talking about the significance. Even Bryan joined the group, lining his ornaments up on the table in front of them. As Tuck watched the scene, he realized how much of their history he knew nothing about, how much he could never be a part of.

His earlier confidence slowly dwindled. There was a lot more to being a father than a few days spent in the company of Grace's children. And there was even more to being a husband. He would have to be there for the long run, through years and years of Christmases, bad times and good.

But despite his doubts, Tuck knew one thing for certain. Someday, he wanted ornaments of his own in a box. Hell, he wanted ten or twenty or thirty. That's what would make him happy. That's what his life should really be about. Families. Forever. And lots of Christmas ornaments in a box.

GRACE YAWNED AS SHE slowly opened her eyes. The clock on the mantel told her it was nearly eleven. She'd snuggled up on the sofa beneath an afghan when Tuck and Bryan left to take care of the animals. She hadn't meant to snooze, but she'd had a busy day—church, play practice and then decorating the tree. Never mind the huge amount of energy spent trying to stop thinking about Tuck, trying to stay far enough away from him for the entire afternoon so she wouldn't be tempted to touch him or kiss him.

The moment he and Bryan had walked out the door, she'd dropped to the sofa in an exhausted heap. Something had to be done and soon. She felt as if she were walking on eggshells, trying her best to make Tuck feel at home, yet avoiding any move toward further intimacy.

Just the thought of their little interlude in the kitchen brought a blush to her cheeks. What had she been thinking? This was all Maureen and Rowena's fault. They were the ones who had convinced her to throw caution to the wind. And now she could barely look at Tuck without thinking about what they might have shared had that phone not rung.

Why couldn't things remain exactly as they were? They kissed, they touched. There didn't have to be more, did there? What came next would only complicate both their lives. But that didn't stop her from wanting to share the most intimate experiences with him. She pulled the afghan up to her nose. She was a sensible woman and she'd do the sensible thing.

"Are you awake?"

Grace pushed up on one elbow and looked toward the dining room. Tuck stood in the doorway, his shoulder braced against the doorjamb. "You're back," she said.

"I have been for a while. I wasn't sure whether I should wake you or not. You've had a busy day."

She swung her legs over the edge of the sofa. "I should get the kids to bed."

"They're already there. Susan put her Cinderella pajamas on and I read her two stories. Bryan showered, brushed his teeth and crawled into bed with a minimum of grumbling.''

''You put them to bed?''

''It wasn't brain surgery. Although discussing Susan's choice of pajamas taxed my intelligence. Holly Hobby, Snow White, Scooby-Dog, or—''

''Doo,'' Grace corrected. ''Scooby-Doo. He's a dog. A cartoon dog. Didn't you watch Scooby-Doo when you were a kid?''

Tuck shrugged. ''My childhood didn't leave much time for cartoons.'' He glanced around. ''I saw some eggnog in the fridge. Would you like a little?''

Grace nodded. She listened to him rummaging around in the kitchen for the next few minutes. When he returned to the fire, she'd smoothed her rumpled hair and straightened her clothes.

''I found some brandy and I added a bit,'' he said, handing her a glass of eggnog.

''We had brandy?''

''It was behind the kitchen cleanser under the sink.''

''Hmm. I wonder how it got there.''

Tuck sat down next to her and kicked his stocking feet up on the coffee table. ''This is nice,'' he said, after taking a sip of his drink. ''You promised me a New England Christmas and that's what I'm getting. I'm glad I stayed.''

''I'm glad you did, too,'' Grace replied.

They sat silently, both staring into the dying flames in the fireplace. Grace was almost afraid to speak, knowing that sooner or later they'd have to address the sexual attraction between them. Or maybe they didn't have to say anything. If they didn't talk about it, it might just go away. She pressed her lips together and tried to slow her quickened pulse.

But when Tuck reached over and grabbed her hand, Grace nearly cried out in surprise. He carefully wove his fingers through hers, then drew her hand up to his mouth and kissed her wrist.

"Thank you for your help," Grace said. "I know I say that a lot, but I'm not sure how I would have gotten through these last few days without you." She drew a deep breath. "You'll make a good father someday."

"Someday," Tuck repeated softly. "I'd like that."

Grace tried to imagine Tuck with a family of his own, a pretty wife and two adorable children. But whenever she tried to create the image in her mind, the wife looked exactly like her, and the children like Bryan and Susan as toddlers.

"Do you ever think about getting married again?" Tuck asked.

The question came completely out of the blue. At first, Grace wasn't sure what to say. Was he asking because he wanted to fill the position of husband himself? Or was he just making idle conversation? Either way, she would have to give him a coherent answer.

"I don't know. I guess I haven't thought much about it," she lied. In truth, that's all she thought about lately. "It would be difficult to find someone."

"I suppose there aren't many eligible bachelors in Cooper's Corner."

"It's not that. I have two kids that come along in the deal."

"Anybody who loved you couldn't help but love your children."

Grace gave him a sideways glance. For a moment, it seemed as if they weren't talking about hypothetical husbands and imaginary marriage proposals anymore. Had he thought about applying for the position? She turned back to the fire again. This was all so confusing. With Dan, it was just assumed that they'd get married and have a family. She'd never had any doubts.

Was this what falling in love was supposed to be—indecision and fear? All these crazy emotions and wild desires? She felt as if she'd been riding on a roller coaster since the moment Tuck McCabe had walked into her life. And she wasn't sure whether she wanted to get off or yell for the operator to crank up the speed.

"I suppose you're going to be glad to get back home," Grace commented.

"Why would you say that?"

She shrugged. "It's hard to be away for such a long time. Giving up your normal routine for someone else's. We're not exactly an easy family to live with." She waited for him to disagree, hoping that he'd say her family was exactly the kind of family he wanted for his own.

But he only nodded. "I've got a lot of work waiting for me. Enough to keep me hopping for the next few months."

The silence stretched out between them. Grace didn't know what else to say. Conversation had always come so easily between them and now she couldn't come up with another subject to discuss if her life depended upon it. She was almost ready to excuse herself and go to bed when he spoke again.

"About last night," he began.

"We don't have to talk about it," Grace said. "We just got carried away. That happens sometimes." She swallowed hard. "I mean, never to me. But I'm sure to you."

"Gracie, I care about you. But I'm not sure I can make you the kind of promises you deserve. You have your kids to think about, as well as yourself. I don't want to do anything that might hurt you."

"I know what I want," Grace said. "You don't have to worry about me. I'm an adult. I make my own choices."

"I know," Tuck admitted. "And this has got to be your choice. If you want anything to happen, you'll have to come to me. Because if it was left up to me, we'd be up in your bedroom finishing what we started last night."

"Then—then you do want me?"

He placed a finger under her chin and forced her gaze to meet his. "I want you more than I've ever wanted anyone in my life. There's just one thing. I want you to be happy, and if I did anything to hurt you, I'd never forgive myself." He paused. "I don't have a great track record with women. And I'm not sure I could ever be the kind of guy that could make you happy. I had a crappy childhood and I'm still working that all out. But I do care about you, Gracie, that much I'm sure of." He leaned forward and brushed a kiss across her mouth. Then he pushed to his feet, letting go of her hand. "I'm going to bed. I'll see you in the morning."

He walked out of the room and up the stairs. When Grace heard him climb to the third story, she flopped back on the sofa and groaned softly. Everyone had baggage from their past they were forced to deal with sooner or later. She had her husband and his mistress, the gossip and her reputation. If anyone should be afraid of commitment, it should be her. And yes, he'd had a tough childhood. Every day she saw traces of those old wounds in his gaze, heard it in his voice.

Grace took a deep breath. They were both adults, both afraid to surrender their hearts, yet anxious to surrender their bodies. So it would be just about sex and nothing more. This may be her only chance. She knew what she wanted and she was going to get it. She jumped off the sofa and ran up the stairs. If Tuck was waiting for her to make the first move, then she was about to make it!

She hurried to her bedroom and closed the door behind

her. Then she yanked open her dresser drawers, looking for something, anything that resembled lingerie. She found the nightgown she'd worn the night Susan was born. "Too maternal," she said, tossing it aside. Next, she pulled out a black contraption with garters and lace, something Dan had given her for one of their anniversaries. "Too slutty," she said, adding it to the pile on the floor.

At the bottom of the drawer she found exactly what she was looking for. A simple cotton batiste nightgown, sleeveless, with fine embroidery around the scoop neckline. She'd seen it in a shop in Pittsfield and bought it on a whim. The fabric was so thin, almost transparent, like wearing a summer cloud. She'd forgotten all about it, but now Grace pulled the nightgown out and unfolded it, then smoothed her hands over the fabric. "Perfect," she decided.

She took a deep breath, then began to tug off her clothes. When she was completely naked, she slipped the nightgown over her head, then hurried over to the mirror to check out the effect. In the low light of her bedroom, she could see the fabric clinging to her curves, leaving just enough to the imagination.

"The glasses have got to go," she said, taking them off. She ran her fingers through her hair, mussing it even more. Then she pinched her cheeks and pasted a sexy smile on her face. "I'm ready," she said. "Let the seduction begin."

She walked into the hallway and opened the door to the third-floor stairway. When the hinges groaned, Grace winced. The stairs were dark but she didn't dare turn on the light. The element of surprise was on her side. If Tuck knew she was coming, he might find a reason to turn her away.

The first step squeaked and so did the second, so she moved quickly up the stairs. But in the dark and without her glasses, she misjudged, and her foot slipped midway up the flight. Grace felt herself falling, but she didn't have a point of reference, no way to know where the rail was, where to find solid footing.

She sprawled onto the stairs and then slowly began to slide down, thumping all the way. Grace bit her bottom lip to keep from crying out. The pain in her knee, the spot where she'd hit the edge of the step, made her eyes water, but still she kept quiet.

When she reached the bottom of the stairs, she waited, frozen in place, her heart slamming in her chest, certain that Tuck would appear at the top any second now. But the house remained completely silent. Slowly, she pushed to her feet, shoving her nightgown down from around her hips.

Even though no one had seen her clumsy descent, her face was still warm with embarrassment. Grace hurried back into the hallway, closed the stairway door and leaned back against it. "So much for seduction."

She limped to her bedroom. If she didn't know better, she'd think fate was stepping in to keep her from sleeping with Tucker McCabe. Whenever she decided to go ahead, something would just as quickly set her back. "Maybe I'm destined to live the rest of my life as a celibate," she said. "Sister Grace of Perpetual Frustration."

In seconds the pretty nightgown was pulled off and tossed onto the pile with the others. Grabbing her faded flannel pajamas, she tugged them on and crawled into bed. As she closed her eyes and forced herself to relax, Grace couldn't help but wonder what she might be doing now if she hadn't fallen down the stairs. Would she be lying in Tuck's arms, touching his naked chest and running her hands through his hair? Or would he be caressing her body and making her ache with desire?

"I guess I'll never know," she murmured, grabbing the edge of the quilt and pulling it over her head.

TUCK LOOKED BOTH WAYS before he crossed the slushy main street of Cooper's Corner. The midday sun had melted the snow on the street, but he was happy to see that Grace's snowbanks were surviving. They had shrunk a bit, but according to the old guy at Tubb's Café, there was more snow coming tonight.

He'd always loved the solitude and the wide-open spaces of Snake Creek Ranch. Living in a city, or even a small town, had been unthinkable. But now that he'd been in Cooper's Corner for a week, he was surprised at how comfortable he felt. There were beautiful forests and rivers and lakes just a few miles from town. The air was fresh and the sky blue. And Grace's house was much cozier and homier than the very masculine surroundings of the ranch house.

He reached his pickup and pulled open the door, but a shout from down the street caused him to turn and look. A tall man approached with a long stride. He wore a canvas jacket much like Tuck's and a pair of Wellies that reached the knees of his jeans.

"Hey," he said in a cheerful voice. "You wouldn't be Tuck McCabe, the cowboy staying over at Grace's place, would you?"

Tuck blinked. Grace had been right. Lori and Burt had been talking. He'd barely been introduced to a handful of people in town and suddenly everyone knew his name. "I am," Tuck said.

The guy held out his hand. "I'm Alex McAlester. Nice to finally meet you."

From what Tuck could see they were about the same age. Or maybe McAlester was a few years older. Tuck always found it hard to judge city boys, with their unweathered skin and neatly shaved faces. The guy was a few inches taller, but Tuck figured he could take him in a fair fight.

So who was this guy and what did he want? Tuck shook the man's hand. "Tuck McCabe. Snake Creek Ranch. Stillwater county, Montana."

"Yeah," Alex said. "You bought Silas's horses. The four Morgans. I'm the local vet. I took care of those horses."

Tuck's curiosity immediately dissolved. "Nice to meet you," he said. "I have to say, those horses were a great buy. A buddy of mine at Tufts knows Silas and he's the one who put me in touch."

"Jim Wallace?" Alex asked.

"Right. He was my advisor when I was in vet school. He got me through fungal infections."

"I know Jim well," Alex said. "He and his wife vacation around these parts. But I didn't know you were a vet. What kind of practice do you have?"

Tuck braced his arm against the pickup. "I don't have a traditional practice. I work off my ranch, kind of freelance. When anyone needs help, I give them a hand. It helps pay for feed. I guess you could say I've become a specialist in range cattle and working horseflesh."

"Can I buy you a cup of coffee?" Alex asked. "I don't get much chance to talk business in Cooper's Corner. And I could use some advice on a case of chronic colic with a mare I'm treating."

"All right," Tuck said, slowly closing the door to his truck. "A cup of coffee would be great."

They walked over to Tubb's Café and took a place at the counter. Lori Tubb bustled up. "Hey, there, boys, what can I get for you?'' Alex ordered a couple of coffees and they sat in silence for a while.

"So, how are the Morgans?'' Alex asked.

"Good. I've had two of them out pulling one of Grace's cutters and they're well trained for the harness.''

"I drove one of the sleighs for Grace last year. She asked me to help her out again this year. A guy doesn't get much chance to do something like that these days.''

"She's got a way with a request,'' Tuck said, smiling wryly. "You should have seen the fuss she put up when she thought I was taking *her* horses back to Montana before the festival.''

"What are you going to do with them on your ranch?'' Alex asked. "Morgans aren't much for herding cattle or roping calves.''

"We've never had harness-broke horses at Snake Creek. I think it will be fun for the boys to learn to drive a team. We've got an old buggy and I'd like to have them build the tack from scratch.''

"Boys? You have sons?'' Alex asked.

Tuck shook his head. "No. My boys are…juvenile delinquents. They come to the ranch to work and get their lives together. We teach them everything they need to know to work on any one of the ranches in the state. I guess I'd be considered a social worker or an occupational counselor. I just make them focus on work and try to keep them from getting in trouble.''

"Must be nice to make a difference like that,'' Alex said.

"I owe a huge debt to that ranch. If it weren't for Snake Creek, I wouldn't be a vet. Hell, I wouldn't have a life.''

"So, you're anxious to get back?''

Tuck shrugged. "I don't know. I was just thinking how much I liked it here. This is a nice town, as towns go.''

"Is it just the town you like?'' Alex asked.

"The town," Tuck murmured. "The woman."

Alex nodded. "Ah, so the gossip is true. I heard down at the barber shop that you and Grace Penrose were running around in your underwear in the snow at midnight the other night. And someone saw you buying condoms over in New Ashford. And Phyllis Cooper is certain she saw you on *America's Most Wanted,* so you can expect a visit from the FBI any day now."

"Geez," Tuck said. "Are the rumors ever true?"

"Hey, I don't believe any of it. But it is interesting to listen to. Most of us lead pretty ordinary lives here. When one of our residents experiences a little excitement, we all feel compelled to enjoy it."

Though he hadn't known Alex McAlester long, Tuck felt he'd made a new friend. It was nice to talk to another guy, someone with the same interests as he had. And Alex seemed like the kind of person he could trust to give him good advice. "Gracie thinks all the talk is ruining her reputation. I'm worried that when I go home, she'll be left with some regrets."

"I don't know Grace very well, but—"

"I thought everyone knew everyone in this town."

"No pets," Alex explained. "But most everybody in Cooper's Corner thinks she's really nice. I've never heard anyone say a bad word about her. I was here when Dan Penrose walked out on her. Boy, there was some talk then. People took sides. But it wasn't long before everyone came over to Grace's side and supported her and the kids."

"She's quite a woman," Tuck said, then decided a change of subject was in order. "So tell me about this colic. I think I've used every known remedy and a few unknown. I've even got some herbal remedies from a Native American cowboy who used to work at the ranch."

They talked business for close to an hour. Lori kept the

coffee coming, and as noon approached, she brought out cheeseburgers and fries. They moved to a booth where they could scribble notes on the backs of placemats. Tuck came away with a new formula for liniment and advice on the latest antibiotic salves. Alex got advice on nearly every common hoof ailment, along with a few breeding techniques for recalcitrant stallions.

By the time Tuck checked the clock, it was already 1:00 p.m. He'd meant to go back to Grace's for lunch. She had play practice that afternoon, so Tuck probably wouldn't see her now until late that night. But maybe that was for the best.

Two nights had passed since he'd laid out the terms of their relationship. She hadn't come to him the first night or the second. In truth, she'd been so busy they'd barely seen each other. But if she didn't come to him tonight, didn't make some sort of move, then he might as well consider the whole thing done and buried. Maybe that was for the best. After all, both of them knew the barriers standing between them. And he was beginning to believe that sex with Grace Penrose would be more than just a one-night stand—for her and for him.

"Too bad you're going back to Montana," Alex said as he paid the check.

"Why's that?"

"I've been looking to take on a partner. Someone who might carry the large-animal work. I've got all I can do with the small animals. And it's just not cats and dogs anymore. I took a continuing education course on ferrets last month. And in the past year I've treated five iguanas and twelve exotic birds. You've got to be a specialist in all species to keep a country practice like mine."

Tuck grabbed his Stetson from the chair next to him and fiddled with the brim. "Hey, I'd like to help you out, but

I have responsibilities back at the ranch. One of our boys is about to graduate from Tufts. We've been working hard to put him through college. And we've got two more boys ready to go. Their scholarships usually don't pay for room and board so we've got to come up with that from ranch profits.''

"This kid at Tufts, he wouldn't be interested in the Berk-shires, would he?"

Tuck pushed his chair back. "Naw, I think he'll be coming back to Montana. But if I'm wrong, I'll be sure to let you know.''

They walked outside together. Tuck pushed his hat onto his head and adjusted the brim against the bright sunlight. Then he held out his hand. "It was good to meet you, Alex. I'd like to stop by and see your practice sometime, if that's all right. I'm going to be here until Christmas.''

"I'd like that," Alex said. "Anytime. Maybe we can do farm visits together. Grace can give you directions.''

They parted ways in front of Tubb's Café. As Tuck walked back to his truck, he mulled over his conversation with Alex—and the job offer. Of all the things standing between him and a future with Grace, that had been the biggest problem—what he'd do for a living if he stayed in Cooper's Corner. Now, over a simple cup of coffee, he'd been offered a solution.

But there were still so many other problems to overcome, so many doubts and hurdles. Tuck opened the door of his pickup and slid behind the wheel. But he didn't reach for the ignition. Instead, he sat for a long time, staring out the window at the street.

Damn it, he didn't want to leave Cooper's Corner. The more he tried to tell himself that his life was in Montana, the more he believed that his future was really here. He was falling in love with Grace Penrose. And it didn't make a difference that she had kids. He was fast feeling the same about Bryan and Susan.

Tuck rubbed his forehead, trying to make sense of his thoughts. What made him so sure that he loved her? He tried to put it into words, but it wasn't something he could verbalize. He just felt it, in his heart and in his soul. Grace had changed something deep inside of him. She'd given him hope, the chance to believe in something more than just a solitary future.

But was she ready for another man in her life? Even if he did decide to stay, would she want to make him a part of her family? Those were the questions that needed answering. And Tuck was determined to make sure he got the answers he wanted to hear.

CHAPTER EIGHT

"WE WANT A FULL REPORT," Maureen said, slipping her arm through Grace's and pulling her toward the church.

"All the details," Rowena added, grabbing Grace's other arm.

Maureen smiled. "Lori Tubb told me that you and your cowboy were in for dinner the other night and then you decided on take-out."

They dragged Grace along with them, but Grace stopped at the church door, digging in her heels. She'd merely been walking down the street, minding her own business, mulling over the parade order, when Rowena and Maureen appeared out of nowhere with absolutely nothing to do on a Tuesday afternoon.

"Don't you two have jobs?" Grace said with a smile.

"Nobody gets a haircut on Tuesdays," Rowena said.

"Clint is minding the inn," Maureen explained, opening the front door of the church.

"Oh, no. I'm not talking about my sex life," Grace objected. "Especially not in church."

Rowena frowned, hitching her hands on her hips. "Tubb's?" she asked, her amethyst eyes sparkling with mischief.

Maureen nodded.

But Grace shook her head. She was not going to fall into their trap again. Her private life was private, and now that she had something to talk about, she darn well was going to keep it to herself. "Gossip central? Absolutely not. Lori Tubb could hear a pin drop in Pittsfield. I'm not baring my soul within earshot of her. Hey, I'm not baring my soul at all. Not that there's any soul to bare. I'm keeping my soul completely dressed, thank you very much."

"Don't be ridiculous," Maureen said, taking on an authoritative tone. "We gave you perfectly good advice and now we want to see what you did with it. You owe it to us. Twin Oaks. We'll go to Twin Oaks and I'll pour us all a nice glass of wine and we'll chat."

"It's not even three o'clock," Grace reminded them. "And we've got play practice later. Getting me drunk is not going to make me spill my secrets."

"Just one glass," Rowena promised. "I want a clear head when I kiss Clint Cooper this evening. He's fantasy material for at least a month and I'm not going to lose it in an alcohol-induced haze."

They walked quickly, or rather Maureen and Rowena raced, and Grace had no choice but to keep up with them. By the time they reached Twin Oaks, they were all breathing hard. They headed directly to the kitchen and Maureen pulled out some crackers and cheese from the fridge and sloshed wine into three crystal goblets.

"To men," she said. Then, without taking a drink, she sat down next to Rowena and turned her gaze on Grace. "All right. We're listening."

"You know, you'd make a very good cop," Grace muttered. "All you need is the bright light overhead and one of those nightsticks."

Maureen blinked in surprise, her expression suddenly shifting. But then she forced a smile. For a moment, Grace thought she'd insulted her.

"There's nothing to tell," Grace said, hoping to put a

quick end to the conversation. "Maybe we should discuss the play. How are things going with the—"

"Don't start with that," Rowena interrupted. "The play is fine, the costumes are made." She stared at Grace for a long moment. "I can see it on your face. Something has happened. You're…glowing."

Grace groaned softly and covered her cheeks in embarrassment. "All right. We almost had sex. Saturday night. There, are you two happy now?"

"Almost?" Maureen and Rowena asked in unison.

She waved her hands in the air. "We were rolling around on my kitchen floor, in the gravy and the meat loaf and the mashed potatoes, and things were getting pretty…hot." Grace swallowed hard, her face flushing with heat at the memory. It really had been one of the most exciting moments of her sex life. Heck, of her *entire* life.

"And?" Maureen asked.

"And the phone rang. And then it was over. Susan was coming home and I had coleslaw in my hair and we had to stop." Grace sighed wistfully. "But it was really great while it lasted. Like something you see in a movie."

"I can understand the phone call," Rowena said. "And the rolling around on the floor. But I don't get the meat loaf and the gravy part. I know I've been out of the loop for a while, but is that some kind of new term for—"

"No!" Grace cried. "It was our dinner. We were just about to eat when I swept everything onto the floor and dragged him down onto the table. Then we ended up on the floor with the food. It really was a mess. I was still cleaning up gravy this morning, and it spilled on the braided rug in front of the—"

"Stop," Maureen ordered. "Forget the gravy and repeat that part about rolling around on the kitchen floor."

"Yeah," Rowena said, leaning forward and bracing her

elbows on the worktable. "I like that part. I once played a scene on the soap where we got into it with honey. It was so sticky and sweet and it took me an hour to get it out of my hair. But meat loaf and gravy would be nice. I like meat loaf."

Grace grabbed her glass of wine and listened as Maureen and Rowena weighed the relative sensuality of different food items. Whipped cream, fresh strawberries, expensive cognac, melted chocolate. But neither one of them had ever considered meat loaf an option—until now.

"It *was* wonderful," Grace confessed. "And that's all I have to say."

The trio sat silently for a long moment, lost in their own thoughts. Then a bell rang in the front of the house and Maureen looked up. "There's someone at the desk. I have to go. Don't say a word until I get back."

She hurried out, the kitchen door swinging shut behind her. But Grace and Rowena could hear voices from the gathering room, Maureen's soft, melodious tones, and a low, masculine counterpart. Grace realized that she recognized the voice. She hopped out of her chair and pushed the door open a few inches.

"It's Tuck," she whispered, turning to Rowena. "Tuck is here."

"Maybe he's looking for you," Rowena said, rushing up to the door and peeking over Grace's shoulder. "You should go out and talk to him."

Grace shut the door and considered her options. Though she had been discussing *their* sex life with her friends, he didn't know that. She could have just as easily been discussing the play. She had nearly decided to step out and say "hello" to him when the kitchen door swung inwardly. It hit her squarely in the nose and she cried out, then backed up and watched Maureen hurry in. Grace's eyes watered and she saw stars. She reached for the counter to steady herself.

"Your cowboy is here," Maureen whispered.

"We know," Rowena said. "What does he want?"

"He wanted to check and see if I had any rooms available."

"Why would he do that?" Rowena asked. She looked at Grace inquisitively.

"I don't know," Grace sighed impatiently. "You don't have any rooms, so—"

"I do," Maureen said. "We had a cancellation just this morning. I've got a room right through Christmas night. What should I tell him?"

Grace glanced back and forth between Maureen and Rowena. "I don't know," she said. "Why do you think he wants a room? Did he say?" She spun on her heel and paced the length of the kitchen. "Do you think he's uncomfortable at my house? Maybe I've done something wrong. Maybe he's embarrassed about the meat loaf incident. I just—well, I don't know."

"What do you want me to tell him?" Maureen demanded. "I can't just let him stand out there. Should I give him the room?"

Drawing a deep breath, Grace tried to think. But she couldn't see past her confusion. She'd never played these little games with men, so she hadn't a clue as to what Tuck was thinking. "Maybe he's just checking in case I ask him to leave."

"So I should tell him we have a room?"

"No," Grace said firmly. "Well, maybe. I don't know."

"Don't tell him," Rowena said. "Grace, you can always mention something if you want to, but for now, Maureen, you don't have any spare rooms."

Maureen nodded, then disappeared again, satisfied that

Rowena had come up with a good plan. A few moments later, Grace heard her speak with Tuck, telling him that for now they were still booked, but she'd call him if anything opened up. Grace watched Tuck nod, then put his Stetson back on and walk to the front door. She released a tightly held breath and turned back to Rowena, smiling weakly.

The door flew open again and she jumped out of the way as Maureen rushed back inside. "I told him," she said.

"We heard," Rowena replied.

Grace wandered back to the table and sat down, then grabbed her wineglass and drained it. "I thought things were going pretty well. He told me he wouldn't pressure me and it would have to be my decision if we wanted to— go further. But obviously, he got impatient and decided he couldn't stick around anymore. Maybe I wasn't woman enough for him."

Maureen slipped her arm around Grace's shoulders. "I'm sure that's not it."

"Then why is he looking for a room? Give me one good reason."

"The bed in his room is too short?" Rowena suggested.

"The kids are too noisy in the morning?" Maureen added. "See, there are two reasons and they don't have anything to do with you."

"This is all my problem, then," Grace said. "If I really had the situation under control, I wouldn't feel this way. It shouldn't make a difference that he doesn't want to stay. But I've been stupid, and now I've fallen in love with him, and if I don't stop talking now, I'm going to cry."

The words came out without pause. Why not admit it? She was falling in love with Tuck McCabe. Grace drew a shaky breath and tried to regain control of her emotions. At least she hadn't made love to him. How would she have felt if he'd decided to leave after something so intimate?

She would have been completely devastated. Now she was just slightly devastated.

"You're in love with him?" Rowena asked.

Grace nodded. "I think so." She wiped away her tears and pasted a smile on her face. "This is all for the best. It never would have worked out, anyway. He lives in Montana. There's no way he could live here. And I'm not sure I could move my kids to Montana, so there really is no future in it. Besides, I don't know if I ever want to get married again, not after the nuts-and-bolts girl." She glanced around. "I should go. I have a lot of work to do before play practice. I've got to confirm the ice order for the carving contest. And I've got to meet with the people who are going to judge the floats in the parade." She brushed an errant tear from her cheek and drew a shaky breath. "I'll see you both later."

With that, Grace hurried through the kitchen door. Luckily, there were no guests in the dining room or the gathering room, so she made her escape without being seen. When she reached the end of the long drive, she stopped, fighting back a wave of frustration.

She should never have invited Tuck to stay. Or maybe she should never have kissed him that very first time. Or the second or the third. And Saturday night's dinner was definitely a major error in judgment. And she probably shouldn't have said anything to Rowena and Maureen about Tuck, either.

For someone who had promised herself there would be no regrets, Grace had plenty of them now.

TUCK TWISTED HIS BODY into the tiny crawl space beneath the eaves and scraped at the drainpipe from the third-floor shower. Grace had been right. There was a pretty nasty leak coming from the joint. The pipe had corroded so badly that there was no repairing it. He'd have to replace it.

He made a mental list of the tools he'd need, knowing he wouldn't find a pipe wrench and plumber's putty in Grace's basement. But it shouldn't be a complicated job, and he'd become a pretty fair plumber over the years, installing windmills to pump water to the cattle at Snake Creek and putting in a shower in the bunkhouse. Between Ray's skill as an electrician and Tuck's plumbing abilities, they'd managed to keep most everything running smoothly at the ranch.

Once he'd pushed himself out of the crawl space, he scrambled to his feet. To his surprise he found Grace standing in the bathroom doorway. "Hi there," he said, wiping his hands on his jeans. She looked beautiful today, the color high in her cheeks, her hair falling in soft waves around her shoulders. In a few short steps, he could have her in his arms, kissing her until her lips were swollen and her eyes sleepy with passion. But Tuck resisted the urge, determined to keep his promise to her. "I was just fixing the leak."

"You don't have to do that," she said, her voice cool and distant. She crossed her arms beneath her breasts and refused to meet his gaze.

Tuck took a step toward her. "What's wrong?"

Grace shook her head. "Nothing. It's just that you're under no obligation to fix my plumbing. Or my refrigerator light. Or the hinge on the back door."

In a single stride he crossed the tiny bathroom and stood in front of her. "I want to do this for you, Gracie. It's no problem. I've got the time and I—"

"That's not the point," Grace said, turning and walking into the bedroom. "I don't want to depend on you. After you leave, I'm going to have to deal with these same problems and I don't want to constantly be saying that I wish Tucker McCabe were here to help out. This is *my* life and *my* leaky pipe. I'll deal with it myself.''

He'd never encountered this mood before, Tuck mused, scanning her face for clues to her distress. Her expression was a mixture of anger and hurt—and suspicion. ''I want to do these things for you, Gracie. I want to help out.''

He reached out and skimmed the back of his hand over her cheek. Her skin was so soft, like nothing he'd ever touched before. Tuck closed his eyes for a moment and tried to remember the sensation, knowing that he might want to bring it to mind later. When he opened them again, her obstinate gaze was still fixed on him.

Tuck bent nearer, needing to taste her mouth, to reassure himself that she wasn't upset with him. Just one kiss. What could be the harm? He teased the crease of her lips with his tongue and she reluctantly opened beneath his gentle assault. A soft sigh slipped from her throat, then suddenly, she drew away. Grace pressed her fingertips to her lips.

''What?'' Tuck said, frowning. ''What's wrong?''

She cleared her throat nervously. ''I—I've been thinking…about everything you said the other night. And I'm just not ready.'' She turned around and walked to the door, then turned back. Indecision was etched on her pretty face. ''There are so many things to consider. The distance, the kids, mistakes I've made in the past.''

His jaw went tight. This was not what he wanted to hear. But he couldn't say that it came as a surprise. ''I understand, Gracie. Hell, we've only known each other a week. It's the right thing. You don't have to give me any explanations.''

His words sounded sensible, but in his heart, deep in his soul, Tuck knew they were a lie. Damn it, he wanted Grace, whatever the terms—forever or for just a night. He didn't think he could live the rest of his life not knowing what it felt like to hold her, to touch her.

"It's just that I don't want to have any regrets after you leave."

Tuck nodded, praying that she'd stop with the explanations before he lost all control, crossed the room and kissed her senseless.

"And that's why I think you should get a room at the inn. Maureen says there's been a cancellation and she has space for you now. You could get your things packed up and stay there tonight."

He blinked in surprise, wondering just how Grace had found out about his inquiry at the inn. "Is that what you want, Gracie?"

She nodded. "I think that would be best."

For a long moment he stared at her, but he still couldn't read her expression. "Did Maureen Cooper tell you I stopped by earlier today?" She hesitated and Tuck knew in that instant that Maureen had. And in that same instant, he knew how much the revelation had hurt Grace.

"She mentioned it," Grace said.

"Grace, I was just asking in case we—"

"There's no need to explain," Grace said. "I understand. And I think it's for the best. When you're around, I can't think clearly."

Tuck laughed softly. "I know what you mean." He drew in a deep breath. "So, I guess I'll be leaving then." The words seared into him like a hot branding iron. "Like you said, it's probably for the best. I don't want you to have any regrets." He rubbed his hands together, then dragged his gaze from hers. "Well, I'm going to go get packed and I'll get out of your hair."

"I wouldn't blame you if you wanted to go home," Grace said. "I mean, to Montana."

"No. I made a promise. I'll stay until after the festival."

A tiny smile of relief touched her lips and she nodded. "I'll call Maureen and let her know that the festival budget will pay for your room. And we'll pick up your tab at Tubb's."

With that, Grace hurried out the door, as if staying in the same room with him was dangerous. Tuck listened to her footsteps recede down the stairs, and when he was sure she was out of earshot, he cursed out loud. "Perfect. You did your best to make her want you and all you could manage was to drive her further away. Smooth, McCabe. Really smooth."

He grabbed his duffel from the closet floor and began to stuff his clothes into it. Where had things gone wrong? Just the other night, he and Grace had been so close...on the verge of surrender...until the phone rang. He thought they might just pick up where they had left off, but somewhere between then and now, Grace's feelings had changed.

If Tuck knew one thing for sure, he knew that his own feelings hadn't changed. He was falling in love with Grace Penrose. Hell, he *was* in love with her, no questions, no doubts. How he was certain, Tuck really didn't care. He wanted a future with Grace—but only if she wanted the same.

"Just tell her how you feel," he muttered, as if saying it out loud would make it easier to accomplish.

But some instinct warned him off. She had to say it first. He couldn't risk rejection, not with Grace. If he opened his heart and she stomped all over it, Tuck wasn't sure he'd ever be able to forget. Maybe he was wrong, maybe he'd grown up too tough and cynical, but he'd always survived by listening to his instincts. He wasn't going to stop now.

"What are you doing?"

Tuck glanced up to find Susan standing in the hallway.

She had her Barbie dolls in her hands. Her gaze shifted to his duffel bag, then back up to his face.

"Hi, Susie Q," Tuck said, trying to keep his voice light. "I'm just packing."

"You're going away?"

"No, I'm going to stay at Twin Oaks. I was supposed to stay there right away, but they didn't have a room for me. Now they do."

"But you're staying with us. Mom said it was all right."

He dropped the flannel shirt he was folding onto the bed, then slowly approached Susan. He bent down on one knee. "Sweetie, your mom is very busy right now. She doesn't need to take care of me along with you and Bryan. It's just too much work. So I'm going to stay at the inn. To make things easier for her. But you can always come and visit me."

Susan thought about this for a while. Tuck could tell she didn't buy his explanation. "But I like it when you live here. We get to play together. And you're the only friend I have who does fashion show right."

Tuck's heart twisted. He reached out and drew Susan into his arms, giving her a fierce hug. Maybe Grace knew best. Susan had become too attached, and given another week together, leaving would be even more difficult. "You bring your Barbies down to the inn and we'll have ourselves a real nice fashion show."

Susan drew back, then gave him a sloppy kiss on the cheek. "You're the best cowboy in the world," she said. "Even if you don't have a sick-shooter."

"And you're the best little girl in the world. Now, why don't you run along so I can finish packing."

She ran to the door, but then at the last moment hurried back to him. She threw her arms around his neck. "I love you," she whispered in his ear.

Then she skipped out of the room, still clutching her dolls.

Tuck rubbed his chest, trying to push away the ache that had settled there. He loved that little girl just as much as he loved Grace. And if walking away from Grace wasn't enough to break his heart, then walking away from Susan would be.

He straightened and went back to his packing. It didn't take long. He'd only intended to be on the road for a week. When he'd collected all his belongings, Tuck slung the strap over his shoulder. He took one last look around the cozy room, then headed downstairs.

Bryan was in the library, playing a video game. Tuck poked his head in the door. "I'm leaving," he said.

The boy twisted around on the sofa. He noticed Tuck's duffel bag, a look of confusion coming over his face. "Leaving?"

"I still expect you to work off our little deal, so I'll pick you up every morning and evening at six. Be ready and waiting on the front porch. I don't want to have to come in and get you."

Bryan opened his mouth to protest, then thought better of it. "Okay," he said. "See ya."

Tuck grinned. "Yeah, I'll see ya."

He walked into the living room and found Susan there. She silently waved goodbye, her gaze shifting over to the kitchen. The sound of supper preparations drifted through the house. Grace was in there. Saying goodbye to her seemed so final, and he wasn't sure that once said, he'd be able to take it back. "Tell your mom I'll see her around."

Susan nodded, her brown eyes filled with confusion. Tuck grabbed the door and pulled it open, then slipped outside. His truck was parked out front, and every step he took toward it was a step away from what he really wanted.

From the moment he'd met Grace, he felt as if they'd been moving toward something.

Now they were moving away, putting a distance between them that seemed impossible to bridge. Tuck adjusted the brim of his hat against the low afternoon sun. He hadn't had a lot of experience with relationships and he was at a loss to know what to do. There had to be a way to convince Grace that they belonged together.

He just hoped he could figure it all out before it was time to go back to Montana.

THE HOUSE WAS SILENT and dark. Grace sat on the sofa, her feet tucked beneath her. No fire burned in the fireplace. That had become Tuck's job, and since he'd left two nights ago, Grace didn't have the heart to drag the firewood inside and mess with the kindling. The cold hearth matched the feeling that had set into her heart.

The Christmas tree they'd put up together twinkled in the corner. The season was supposed to be happy—harried, yet happy. But her Christmas spirit was in serious jeopardy. Even watching the Grinch video with Susan and Bryan hadn't lifted her mood. All she could think about was how much she wanted Tuck to share in the fun.

She'd caught sight of him a few times, when he'd picked Bryan up in the morning and the evening to work with his horses and goats. Susan had begged to go along and she had no choice but to relent. Both her children returned with stories to tell about their adventures with Tuck, how much fun the horses were. Grace listened, but all the while her heart was breaking. This was worse than a divorce, sharing custody of her children with a man she'd never even been married to.

But she'd let him walk out of her house for all the best reasons. Suddenly, those reasons didn't matter. All that mattered was the strange, empty void in her life that nothing seemed to fill—not even three candy bars, a pint of gourmet ice cream and half a bag of nacho chips. She wanted Tuck back in his bedroom on the third floor, back in her kitchen first thing in the morning, back on her sofa late at night.

Susan hadn't been happy with her decision to have Tuck move out. She was still obsessed with turning him into her new father and regularly tried to reassure Grace that he'd be back the next day. That he wouldn't like staying at Twin Oaks because they didn't have good toys there and he'd miss them all too much. Bryan, reverting to his usual sullen self, had no immediate reaction. Grace couldn't tell if he cared one way or the other.

In an attempt to push thoughts of Tuck out of her mind, Grace focused on the Christmas tree. Now was a good time to count her blessings. She had a nice job, two healthy children. A wonderful place to live, food on the table, clothes in the closets. It should be enough, she told herself. So why wasn't it?

She climbed off the sofa and headed for the stairs. Maybe a hot shower would make her feel better. But she stopped halfway up the stairs, then turned around and came back down. Grace knew what she had to do. She could stay in the shower for the next three days and she still wouldn't be able to wash Tuck McCabe out of her life.

The sitter's number was taped to the refrigerator door. Grace picked up the phone and dialed Mrs. Girard. The woman answered after two rings. "Mrs. Girard? This is Grace Penrose. I'm wondering if you could come over and watch the children… Yes, I know it's late, but an emergency has come up with the festival plans and I'm going to have to leave… Yes, I may be a little late…maybe midnight?"

Estelle Girard, a spritely widow, was one of the town's favorite baby-sitters. She lived just one house away from Grace and would be at the front door in a matter of minutes. Grace raced upstairs, ran a comb through her hair, dabbed on a bit of lipstick and then took a moment to convince herself that she was doing the right thing. She just couldn't stand all this indecision and doubt.

When the doorbell rang, she didn't have any more time to consider her options. Maybe that was for the best. If she just operated on impulse, she wouldn't be so nervous.

Grace let the older woman in. "Thank goodness you could come," she said as she closed the door behind Estelle. "I wasn't sure what I was going to do. There's an emergency with the—"

"What could be so important that takes you out this late, dear?"

Grace bit her bottom lip. She hated lying, but if this wasn't a good cause, what was? "Elves," Grace said. "And with the parade just days away, if I don't take care of this immediately, there's no telling what might happen. They might revolt." She grabbed her jacket and tugged it on. "If there are any emergencies, you can call me at—" She hesitated then drew a deep breath. "Just dial 911."

With that, Grace turned and hurried out of the house. She decided to walk to the B and B. The sight of her car parked out front would probably cause a few tongues to wag. The whole town already knew that Tuck was now staying at Twin Oaks, and speculation was running rampant as to what had put him there.

The night was chilly, but a wispy fog hung in the air, creating halos around each of the streetlights. Christmas lights twinkled from windows and eaves and the snow crunched beneath her feet. Grace shoved her hands in her pockets and kept her head down. She didn't allow herself to think about what she was going to do when she got to the B and B. Thoughts like those might cause her to turn tail and run back home.

"I'm an adult," she said. "A woman who can make her own choices. And if this is what I choose, then so be it."

When she reached the inn, she stepped up to the front door, smoothed her hands over her hair, said a silent prayer, then went inside. Two guests turned to look at her as she came in, then went back to their conversation. Maureen smiled an automatic greeting, assuming she'd stopped to talk about the play.

But then she realized what Grace had come for and grinned. "Room three," Maureen said. "He came in about fifteen minutes ago."

"Thanks," Grace murmured, her face warming with a blush. She climbed the stairs quickly, and when she reached the door, she hesitated for only a moment. "This is what you want," she whispered to herself. "This is what you've always wanted from the moment you saw him."

The volume of her knock echoed in the empty hall. She heard footsteps on the other side of the door and her tummy did a little somersault. The instant Tuck opened the door, Grace felt a twinge of anxiety, but she brushed it aside. He was dressed only in jeans and they were unbuttoned at the waist. A towel was draped around his neck, brushing against his naked chest as he moved.

"Grace."

She reached out and placed her finger on his lips. The moment he started talking, Grace knew her resolve would waver. If she could just keep him quiet, she could get through this without humiliation. "This is what I want," she said. "I've decided."

"Are you sure?"

"Please, don't ask me that," she replied, walking past

him into the room. "We're attracted to each other. And whether I want to admit it or not, these opportunities don't come along every day. Or even every year. I live a quiet life here and exciting things just don't happen to me."

"So you're taking advantage of an opportunity?" Tuck asked, closing the door behind her.

She turned around and faced him. "Is there something wrong with that?" she said.

He slowly shook his head. "No. Not if it's what you really want."

"And what do you want?" she asked, her voice barely a whisper.

Tuck reached out and touched her cheek. "I want you."

Without a second thought, Grace threw her arms around his neck and kissed him. Like jumping into a cold lake on a warm day, the sensation was at first overwhelming. But then, as their tongues touched, she relaxed. This was exactly what she needed, this wonderful wave of desire washing around her. Four days without his touch had been too much to bear.

He ran his fingers though her hair, molding her mouth to his. She'd grown familiar with his taste and now craved it. A tiny sigh slipped from her throat as she tried to catch her breath. She'd done the right thing coming to him. He was the only man who could bring forth this passion, and Grace needed to see how far he'd take her.

"God, I've missed you," Tuck confessed, his lips hot against hers. He dragged his mouth to her throat and kissed her there as his fingers fumbled with the zipper of her jacket. When he'd tossed that aside, he started on her blouse. One by one, he opened the buttons, exploring new territory with his tongue. Lower and lower he moved until he was on his knees, his face nuzzling her belly.

Grace tipped her head back and cupped his face in her

palms. His beard was rough against her skin and his hair soft between her fingers. Everything about him made her heart race and her senses spin, and she felt like more of a woman with him, simply because he was more of a man.

Another sigh escaped her throat as he dispensed with the clasp of her bra. And when he moved to her nipple, Grace cried out softly, a flood of warmth racing through her. With his mouth and with his hands, he touched her gently, as if every new spot was a revelation to him, something to be savored slowly.

Life had played a cruel trick on her, leaving her unfamiliar with such overwhelming desire. She felt like an untried girl, experiencing intimacy for the first time, plumbing the depths of her own passion. But then, maybe this was fated to be. Maybe she was destined to wait until Tuck came into her life.

"We can't do this," he murmured, his breath warm on her belly. He gripped her waist and trailed kisses along the waistband of her jeans.

"Don't say that," Grace replied. "You don't know how hard it was for me to—"

"No," Tuck interrupted. "I just got back from the Rawlings place and I need a shower." He stood and looked down into her eyes, his gaze lingering for a long moment. "Aw, hell," he said. In one quick motion, he slipped his hands underneath her blouse and brushed it off her shoulders. "You're coming with me."

"In the shower?" Grace said with a gasp.

He reached for the top button of her jeans. "I'm afraid if I leave you here, you'll be gone when I get out."

Tuck brought his mouth down on hers again, but this time his hands frantically worked at her clothes. Bit by bit, he undressed her, his mouth never leaving hers. And bit by bit, Grace felt her shy nature dissolve beneath the touch of his hands. She wanted Tuck to know her, to see her as a sexy and desirable woman. Clothing had become a barrier between them.

As he stepped back and tossed aside the last of her clothes, Grace didn't worry about her flaws. She knew that in Tuck's eyes, she was nothing less than perfect. She watched as he skimmed out of his jeans, then his boxers. He stood in front of her, naked, completely unaware of what the sight of his body was doing to her.

For a moment, Grace couldn't breathe. He was so beautiful, so perfect…so aroused. What incredible luck had brought a man like this into her life? She reached out and placed her hand on his chest, then smoothed her palm over his skin. Hard muscle rippled beneath her touch, and beneath that, his heart beat strong and sure.

Slowly, she let her hand drift down, to his flat belly and then his hip. Drawing a deep breath, she moved to his hard shaft. A low moan rumbled in his chest as her fingers encircled him. Amazed at the effect her caress had on him, Grace allowed her fingers to slide up and then down, so softly that she was barely touching him at all.

But he didn't let her go much further. A few moments later, Tuck reached down and laced his fingers through hers, then pulled her along toward the bathroom. "If I don't find another way to occupy your hands, this is going to be over before it even begins," he warned her. "Come on. I'll let you wash my back."

Warm water rushed over her as she stepped into the shower. Tuck followed right behind, then wrapped his arms around her waist and pulled her against him. The water, gliding over her skin, heightened the effect of his touch on her, and the exploration he began in the bedroom started anew. Sensation pulsed through her and his hands turned to liquid heat on her body.

Grace gasped as his fingers slipped between her legs. His caress was electric, sending a current through her body, stealing the breath from her lungs and the thoughts from her head. "Oh, my," she murmured as the water spattered down on her.

On and on he went, bringing her close to the edge before drawing her back again. Grace had never been seduced like this, with such exquisite pleasure and addicting torment. In a very short time, Tuck had learned her body and knew just where to touch to make her ache with need.

He stopped for only a moment, to find a condom and sheath himself. Grace knew what was coming. She wasn't exactly a virgin. But as he picked her up and pressed her back against the wall of the shower, she realized that this might as well be the first time for her. And as he entered her, Grace knew in her heart and in her soul that she'd never made love to a man. Not really.

And as he moved inside of her, bringing her to a shattering release, Grace knew something else. It was the first time. Tuck was the only real man she had ever had. And the only man she might ever love.

CHAPTER NINE

Somewhere in the depths of the old house, a clock chimed. Tuck counted until it stopped at twelve. Then he sighed softly and nuzzled his face into Grace's hair. They hadn't slept. After they'd made love in the shower, they came back to his bed and did it all over again, only slower and with greater care, lingering over each moment, savoring each new sensation until they were both spent.

Tuck had known it would be good between them. From the moment they'd met, he'd wondered if they'd come to this place. But at the start, it was simply raw lust that had occupied his thoughts. Now, as Grace lay curled in his embrace, sated by what they'd shared, lust was the last thing on his mind.

They belonged together. He might not have been ready to admit that just a few hours earlier, before she'd knocked on his door. But there was no denying the truth now. Grace had made a place for herself in his heart, a heart that he'd considered immune to love. And now he wanted nothing more than for Grace to want him, to need him, for the rest of his life.

He loved her. For some reason, Tuck thought that if and when that emotion finally struck, he'd be stunned or caught unaware. But with Grace, it was simple. Maybe he'd known all along she was the one, from the very first time they met on Silas's back steps. He tried to trace the start of his feelings, but they were like a long thread that wound its way around his heart, with no beginning and no end.

The traditional images flashed through his mind, like a newsreel of the life he wanted to live. There were holidays and vacations, children and grandchildren, anniversaries and birthdays, all the things that families were supposed to be. His notions of family, the ideas that his drunken mother and absent father had unknowingly instilled, were suddenly gone. Now, in the middle of each scene, Grace was there, standing at his side. And they were happy.

But how did she feel? Were the same thoughts running through her mind? Tuck didn't believe for a second that Grace was only interested in a one-night stand. She wasn't the kind of woman to take intimacy so lightly. So why had she really come to him? Was it a surrender? Or a test? Or had her emotions overwhelmed her common-sense approach to life?

Damn Dan Penrose and his wandering libido! He was the one to blame, the one who had made Grace so wary around men. Her ex had destroyed her confidence. He'd made Grace doubt herself, her beauty, her passion, her ability to know desire and to deserve love.

Tuck pressed a kiss to her temple as he twisted his fingers through her still-damp hair. He wanted to tell her how he felt, to open his heart to her, to trust her with his soul. But something still held him back, some primal instinct to protect himself. If he said those words and she didn't respond, he'd never be able to take them back. For the rest of his life, he'd know that Tuck McCabe had loved Grace Penrose, but that love hadn't been returned.

His thoughts were distracted by the feel of her fingers gently tracing a path from his collarbone to points south. When she brushed against his sex, he felt desire stir again. Already, she knew how to make him ready and able, and with barely a caress. He growled playfully. "I'll give you exactly an hour to stop that," Tuck warned.

Her hand stilled and she looked up at him. "We don't have an hour," she said. "I left the kids with a sitter and she needs to get home. I told her I'd be back before midnight."

Tuck groaned and pulled her tightly against his body. "You underestimated me," he teased. "You should have told her you'd be back next week." Now that he had Grace exactly where he wanted her, he never wanted to let her go. "Someday, you and I are going to have time," he said. A worried expression etched her flushed features and he tried to smooth it away with his fingertips. "What? Tell me."

"You don't have to say that," she said.

He frowned. "I want to say that."

"But you don't have to. I understand what happened here and I want to be adult about it."

"What is that supposed to mean, Gracie? You don't have to *be* adult, you *are* an adult. We both are."

Grace took a deep breath, then let it out slowly, focusing her gaze on his chest, all the while drawing circles with her fingertip. "When I was a teenager, I fell in love with Dan and we…were intimate. I believed that because we were, that meant that we were in love and we should get married. I confused love with lust, at least on his part." She paused. "So we did—get married. It was only afterward, when I got a little older, that I realized I wouldn't have had to marry him. I tried to make it work, but we had just begun the wrong way."

"I'm not asking you to marry me," Tuck said, frustrated by the direction of their conversation.

She reached up and touched his face. "And I'm not waiting for a marriage proposal, Tuck. You don't have to worry.

After you go home, I won't be calling and bothering you.'' She drew a ragged breath. ''Clinging to some silly fantasy is childish. I'm not going to do that again. This is just one night, and when it's over, you and I can go back to our lives. No regrets.'' She pressed her forehead to his chest. ''When Dan told me he was leaving, I pleaded with him to stay. I cried and I begged and I pushed aside every shred of pride that I possessed in order to keep our family together. I'm never going to do that again, Tuck. It took so much out of me.''

Tuck didn't know what to say. Before he met Grace, this was his dream date—great sex with no strings. But damn it, he wanted more. He wanted a future, he wanted to fall asleep with Grace in his arms every night and wake up next to her every morning. He wanted to take care of her children and make a family with her. That's what *he* wanted.

''If that's what you want,'' he said, his instinct for self-preservation kicking into high gear.

''That's what I want,'' Grace said firmly.

An uneasy silence hung between them. The conversation didn't have anywhere else to go and they both knew it. She slipped out of bed and slowly began to gather her clothes. Tuck watched her in the light filtering out of the bathroom, well aware that he might never have the chance to look at her again. Over the past two hours, he'd touched every spot on her body and committed her form to memory. He knew exactly what brought her to the edge and what piqued her desire.

''Gracie, I want you to know that—''

''Don't,'' she whispered, stiffening. She turned, clutching her clothes to her chest. ''This was the most incredible night. Let's not try to make it more. Let's keep things simple and easy.''

Tuck threw back the covers and crawled out of bed, the

cool air hitting his hot skin. He gently took the clothes from her hands and set them on the bedside table. Then he started to dress her, taking one last chance to touch her body, to appreciate every curve, every soft inch of skin, all the places that tasted so good and felt so right.

When he got to her jacket, he held it out as she slid her arms inside. Then she turned and he zipped it up, pulling her collar up around her chin. Her hair was still damp from the shower, but she hadn't brought a hat. "It's cold outside," he said. "Are you sure you don't want to stay here with me?"

He knew what the answer would be. Removing the clothes from her body had been akin to stripping away the last barriers that stood between them. And now, with her fully dressed again, the barriers had returned.

"I can't," Grace replied. She pressed her palms against his chest, then pushed up on her toes and kissed him. "Thank you," she said.

He cupped her face in his hands and gave her a proper kiss, a kiss she'd remember. A kiss he hoped would bring her back to his door tomorrow night and the night after that. A moment later, she was gone, the door closing behind her with a loud click. Tuck stood in the middle of the room, feeling very naked and oddly vulnerable. It took him only ten or fifteen seconds to decide to go after her. With a low curse, he snatched up his clothes and began to tug them on.

"Thank you?" he muttered. "Like loving her is some kind of chore? Where the hell would she get an idea like that?" He shook his head. "I should hunt down her ex and tell him exactly what I think of him. With my fist."

By the time he pulled on his boots, his temper had cooled and reason superseded emotion. Maybe it was time he took a risk. He'd tell Grace how he felt and take his chances.

He grabbed his jacket from a hook on the back of the door, then stepped out of his room.

When he got downstairs, he found Maureen sitting at the front desk, perusing a magazine. "Did she say anything to you?" he asked.

Maureen looked up and shook her head. "This is all pretty new to her," she said. "I think you're going to have to give her a little time."

His jaw tightened. "I don't have time," he said, heading toward the front door.

When Tuck stepped outside, he breathed deeply of the night air, trying to look at what had happened objectively. But everything was still surrounded by a haze of passion. As he walked, he considered what he was going to say. First, he'd try to convince Grace that what they'd shared wasn't just a one-night stand. Then he'd tell her there was every chance that they deserved a future together. And then he'd have to figure out how to make that happen with her in New England and him in Montana.

He wandered through Cooper's Corner, taking the loop down Main Street before walking toward Grace's house near the corner of Oak Road and School Street. When he reached her front gate, he stood on the sidewalk and stared up at her house. A light shone in her bedroom window.

He closed his eyes and tried to imagine the scene behind the lacy curtains. He saw her slowly undressing, unbuttoning her blouse, casting aside her bra, slipping out of her panties. But his visions were no longer fantasies. Their time together had made them a reality. He knew the way that light shone on her silken skin, knew the sweet curve of her back and the arch of her neck. And he knew so much more—how to make her cry out with desire and shudder with release.

But he didn't know how to make her love him the way

he loved her. Not yet. Tuck sighed, his warm breath clouding around his face. Until he did, he didn't want to push his luck. He suspected he'd only have one chance to convince Grace Penrose that she belonged in his life—forever. And he wasn't going to waste that chance tonight.

In the end, Tuck turned and walked back the way he came. For now, he'd wait, content with the fact that this wasn't the end. But he wouldn't wait long. Things would be settled between him and Grace soon. And then he'd finally know if they'd begin a new life together or he'd be left to pick up the pieces of his old life alone.

GRACE SAT AT THE KITCHEN TABLE, index cards spread out in front of her. Each color-coded card represented a single entry into the Christmas Eve parade. Blue cards were for floats, green for musical acts, yellow for civic groups. Though she only had twenty-nine cards, there was a definite art to the arrangement. If the American Legion band marched too close to the senior center's kazoo band, the kazoos would be drowned out. And then there was Dabney Archer's Apple Orchard float. Dabney, who insisted on participating, was known for his shabby float construction. After his float collapsed in the middle of Main Street last year, dumping bushels of apples on the ground, the parade was held up almost fifteen minutes while the debris was cleared.

She yawned and rubbed her eyes, trying to push aside the exhaustion that muddled her mind. For a moment she allowed her thoughts to drift, and the direction they drifted didn't surprise her. Tuck. She'd been thinking about him since she left Twin Oaks last night.

Grace had known that making love to Tuck McCabe would be memorable. But she'd never anticipated that she would enjoy the memories so much. Last night, after she returned from his room, her senses were filled with him.

The scent of his shampoo was still strong in her hair, the warmth of his hands still tingled on her skin, and she could taste his kisses on her lips. Every sensation she had shared with him was still fresh in her mind.

When she'd crawled into her empty bed, she'd expected sleep to come after being so completely sated. And then the sun would rise and she'd put their night together behind her. But instead, she lay awake all night long, plagued by doubts and indecision. What had seemed like such a simple solution to their attraction didn't feel like a solution at all. It had merely made her desire for Tuck more acute. Before this, she could only guess at what they might share. Now she knew exactly what she'd have to learn to live without.

With a soft groan, she buried her face in her hands. Yes, she was an adult and she'd made an adult choice to tumble into bed with Tuck McCabe. Yet she felt like a naive girl when dealing with the consequences. Making love to Tuck had been the most wonderful experience of her rather inexperienced life. She couldn't help but want to repeat it—over and over and over…

"How's it going?"

At first she thought she'd imagined his voice. It hadn't been the first time that day. Then she looked up and saw him standing at the back door. He was so handsome, his cowboy hat pulled low, his long legs covered in faded denim. He took her breath away. She stared at him for a long moment. And then a cold draft blew through the kitchen. An instant later, her index cards flew off the table.

She cried out in dismay and attempted to gather them in her arms. But it was no use. All her work had gone to waste. She pushed off her chair and knelt down on the floor, picking up each card and trying to remember where it belonged in the order.

"I'm sorry," Tuck said, joining her on the floor.

"It's all right," Grace replied, not looking at him. "It probably doesn't make a difference. The parade usually has at least one disaster. Perhaps this is it."

When they'd collected all the cards, Tuck helped her to her feet. He smiled apologetically. "Maybe I should come in and we can start again."

"It's all right," Grace murmured, her gaze drawn to his. Her heart skipped and she felt a bit dizzy. Why did he have to be so gorgeous? His cheeks were ruddy from the cold and his hair stood up in unruly spikes, as if coaxed by his fingers. And he hadn't shaved, the shadow of his beard giving him a rugged look. Even though he was fully dressed, he moved exactly the way he had when he was completely naked. "Wh-what are you doing here?"

"Would it be a problem if I came to see you?" Tuck asked.

Grace swallowed hard. "Did you come to see me?"

He grinned. "Of course."

"Why?" she asked with a frown.

This time her question brought a laugh. "Gracie, are you going to pretend that nothing happened last night? Because I was there. And I can tell you, without the least bit of male ego, I wasn't that forgettable."

"Oh, no," she said. "I didn't mean—you were very—well, good." She bit her bottom lip. "Do we have to talk about this now?" She turned back to her cards. "I really have to get this parade organized."

Tuck shrugged. "We don't have to talk at all." He reached out and grabbed her around the waist, pulling her against him. "I've always believed actions speak louder than words."

Without pause, he brought his mouth down on hers and kissed her, gently but thoroughly. In a sudden rush, all the feelings she'd experienced the night before came back. Her knees went weak and her thoughts began to swirl. For a moment, she could do nothing more than focus on the taste of him, how his tongue gently teased at hers, how his kiss was sweet yet provocative, promising so much more if she'd just surrender.

But he couldn't stop there. He skimmed his hands over her body, finding familiar curves beneath Grace's clothes. A tiny moan slipped from her lips and he froze for a minute—until she wrapped her arms around his neck and sank against his chest, allowing herself to enjoy the feelings that rushed through her.

Her hands explored his body with a frantic touch, fumbling with the buttons on his shirt. But when she finally found skin, Tuck drew back and looked down into her eyes. "I like the way you kiss," he said.

Grace opened her mouth to respond, then snapped it shut, reality crashing back. Why couldn't she control herself around him? These feelings were supposed to go away, but they were more intense than they had been last night. "I— I have to go," she murmured.

"So, what are you doing tonight?" he asked. "Can I take you and the kids to dinner? It's fried chicken night at Tubb's."

She frowned. Hadn't she made her intentions clear? What they'd shared was one night only. Maybe he hadn't heard her. Or perhaps Tuck was just ignoring her wishes. "Once the kids are home I have to run to Pittsfield to the printers. Then I have our final rehearsal for the play. I really won't have time for dinner."

"Actually, I can help you out with the kids so you can go to Pittsfield now," he said. "We'll come and pick you up after your rehearsal and have a late dinner."

"No," Grace said firmly. "I don't want you to do that."

"I hoped they'd help me decorate the sleighs tonight,"

he explained in an even voice, as if he were trying to school his temper. "I picked up some garland and ribbon and I thought we might have some fun. Get into the Christmas spirit."

Grace knew her kids would rather spend the evening with Tuck than with Mrs. Girard. And decorating the sleighs sounded like an awful lot of fun. But once again, Tuck was making himself indispensable—to her and her children. Still, she felt her determination waver. "All right," she said. "They'll be home from school in an hour. But don't wait on dinner. I might be late and they'll get hungry."

"Good," Tuck said. "If you're late, I'll put them to bed. And after you get back from play practice, we'll talk."

"Fine," Grace agreed, lacking the energy to fight him anymore. It was just less trouble to let him be a part of her life until he left. He made it so easy for her to need him. "I have to go."

"Then, I'll see you later," he said with a smile.

She nodded, grabbed her jacket and left. When she got inside her car, she paused before starting it. Touching her lips with her fingertips, she realized they were still moist from his kiss. "Oh, damn," she cried. "What are you doing? You can't let yourself love him, you just can't."

She wouldn't think about all that now. She was going to the printer's and then she was going to play practice. She was going to concentrate on the festival and push all thoughts of Tucker McCabe from her head. Reminding herself that she was Grace Penrose, prim-and-proper resident of Cooper's Corner, would probably help. "I'm not a wanton woman," she said. "Not some nymphomaniac who can't control her desires. I'm Grace Penrose." She drew a ragged breath. "Supermom."

She threw the car into gear then hit the accelerator. The tires spun on the snow and she swerved as she pulled onto

Oak Road. When she drove past the drive to Twin Oaks, she thought about turning in. Right now, she could use a little advice. But going to Maureen or Rowena would require a full accounting of the facts and even she couldn't recall her night with Tuck without blushing.

A delicious memory drifted through her mind and an unbidden smile quirked her lips. He had such a way of making her feel sexy. When she thought about their night together she got all shivery and fluttery. And she automatically thought about what secret pleasures they might share the next time and the time after that.

"There won't be a next time," Grace muttered. She reached for the radio and cranked the volume up until it nearly drowned out her thoughts.

How could she possibly trust herself again? She'd made one mistake and spent the last seven years paying for it. Seven years without a man in her life. Seven years until she was brave enough to share her soul again. If things didn't work out with Tuck, she'd be forty-three years old when the next man entered her life!

Grace sighed. What did she really want? She wanted to believe she could love again, didn't she? And she thought it would be easy once she found the man of her dreams. But the man of her dreams was some love-besotted fool who was willing to fulfill her every wish. Tuck was a real man, with real flaws, a man more afraid of commitment than her ex-husband.

Why did it always have to come back to Dan? His desertion had cost her so much—her confidence, her ability to trust her instincts. And looking back on it, she'd never truly loved him. She'd thought she had, but then that love faded. Would it happen with Tuck as well?

"You don't love him," she said to herself as she pulled

out on the road. "You only think you do. You've always mixed up lust and love."

Always, Grace mused. Even though always was only one time. But no one could say that Grace Penrose made the same mistake twice.

TUCK SAT OUT ON THE FRONT porch of Grace's house and waited for the kids to come home from school. It was a beautiful day, the afternoon sun shining bright through the leafless oaks in the front yard. But his mind wasn't on the weather.

Grace really could be the most exasperating woman at times. When he first met her, he thought she was honest and uncomplicated. But now, it would take a road map to navigate the twists and turns of her behavior. "She loves me, she loves me not," Tuck murmured.

He stretched out his legs and stared down at the toes of his cowboy boots. Well, they'd get things straightened out between them tonight. He didn't intend to go back to the inn without some serious answers to his serious questions.

He glanced up when he heard a shout and saw Susan first. She was running ahead of Bryan, her dark hair flying out behind her, her backpack swinging at her side. When she opened the gate, she stopped short at the sight of Tuck. Then she gave Bryan another shout and ran up the walk.

Tuck stood and held out his arms and she threw herself at him, giving his legs a hug. "Tuck!" she cried.

"Hey there, Susie Q." He ruffled her hair. "How was school today?"

She gazed up at him with that same adoring expression he'd come to crave. "Martin threw up in gym and Mrs. Elliot read us a story about a boy who got squished by a bulletin board and I got a blue star on my printing. How was your day?"

He chuckled. "It was pretty good." Bryan still stood at the end of the walk, watching him suspiciously. "Are you going to stand there all day?" he called.

Bryan shook his head, then grudgingly walked up to the porch. "You're early," he said. "I've got homework."

"I'm not here for the animals. And forget your homework," Tuck said. "We've got more important things to do."

"Like what?" Bryan asked, his mood brightening considerably.

"Your mom is working on the festival. She has play rehearsal. And we're going to decorate the sleighs for the parade. I hauled the sleighs back from the Rawlings place so they're both in the coach house now. We'll get them all fixed up and looking pretty, and then, before the sleigh rides start, I'll bring the horses over here in the trailer and we'll be all ready to go." He glanced at Bryan. "Of course, you'll have to take them out on a test drive sometime this weekend, just to make sure none of the decorations fall off."

A reluctant grin split Bryan's face. "Yeah, all right. Maybe I could do that."

"That'll be fun," Susan said. She sat down on the top step and patted the spot beside her. It had become their little sign for when they had something to discuss. Tuck plopped down next to her, resting his elbows on his thighs.

"Is there a problem with my plan, Susie Q?" he asked.

Susan shook her head. "We have to talk," she said in a very mature tone.

"Susan," Bryan warned. "Just shut up."

She gave her brother a withering look. "Mommy says we should always be honest," she said. "I can tell if I want."

"You don't have to blab everything that comes into your

tiny little brain,'' Bryan shouted. ''There are such things as secrets, you know.''

''Hey,'' Tuck warned. ''Don't talk to your sister like that.''

''It's my idea and I can say it if I want,'' she countered.

''It's your idea, but it's dumb. Just like you.''

''All right, all right,'' Tuck said, holding up his hands. ''Why don't you tell me this idea you have and we'll talk about it?''

''I think you should marry our mommy,'' Susan said. ''And so does he,'' she added, pointing to her brother. ''He said it would be all right.''

Tuck gasped, then coughed to cover his surprise. If he thought Grace's appearance at Twin Oaks was a surprise, it was nothing compared with this. ''Well, that's an interesting request.'' He looked at Bryan. ''I thought you didn't like me.''

Bryan shrugged. ''I don't,'' he muttered.

''We promise we'll be really good,'' Susan said.

''Speak for yourself,'' Bryan said.

''And we won't run in the house or fight or leave the water running in the bathroom.''

Tuck slipped his arm around Susan's shoulders. ''Darlin', I'd love to be your daddy. But things are a bit more complicated than that. Daddies and mommies are supposed to love each other.''

''Couldn't you love her? She's really nice,'' Susan said. ''I know she doesn't cook so good and sometimes the house is messy, but she's a good mommy.''

''Yes, she is,'' Tuck said. ''You know how I can tell? Because she has such a sweet daughter.''

''We could live in Montana,'' Bryan muttered.

''What?'' Tuck wasn't sure he'd heard right.

''I said, we could live in Montana. That's the problem,

isn't it? My mom won't want to move because she thinks we won't want to move.''

"Bryan, I don't think your mom has ever considered marriage to me. Or moving to Montana. We've only known each other for a week or so. That's not long enough to make such an important decision.''

"You don't know her," Bryan said. "Until you came along, she didn't have anybody. And now she has you. You can take care of her—and us.''

"You can," Susan pleaded.

This was just too much to deal with right now, Tuck realized, and he wanted the conversation to end before Bryan got mad and Susan burst into tears. "All right, I promise I'll think about it," he said, pushing to his feet. Hell, spending the rest of his life with Grace was all he had been thinking about lately, so it wasn't much of a promise. "Come on. Let's go work on the decorations. Go inside and change and I'll meet you both in the coach house.''

"Have you even asked her?''

The usually cynical look on Bryan's face was gone, replaced with a hopeful expression. "No," Tuck said.

"You could ask her later," Susan suggested. "When she gets home from play practice. It's not that hard. You just gotta have continents.''

"Continents?" Tuck asked.

"Maybe you should just ask her," Bryan suggested. He reached down and grabbed Susan's hand and dragged her toward the front door. "You shouldn't have said anything," he hissed. "You probably wrecked everything. And it's confidence, not continents. That's like Africa and Australia.''

Tuck waited until they disappeared inside, then released a tightly held breath. "Maybe I should just ask her," he said to himself. He'd never really considered that option.

But it could be the perfect solution. They simply needed to make a commitment, a promise to love each other forever. Once they did that, they'd have all the time in the world to make it work.

Either he and Grace loved each other or they didn't, either they'd get married or they wouldn't. Tuck frowned. Maybe it was that simple. After all, what did he really have to lose? Sure, rejection wouldn't be a barrel of laughs. But compared with what he had to gain—Grace, a family, a future—wasn't it worth the risk?

He turned and walked inside Grace's house, heading to the kitchen. He picked up the phone and punched in the number for the ranch. Ray's wife, Annmarie, answered after two rings and Tuck spoke with her for a minute, chatting about the holidays and the baby, before asking for Ray.

A few seconds later, his partner came on the line. "Hey, buddy. How's it going?"

"Great," Tuck said. "Things are going good. How about the ranch? Did that feed get delivered all right?"

"It was fine," Ray told him. "Is that why you're calling? To ask about the feed?"

"No. Actually, Ray, I'm thinking about staying out here a little longer. Can you do without me at the ranch for a while?"

"What's going on?" Ray asked.

Tuck raked his hand through his hair and leaned up against the wall. "I'm not sure. I wish I could tell you, but I haven't figured it out yet."

"Jeez, Tuck, are you in some kind of trouble? Did something happen?"

Ray had always been like a big brother to Tuck. "That depends upon what you'd call trouble. I haven't stolen a car or been caught vandalizing mailboxes."

"What is it, then?"

"I think I might—" Tuck paused. "There's this woman who—" He cursed softly. "What would you think if I brought someone home to live on the ranch?"

"Someone? Another kid?"

"A woman. Actually, Grace Penrose. And her two kids, Bryan and Susan. Could we make that work? We'd have to live at the house for a while, until I found another place."

The line was silent for a long moment. "Yeah," Ray said with a chuckle. "Yeah, we could make that work."

"I think I might want to marry her," Tuck added, without a single ounce of doubt in his voice. He didn't give Ray a chance to respond. "So, I guess I'll be home whenever I get there."

"Hey, Tuck. I'm happy for you. You deserve a good woman in your life."

Tuck hung the phone up, then smiled. "I'm going to marry her," he repeated. "See, Susan was right. All I needed was a little continents."

But there was one other option he had to cover. He'd have to talk to Alex McAlester. If Grace didn't want to move to Montana, he'd have to have an alternative plan, and staying in Cooper's Corner as a partner in Alex's practice would be part of that plan. He could buy the Rawlings place and keep the Morgans and the goats, maybe get a few more animals. He could teach Bryan everything he knew about horses, and maybe get Susan a pony.

"I'm ready!"

Susan bounded into the kitchen. She wore a mismatched outfit with her pink jacket, two different mittens and a goofy-looking hat pulled low over her eyes. "I have a surprise in the coach house," she said, grabbing his hand and pulling him toward the back door. "Come on, I'll show you."

Tuck followed her to the back of Grace's property, the two of them trudging through the snow. Susan helped him pull the large doors open, then scampered inside, her little feet kicking up dust motes. "It's over here," she said, motioning him to a dark corner. "Under here. It's a little sleigh."

He drew the dusty canvas back and found a children's sleigh, fashioned much like a buggy, so that an adult could push it. "This is nice," Tuck said.

She hopped up inside of it. "It's just my size. My mom used to ride in it when she was little. Her daddy would push her all over town."

"How would you like to ride in this sleigh for the parade?"

"Can I?"

"We'll make a surprise for your mommy," Tuck said.

"What kind of surprise?"

He bent down and examined the rusty runners. "We can turn my goats into little reindeer. There are nine of them. How many reindeer does Santa have?"

She frowned and silently counted on her fingers. "Eight, plus Rudolph." She clapped. "Just right!"

"And we can fill the little sleigh with presents and candy and Bryan can lead the goats and you can ride in the sleigh and throw candy to all the children. How does that sound?"

"I'll have my own sleigh with real reindeer?"

"Goats," Tuck said.

"Yeah, goat reindeer. That would be so cool."

"Then let's do it," Tuck said. "We'll make it our own little secret, me, you and Bryan." He paused. "And that other thing we talked about? I think we should keep that our little secret, too, all right?"

"You mean about marrying my mommy?" Susan asked.

"Yep, that secret."

''We have to pinkie-swear.'' She held out her little finger, crooked slightly, and hooked it through his. ''Pinkie-swear,'' she vowed.

Tuck grabbed her up from the sleigh and spun her around until she screamed in delight. When Bryan appeared at the door to see what all the commotion was about, Tuck pinkie-swore him to secrecy, too. He had six hours until Grace got back from play practice. That was just enough time to decorate the sleighs, have some dinner and fashion a decent marriage proposal. Not hard to do when a guy had continents.

CHAPTER TEN

TUCK POKED AT THE EMBERS in the fireplace, then tossed another log onto the grate. The birch bark crackled and spit before the wood caught. He stared down at the flames, his hand braced on the mantel, lost in his thoughts.

He and the kids had finished decorating the sleighs that afternoon and later walked down to Tubb's for burgers and shakes. When, they returned to the house, they'd spent the rest of the night learning the finer points of draw poker. Throughout the evening, he found himself slipping into the role of father without even realizing it. In arguments, he became the arbitrator. When confusion reigned, he became a teacher. And when questions were asked, he was a friend and adviser.

I can do this, he thought. I can be a good father.

It seemed to come so easily, but Tuck was sure there must be more to it. If it was so simple, why had his mother been unable to master even the most basic parenting skills? Had she ever loved him? And if she had, what had made her stop? What had he done? Tuck tried to think of something that Bryan or Susan could do to completely change his feelings for them, but he couldn't come up with anything.

But Bryan and Susan had become the easy part of the equation. It was Grace he wasn't sure about. What would she say to his proposal? Would she understand how practical it was? That marriage would be their promise to each other to make it work between them? There might be some uncertainty at first, but if they loved each other, then this was the right thing to do.

Tuck turned at the sound of footsteps on the front porch. The hinges groaned as the front door swung open, and a moment later, Grace walked into the living room. She stopped as soon as she saw him, set her bag down on a nearby chair and slowly slipped out of her coat.

"Hi," she murmured. "I'm sorry I'm late. Play rehearsal ran over. I think everyone is getting a little nervous. Our first performance is just a few days away."

"No problem," Tuck said as he stood.

Grace rubbed her hands together, then walked over to the fire. "Are the kids asleep?"

"Bryan might be reading. Susan fell asleep on the sofa and I carried her upstairs. She's still in her clothes. I didn't have the heart to wake her."

She nodded and held her fingers out to the warmth. "Thanks for taking care of them. I know they like being with you." She smiled ruefully. "Too bad their father doesn't take such interest. You could give him a few lessons, I think."

"That's kind of what I wanted to talk to you about. There's something important I have to say and I—"

She shook her head. "I know. I've been meaning to talk to you, too."

"You first," Tuck said, curious to know what was on her mind.

"I suppose I should start with an apology. I've been giving you mixed signals and that's not fair. After our…interlude at the inn, I've tried to handle things the right way and I keep messing up. But I understand what I need to do now and things will be easier. I promise."

"And what do you need to do?" Tuck asked.

"To face the reality of the situation," she said. "To put our night together in perspective. You came here to get your horses and I convinced you to stay in Cooper's Corner. And then I allowed you to become a part of our lives. That wasn't fair to you. And I shouldn't have taken advantage the way I did. I was treating you like a husband, and I know that's the last thing you want to be. If there are any hurt feelings, they're my fault."

"Funny," Tuck said. "The way you're talking about our night at the inn, it doesn't sound like you have any feelings about it at all."

"That's not true." Grace sounded defensive.

"Then tell me," Tuck urged, grabbing her shoulders and forcing her to face him squarely. "Tell me how it made you feel, Gracie. Tell me that you enjoyed it as much as I did. That we were good together. Tell me that you want to share that all over again. It doesn't have to be just one night, you know."

She twisted out of his grasp. "Yes, it does. We can't let that happen again." She stepped away from the fire and forced a smile. "Can we stop talking about this?"

"No," Tuck said. "No, we can't." He circled the sofa and grabbed her jacket from the chair, then held it out to her. "Here, put this on."

"Why?"

"Just do it," he snapped.

Grudgingly, she slipped her arms into her jacket, then held it closed. Tuck reached for his own coat, tugged it on, then took her hand. "We're getting out of here," he said.

"We can't leave! The kids are asleep upstairs."

"We're just going outside," he said, dragging her through the kitchen. "Where we can talk without any chance of being interrupted. We won't be far."

"What is so important that we can't talk in here?" Grace asked. "It's freezing outside."

They trudged through the snow in the backyard until Tuck reached a spot underneath a tree. He glanced around. This was perfect. Silent, the moon shining down on the snow, the bare branches rustling overhead, just enough light from the porch for him to see her expression. He pressed Grace's hand between his.

When he dropped to one knee in the snow, her eyes went wide and she gasped. "What are you doing?" she asked.

"What I should have done that night at the inn." Tuck cleared his throat. "Gracie, I know we've only known each other for a short time, but it didn't take me long to decide what I wanted. I want you, as my wife. And I want Bryan and Susan to be my children." He drew a deep breath. "Grace Penrose, I want you to marry me."

"What?" She snatched her hand from his and held it to her chest. Her breath came in quick gasps, clouding around her face. "You can't be serious."

Tuck slowly stood. This wasn't exactly going the way he'd planned. He shouldn't be surprised, though. He hadn't expected her to say yes immediately, but he also hadn't anticipated complete shock on her part. "I'm dead serious," he said. "Over the past few days, it's become quite apparent to me that we belong together. You need me and I need you."

"Well, that—that may be true," she stammered, "but it doesn't mean we should just get married. We've only known each other…" She counted on her fingers. "Ten days. That's all. Ten days. I know the guy who fixes my car better than you! And I don't have any intention of marrying him."

"I figured you'd bring that up," Tuck said, glad that something was going as planned.

"The guy who fixes my car?"

"No, the time thing." He had come prepared with an argument for every point she could possibly raise. "There's something to be said for love at first sight. A lot of people have fallen in love in a matter of days, sometimes hours. And they've had long, happy marriages. There are stories everywhere. I wish we had more time, but I love you, Gracie. I'm absolutely sure of that. And I think you feel the same way. Time shouldn't make a difference."

"We live hundreds of miles from each other," she said.

"Ah, the distance thing. That's the least of our worries. If we love each other, we'll work that out. We'll compromise."

Grace turned and started toward the house. "This is crazy."

"What's so crazy?" Tuck shouted. "I've spent my entire life wondering if I'd ever feel this way, if I'd ever find someone. And now that I have, I don't want to let it go."

"And you know the mistakes that I've made," Grace said, facing him, but continuing her retreat. "I have two children to think about. I can't afford to make another mistake."

"The children thing. Well, I love your children," Tuck shouted. "And they'll come to love me. I'd be a good father to them. And I don't want them hurt any more than you do. If I thought we couldn't make a good marriage, then I never would have asked you."

"It's not just about what you want," Grace said, stamping her foot in the snow.

"Well, what do you want?" Tuck demanded. "Tell me and I'll make it happen."

She shook her head. "I can't say yes. I just can't."

"You can," Tuck countered, walking toward her.

She turned again and started for the house. "Is it the age thing?" Tuck asked.

She stopped, then slowly faced him again. "What age thing?"

"You're older than me."

"I am not!" Grace said, insulted.

"Yes, you are. Seven years. Susan told me how old you are. She said you were thirty-nine."

"I'm thirty-six!" Grace said. "How old are you?"

"Thirty-two," Tuck replied.

"Oh, God," she said, covering her mouth in surprise. "I *am* older than you. I didn't know we had an age thing, too." She wagged her finger at him. "See, there's another perfectly good reason why we can't get married. I'm old enough to be your—your older sister!"

Tuck ran after her and grabbed her hand, spinning her around to face him again. He cupped her face between his palms and kissed her, trying to convince her with his mouth instead of words. She relented, but only for a moment. "Kissing me is not going to change my mind," she said, drawing away.

He kissed her again, this time more deeply, teasing her tongue with his. He felt her soften then surrender, and when she slipped her arms around his neck they tumbled into the snow.

They picked up where they'd left off at the inn, tugging at each other's clothes, trying to find a bit of warm skin to taste. Tuck knew he had to keep control of the situation. He wanted to prove a point to Grace and he wasn't about to miss the opportunity. When he was satisfied that all her defenses were down, he drew back and looked into her flushed face. She blinked, melted snowflakes glistening on her eyelashes. Tuck rolled off her and stood up.

"I guess you don't have any problem with the kissing thing," he said.

Grace scrambled to her feet. "Great sex will only last so long," she said, brushing off her clothes.

"I figure it'll take about sixty or seventy years with us," Tuck replied. "And that's just long enough for me." He reached out and brushed the snow from her shoulder, then ran his finger along her cheek. "I'll expect an answer to my proposal."

"I know my answer," Grace shouted.

"Think about it, Gracie." Tuck held out his finger to silence her. "Don't answer too quickly. Once you say no, I'm not going to ask you again."

He turned and started back toward the house, leaving Grace to stand in the snow all alone. He didn't go inside, but headed for his truck parked out front. He'd give Grace time, keep his distance and allow her to realize the magnitude of what they shared. Sooner or later, she'd have to admit they belonged together.

Tuck smiled to himself. Overall, his proposal hadn't gone too badly. Though she hadn't said yes, he'd managed to keep her from saying no. So there was still hope, and for now, that was enough for him.

"LET THE NINTH ANNUAL Cooper's Corner Christmas Festival begin!"

The crowd cheered and clapped, and butterflies fluttered in Grace's stomach as she handed the bullhorn to the president of the village board and stepped down off the stage. This was it. The official kickoff on the village green. From now on, Grace wouldn't stop running until the parade ended on Wednesday night and everyone left for their own celebrations at home.

This was the first year that the festival was a three-day

event, but Grace had added some special family activities. The first was a father-daughter, mother-son snowman building contest. The idea had been suggested by a member of the village board and he'd promised to coordinate the judging, so Grace had gratefully agreed. It was only later, when she realized her children wouldn't be able to participate—Susan didn't have a father, and Grace was too busy to partner with Bryan—that she regretted her enthusiasm.

She listened distractedly as the rules were read from the stage, then looked down at her clipboard. The snowman contest would last for the next hour and then the band she'd hired would start at the far end of the village green with up-tempo holiday music. A small section of the green had been flooded for skating, and the ice-carving contest was set to begin at five, with huge blocks of ice scattered along Main Street.

After that, she needed to gather her crew of judges to confer the awards for the Windows on Main Street contest. Groups of high school students had taken over the front windows of the businesses around town and decorated them with displays and paint and lights until Main Street positively shouted Christmas cheer.

"Hey, Mom!"

Grace turned and saw Bryan hurrying across the village green. He clutched a piece of paper in his hand and tried to read it as he walked. "Hi, sweetie. I thought you were going to Keegan's after school."

"Keegan wanted to enter the contest," Bryan explained.

Grace frowned. "But he doesn't have a mom."

Bryan shrugged. "It doesn't make any difference. His aunt Maureen is on his team, and his dad is doing it with Randi and Robin. The judges said that since they were so little, they only counted as one daughter."

"Well, that was nice of the judges."

Her son stared down at the toe of his boot and kicked at a mound of snow. "I was thinkin'…I mean, I know you're busy, but if you have time…" He looked up at Grace. "I thought we could be a team."

Grace's breath caught in her throat. For an instant, she saw the little boy she'd once known, the boy who wanted nothing more than to spend every waking minute with his mom, the boy who was so willing and eager to please. Suddenly, her schedule didn't make a bit of difference. "I'd like that," Grace said.

"Good," Bryan replied, holding out the paper. "'Cause I already entered us. We're team number twelve."

"Then I guess we'd better get busy," Grace said with a laugh. She glanced down at the fashionable leather gloves she was wearing. A small price to pay for this experience with her son, she mused. Heck, she'd build a snowman with her bare hands if it meant that she could finally do something to please Bryan. But as they were walking toward their spot, Bryan reached inside his jacket pocket and handed her a pair of his gloves.

"Thanks," Grace said.

She glanced around the crowd of children, looking for Susan, knowing that she'd want to cheer them on. Martha's mom had picked her up from Mrs. Girard's and they'd planned to attend the contest. But her search picked out another figure—tall, broad-shouldered, wearing a cowboy hat. "Tuck."

Bryan looked up at her. "He's going to enter with Susan."

"What?"

"Yeah. He and Susan are challenging us to see who can win a prize," Bryan explained. "I figure we have a pretty good chance since Susan is on *his* team. Her hands will get cold and she'll want to quit. And she can't carry much snow. Besides, she'll want to make something stupid like a kitty or a bunny.''

Grace reached out and slipped her arm around her son's shoulders, warmed by Tuck's generosity. She didn't care if he was behind this little truce with Bryan. She wasn't going to pass on the opportunity to make peace with her son. ''I wouldn't underestimate your sister,'' she teased. ''Susan may be small, but she's quick. And some of the judges might like kitties.''

Bryan rolled his eyes at her joke. ''Yeah, and she can get Tuck to do anything for her.''

They found their spot and Grace wasn't surprised to discover it was just a few yards from Tuck and Susan. Susan was jumping around within the little square that had been laid out for them. She waved at Grace. ''Me and Tuck are a team,'' she called, unable to contain her excitement.

Tuck tipped his hat at Grace and she nodded. A smile curved his lips and a delicious shiver raced up her spine. She'd seen that smile before—charming, boyish and just slightly wicked. He knew exactly what he was doing, aligning her children on his side in order to influence her. Well, it wasn't going to work. She had no intention of marrying Tuck McCabe, no matter how sweet and thoughtful he was.

With a frown, she turned her attention back to the competition. The members of the village board had done a wonderful job organizing the contest. They'd put together mystery boxes for each of the contestants that included a wild assortment of items to use in decorating the snowmen. And they'd hauled in truckloads of fresh snow and piled it along the edge of the green. Each team got two big buckets they could fill with snow, over and over again, until they had enough to complete their creation. They'd even provided water spray bottles to make the snow easier to pack.

''Contestants ready?''

The crowd shouted.

"Go!"

Grace and Bryan tore into their box and pulled out the items they'd have to use in building their snowman. A whisk broom, an egg carton, an old phone book and a stocking cap. Bryan groaned. "What are we going to do with these?"

Grace grabbed the egg carton and began to tear it apart. "Eyes and nose," she said, holding up each section. "And maybe even ears."

"Yeah," Bryan said in amazement. "And we can tear up strips of paper from the phone book for hair."

"And if we bury the top of the whisk broom in his chin, it will look like a beard."

"Yeah," Bryan said. He handed Grace a bucket, and together they headed for the pile of snow. Over the next ten minutes, they returned again and again, adding snow to their growing mound. When Bryan figured they had enough, he and Grace started to build the base of their snowman.

As they worked, Grace took time to observe their competition. Tuck and Susan had decided to build something on a much smaller scale, a snowman that was no taller than Susan herself. Her daughter was chattering the whole time, telling Tuck where she wanted more snow, and he was cheerfully obliging.

Grace was amazed at how well she and Bryan got on together. He didn't get upset when something didn't work out, but merely proposed an alternative and then moved on. Their snowman grew to nearly five feet, and had carefully sculpted arms and feet. The egg carton eyes and nose worked out perfectly, but they were having trouble with a mouth.

In sudden inspiration, Grace grabbed the phone book and

tore out a few pages, then wet them down with water until they were mushy and gray. She handed the mess to Bryan and he fashioned the paper into a wide smile for their snowman. The whisk broom became a beard, and strips of paper turned into hair, which fluttered in the breeze. They'd just topped their creation with the stocking cap when the judges gave the five-minute warning.

A few more refinements were all it took to finish. Then Grace and Bryan stepped back and evaluated their handiwork. "It's nice," Grace said, surprised that they'd been so successful. "Considering your mother has no artistic ability, I'd say we did pretty good."

"I think it's great," Bryan declared, pride suffusing his voice.

The judges wandered from snowman to snowman, discussing each in hushed tones. Grace looked over at Tuck and Susan and smiled. As Bryan had predicted, they'd built a little bunny, complete with snow ears and whiskers made from pencils they'd found in their box. An old pair of shoes made cute little feet and the bunny held a garden trowel in his paws.

After ten minutes of judging, the village board gathered on the small stage to announce the winners. Grace was disappointed when she and Bryan didn't win in their category, but Bryan just shrugged it off, more concerned with her hurt feelings than his own. But when Susan's name was announced for the five-to-seven-year-old group, they both screamed and clapped. Susan and Tuck hurried up to the stage to collect her ribbon, then posed for a photo before wandering back into the crowd.

A few moments later, Susan was beside Grace. Grace knelt down and gave her a hug, but Susan pushed away, anxious to show off her ribbon. "We won, Mommy."

Tuck appeared and he and Bryan shook hands, Bryan

grudgingly conceding defeat. Susan scampered over to Bryan and handed him her ribbon. Grace held her breath and waited for a disparaging comment, but he examined the ribbon, smiled and handed it back to her. And then, to Grace's shock, Bryan ruffled Susan's hair, the same way Tuck had done many times before.

"Thank you," Grace murmured to Tuck as they watched the little scene before them. "I don't think you'll ever know how much this meant to me."

"I didn't do anything," he said. "Except build a very nice, award-winning bunny." He moved closer and kicked at the snow with the toe of his boot. "So, how have you been? I haven't seen you for, what? Three days."

"I've been busy," Grace said, avoiding the obvious subject—his proposal.

"I bet. But this part of the festival looks like a big success."

"Mom, can I have some money? I want to get a hot chocolate."

Grace dragged her gaze from Tuck's, then reached into her coat pocket and pulled out a handful of change. "Take Susan with you," she said.

Bryan frowned. "Do I have to?"

"It's Christmas," Grace said. "Be nice to your sister."

She watched her son and daughter walk across the village green, then sighed. "One step forward, two steps back." She turned to Tuck, then reached into her other pocket and withdrew a pair of tickets. "These are for the play on Wednesday afternoon," she said. "I thought, if you weren't doing anything, you might enjoy seeing it."

"Two tickets? So you think I should take a date?"

"I just had two." She snatched one of the tickets from his hand and shoved it back in her pocket.

"Alex McAlester and Felix Dorn are going to be doing

the sleigh rides that afternoon, so I should be free…if you promise to sit next to me.''

Grace opened her mouth to reply. But Tuck obviously didn't want to know what she had to say. Instead, he bent down and stopped her words with a quick kiss. He let his lips linger for a long moment before he drew away. Grace blushed, then glanced around, but no one was watching them.

''There's only one answer I want to hear, Gracie,'' he warned. With that, Tuck called out to Bryan and Susan. They came running over, cups of cocoa clutched in their hands. ''I can watch Susan if you're busy,'' he said. ''And I was hoping Bryan might help me groom the horses one last time before their big appearance tomorrow.''

Bryan gave her a hopeful look and Grace nodded. ''All right. But I want you two to meet me at the church after you're done in the barn. I've got some last-minute work to do for the play. I'll be there until nine tonight.''

''I'll drop them off there,'' Tuck promised. They set off toward the road and Grace watched the trio, amazed at how perfect they seemed together. Maybe Tuck was right. Perhaps she should forget all the things that stood between them and focus on the positive aspects of his marriage proposal. She did care about him—in truth, she loved him. And her children had come to love him as well—at least Susan had. Bryan just loved his horses.

So why couldn't she accept his proposal? Grace closed her eyes and drew a deep breath of the crisp afternoon air. How was she supposed to know if her feelings were really love or just…relief? Relief that someone had come along to ease her burden, to make her life more secure, to make her feel wanted. That's exactly why she'd married Dan Penrose, because he made her feel safe and needed. And that relationship had collapsed.

What made her believe that she could keep a man like Tucker McCabe happy if she couldn't do the same for her ex-husband? Grace had surrendered her heart once before and it had been returned to her, battered and broken. If that happened again, she wasn't sure she'd be able to survive.

"Grace!"

Her thoughts were interrupted by a shout from the president of the village board. She pasted a smile on her face and hurried over to him. There was no reason to reconsider Tuck's proposal. She'd already made up her mind. And the next time she saw Tuck, she was going to tell him.

THE LAST DAY OF THE FESTIVAL had dawned cold and clear. Grace ran her fingers through her hair and pulled her robe more tightly around her as she padded down the stairs in her stocking feet. She yawned once, then tried to clear the cobwebs from her mind.

She hadn't slept at all last night. Though she'd tried to blame it on the excitement from the festival, she knew that was just an excuse. Yes, this was the final day, the big day. But it was also something more. Today was the last day that Tuck was required to stay in Cooper's Corner. Time had run out, and once the sleigh rides were finished, he had nothing to keep him here.

A strange emptiness had settled around her heart. What was it—loneliness? Or just a faint longing for what might have been? She rubbed her eyes, then continued down the stairs, heading for the kitchen and her first cup of coffee. But as she reached the bottom of the stairs, the scent of freshly brewed coffee teased her nose. A pot had been made already and waited for her. She knew Tuck hadn't come in when he picked up Bryan earlier that morning. She'd heard him beep the horn when he drove up. And Susan didn't know how to make coffee. So her son was the only one who could have put the pot on.

"What has gotten in to Bryan?" Grace wondered as she grabbed the milk from the refrigerator.

As she sipped at her coffee, she stared out the window that overlooked the backyard, her mind swirling with thoughts of Tuck. And then, as if she'd conjured him out of thin air, she saw him walking toward the coach house with Bryan. Their heads were down, as if they were discussing something very important. Bryan nodded, turned and started back toward the house. Tuck glanced over his shoulder at him, and Grace quickly stepped away from the window, reluctant to get caught spying on him.

She cursed softly. "It's my window. I can look out of it if I want to." But by the time she moved back, Tuck had disappeared into the coach house.

The back door opened and Grace spun around. Bryan clomped into the kitchen, his boots covered with snow. "Hi, Mom," he said.

"Hi there, sweetie. You're up early."

"Tuck and I had to groom the horses. And one of the horses was limping so Tuck showed me how to check his hooves. He had a little stone caught in his shoe so we had to pick it out." He moved to the coffeemaker, pulled a mug off the rack and filled it with coffee.

Grace frowned. "Are—are you going to drink that?"

"Nope, it's for Tuck. We're working on something in the coach house."

"Something?"

Bryan nodded. "You'll see at the parade this afternoon." He hurried to the door, then let it slam behind him.

Grace looked out the window again, hoping to catch sight of Tuck when Bryan went back into the coach house. But the inside was too dark from such a distance. She sighed softly, then wandered back through the house to the library. "Morning, Susie Q," Grace said. It was only after the greeting that she realized she had used Tuck's pet name for her daughter.

Susan didn't look away from the television. "'Morning, Mommy."

"Tuck and Bryan are out in the coach house working on a surprise. Do you know what they're working on?"

"Yep," Susan said, still staring at the Grinch.

"Do you want to tell me what it is?"

"Nope." She rolled over and scrambled to her feet. "I'm going to go help." She skipped out of the room.

"Did you have breakfast?" Grace called.

"Yep!"

Leaning back against the doorjamb, Grace took another sip of her coffee. If she really wanted to know what was going on outside, she could just visit the coach house. "It is *my* coach house, after all," she muttered.

She set her coffee cup down in the kitchen, then hurried upstairs to pull on warm clothes. Before she walked outside, she grabbed a few powdered sugar doughnuts from the freezer, prepared to use them as an excuse for her visit. Her coffee sloshed over the rim of the cup as she stumbled through the deep snow.

Grace felt compelled to knock on the door before entering, giving the children enough time to hide their surprise. "Who is it?" Susan called from inside.

"It's your mother," Grace said. "Who do you think it is?"

"Just a minute," Tuck called. There was a general flurry of activity and then Bryan slid the door open, allowing Grace to step inside.

"What's going on in here?"

Bryan grabbed Susan's hand and pulled her toward the

door. "Come on, Susan. Let's go get something to drink. I'll make you hot chocolate with marshmallows."

Susan followed him out. "I wouldn't tell," she protested. "I can keep a secret."

"Yeah, right," Bryan said.

When they'd walked halfway back to the house, Grace turned to find Tuck staring at her. She glanced around. Nothing looked out of place. "This is all very mysterious."

Tuck went back to his work. He laid out a pair of harnesses on the workbench and punched a series of holes in them with an awl. She wandered over to the table he'd set up for the tack. "Is this part of the surprise?" she asked.

When he didn't answer her, she picked up a harness and examined it, the jingle bells on it tinkling softly. "Everyone was very excited about the sleigh rides last night," she said. "Did you have fun?"

He shrugged. "It was all right. Busy. Between me and Alex and Dr. Dorn, we must have given rides to a couple hundred people." He laid out another strip of leather and cut it with a razor knife. "Bryan is going to help me get the horses ready this afternoon and we'll be in front of the church by the time the play is over. We'll do the parade and then give rides until about seven tonight. I have a copy of your schedule. You don't need to worry."

"I—I wasn't worried," Grace said. "I know I can depend on you."

"Yes, I am a dependable guy, aren't I?" he said, allowing a sarcastic edge to creep into his voice.

Grace frowned. He was in such an odd mood this morning, so distant yet edgy, impatient, completely unlike the Tuck she'd come to know. "Are you angry about something?"

"What would I have to be angry about?"

"Why do you keep answering my questions with more

questions?'' Grace paused, deciding to take a different approach. ''So, are you going to make it to the play this afternoon?''

Tuck chuckled. ''That was a deft change of subject.''

''I don't know what you want me to say.''

''Why are you here, Grace?''

Their rather benign conversation had suddenly turned serious. She knew this discussion was inevitable. In truth, she'd been dreading it. But she was tired of all these unsettled feelings. ''You want to discuss your proposal,'' she said.

''No, just your answer,'' he replied.

Grace drew a shaky breath. ''I have thought about it. And I do care about you, Tuck. So do the kids. And I appreciate your proposal, but…''

''But the answer is no.''

''Yes,'' Grace said. ''I mean, no.'' She cursed softly. ''For now, the answer is no. But I was thinking that maybe, if we had more time, the answer could be yes. Someday. We could visit each other. I know the kids would love to come to your ranch this summer. And you must be able to take some vacation time. We could always meet halfway.''

He stared down at the harness he was working on, his shoulders slumped slightly. ''No.''

''No to what? The ranch, the vacations?''

His hands gripped the edge of the workbench as he turned to look at her. His eyes were cool, his expression indifferent. ''It's all or nothing, Gracie. Either you accept my proposal or I go back to Montana and we never see each other again. I've never been good with rejection. Or with commitment. Now that I've stuck my neck out, I'm not going to let you cut my head off slowly. We can't have a long-distance relationship. I want an answer now. I know

I love you. You have to decide how you feel. Yes or no, Gracie. What'll it be?''

Stunned by his ultimatum, Grace wasn't sure what to say. Her heart wanted to accept, but her brain kept telling her it was too soon. Too soon. But could she really let him walk away? And if she did, would she come to regret her choice someday? ''I—I can't,'' Grace said.

Tuck shrugged and smiled coldly. ''Then I guess we have nothing else to talk about. It's all right,'' he said. ''I'm fine with it. And you're right, it never would have worked. We barely know each other. And hell, I'm damaged goods. Who knows how long it would have lasted before I messed up?''

With every reason Tuck gave her for failure, she wanted to give him a reason why it might succeed, if they only had a little more time. ''Tuck, don't say that. It's not you, it's me.''

''Right,'' Tuck said. He rubbed his hands on his jeans. ''So, I guess that's it, then.''

An uneasy silence settled over the coach house. Was this the time they were supposed to say goodbye? Or would that come later? She'd never turned down a marriage proposal before. She didn't know the protocol. ''I guess I'll see you tonight,'' she said. ''At the parade.''

Tuck nodded, still focused on his work. Grace backed away, then slipped out of the coach house without another word. As she walked to the house, a tear slipped from her eye. She brushed it away, but the cold trail it left was still there.

Would she ever be able to forget him? Or would memories of their time together haunt her for the rest of her life? Only time alone would tell. And right now, Grace had plenty of that ahead of her.

CHAPTER ELEVEN

THE INTERIOR LIGHTS OF THE church were dimmed, the stage illuminated by rented spotlights. Grace stood off to the side of the audience, her clipboard clutched in her hands, her gaze fixed on Rowena as she moved about, pretending to prepare a Christmas dinner. She fumbled with a pewter cup, and for a moment Grace was sure she would drop it. But she smoothly covered her mistake and the butterflies that fluttered in Grace's stomach calmed slightly.

She sighed. Why did she always have to think about the bad things that might happen? Life didn't have to be a series of disasters waiting to befall her. She should learn to be more optimistic. Rowena hadn't dropped the cup and the spotlights hadn't blown a fuse and none of the children had thrown up on stage.

"It's wonderful."

Grace turned to find Maureen standing behind her. "Do you think so?" Grace asked.

Maureen nodded. "Look at the audience," she whispered. "They're mesmerized. It's really a shame we're only going to do this once. You should restage this play next Christmas. And do two performances."

Next Christmas. Grace hadn't even thought about it. She just wanted to get through this one. But now that Maureen had brought it up, she felt suddenly depressed at the prospect that she'd have to do this all over again in a year. Was this what her life was supposed to be, one Christmas Festival after another? Year after year until she got old and retired? Until this moment, she'd been satisfied with her life here in Cooper's Corner. Why did it seem so deadly dull now?

"Maybe," Grace replied. "We'll see."

They continued to watch the play together. Maureen fidgeted nervously when Clint entered for the final scene. He wore a tattered soldier's uniform and carried a musket and looked incredibly handsome. Grace held her breath, transported by the story being told on the stage. She listened to each word, forgetting her nerves and losing herself in the emotion of the moment.

And when Clint pulled Rowena into his arms and kissed her, Grace felt the tears well in her eyes. She drew in a ragged breath, then turned to look at the audience. Her gaze fell on a shadowy figure standing near the back and her breath froze in her throat. He stared at her for a long moment, the applause from the crowd fading into the background.

Grace felt as if they were the only people in the church. Her heart beat frantically in her chest and she felt an undeniable need to go to him, to step into his embrace and let her tears flow freely. All the emotions from the past few weeks spilled over, the tension from the festival, her indecision about their relationship, her fears about the future, and she couldn't seem to stop crying.

She reached up and brushed the tears from her cheeks, then took a step toward him. As suddenly as he'd appeared, Tuck was gone, hidden by the standing ovation that the audience offered the actors on stage. Grace frowned and tried to find him again, but the crowd was too large and the lights too dim.

"Oh, Grace, look at the audience. They loved it." Maureen gathered her into a hug, then drew back and began to clap as her brother Clint took his bow. "I'm going to go congratulate Rowena. She was just so good!"

Grace nodded. "I'll meet you out front in fifteen minutes. The parade is scheduled to start in a half hour and I'm going to need your help getting things started."

Maureen nodded, then pushed her way through the crowd to the front of the stage. A moment later, Tom Christen tapped Grace on the back. "It was wonderful, Grace. A great success. We're going to have to do it again next year."

"Right," she said, forcing a smile. "Next year."

One after another, the townsfolk came up to her to offer their congratulations. Grace tried to maintain her enthusiastic facade, but the moment she had a chance, she slipped out the side door into the waning light of the afternoon.

Tears threatened again and she drew a deep breath of cold air to force them back. Just a few more hours and he'd be gone. She'd never turn around again and find him watching her, never feel that little flutter of excitement when their gazes met. He'd never reach out and take her hand or bend down to kiss her. Her life would pass by, from Christmas to Christmas, and nothing exciting would ever happen to her again.

She'd tried to become someone different, an exciting and spontaneous woman who could live out her fantasies. For a brief moment, she'd tossed aside her reputation and risked her heart. And she'd found passion and romance. But now that she had it, Grace didn't know what to do with it.

She couldn't be the woman Tuck wanted her to be, fearless and determined, ready to jump into marriage at the snap of his fingers. She was Grace Penrose, simple, steady, conservative. She didn't fall in love in one week. She didn't run off to Montana with the first cowboy who came into town. And she didn't throw her life away for a love that might not last.

"Grace, are you out here?"

She spun around to find Maureen standing in the doorway. "I'm here. I was just getting some air."

Maureen stepped outside, her expression etched with concern. "Are you all right?"

"The play," Grace said, brushing an errant tear from her cheek. "It just made me all emotional. It was so touching, I couldn't help but cry."

"Is that all?" Maureen asked.

"What do you mean?"

"He's going home soon, isn't he? He's going to take his horses and go back to Montana," Maureen said. "Could that be why you're crying?"

Grace drew a ragged breath. "He asked me to marry him."

A gasp slipped from her friend's lips. "Oh, Grace, that's wonderful!"

"No, it isn't," she said, shaking her head. "I turned down his proposal. I can't marry him. I barely know him."

Maureen reached out and took her hand. "Do you love him?"

That was the question, wasn't it? The very heart of the matter. "I think I do. But thinking isn't knowing. And I can't risk everything if I have any doubts at all. I have to consider Bryan and Susan. And our future. One divorce was enough. I couldn't bear to have another marriage fall apart."

"I understand," Maureen said.

"If we just had a little more time together, maybe I'd know for sure." Grace looked up at Maureen. "Am I making the right decision?"

Maureen considered the question for a long moment. "I

was married. Four years ago. And we married after a very short courtship. He was so handsome and charming, so exciting. But I knew there were problems ahead. Competing careers and unrealistic expectations. I thought love could conquer all. His job took him to Europe and I wasn't willing to follow him there. He demanded I come with him, I said no, and he walked out. That was the end of it.''

"Just like me and Tuck," Grace said.

"Listen to your heart," Maureen suggested, her tone somber. "If you have any doubts, you have to take the time to work them out before you get married."

"I don't have any doubts," Grace insisted, tipping her chin up. "I'm not going to marry Tuck McCabe." She wiped her damp cheeks once more, then pasted a bright smile on her face. "We'd better get going. We've got a parade to start."

ALL OF COOPER'S CORNER HAD gathered along Main Street for the finale to the Christmas Festival. People strolled from the church, where the play had just finished, to find a spot on the sidewalk where they could watch the parade. The sun had just set and all the Christmas lights twinkled brightly. Tuck stepped up into the sleigh and looked down the length of Church Street, where the parade participants had assembled.

With all the noise and excitement, the horses were skittish. Bryan stood at the front of Santa's sleigh, trying to calm them. Alex McAlester squatted near the front of Tuck's sleigh, examining one of the horse's legs. Tuck's sleigh would carry Enos Harrington, the official parade master. The other sleigh would bring up the rear of the parade, carrying Santa and his sackful of presents. Bryan and Susan's entry, pulled by nine goats with little cardboard antlers, would find a spot somewhere in the middle.

In between, there would also be antique cars, an old fire truck, the local American Legion band, and Christmas floats made by local businesses. The floats were pulled over to one side of Church Street and the fire truck sat right behind the horses. The driver of the fire truck blew his horn, anxious to get the parade started. The horses jumped. "Hold 'em tight, Bryan," Tuck called. "Talk to 'em. Calm them down."

He glanced over at Susan. She was standing near the goats, which were all harnessed together and causing a ruckus. Tuck had wondered how they'd react with the noise of the crowd, but even the blast from the fire truck hadn't put them to sleep.

As he scanned the street again, his gaze caught a movement in some bushes near the turn onto Main Street. He wondered if a dog was loose. That was all he needed, some mutt running out and startling the horses. He made a mental note to take care around that part of the parade route, just in case.

"We're here," a voice called.

Grace appeared from the crowd along with Maureen Cooper, both of them carrying a large piece of bright red cardboard. Grace was breathless, the color high in her cheeks. Though she appeared outwardly calm, Tuck could tell from the tight set of her shoulders that she was uneasy. He wrapped the reins around the brake, then jumped down from the sleigh.

"Mommy, Mommy!"

Susan ran over from her spot next to the goats and grabbed Grace's hand. "Come and see our surprise!" she cried.

Distracted by her duties, Grace patted her daughter's head. "Honey, I have to put these signs on the side of Mr. Harrington's sleigh. Then I'll come and see your surprise."

She stepped up into the sleigh and Maureen handed her a roll of tape. But Susan wouldn't be deterred. Tuck reached to grab her, but she crawled up into the sleigh behind Grace.

One moment everything was fine, and the next, all hell broke loose. A flash caught his eye and then a sharp crack split the night air. The horses reared and then bolted. Before Tuck could even move, the sleigh jerked, sending Grace and Susan tumbling onto the seat. Alex tried to grab the horses from his spot near the front of the sleigh, but he had no choice but to jump out of the way or get trampled.

Tuck shouted at Grace to grab the reins, but it was too late. The sleigh skidded and Grace and Susan tumbled off the seat onto the floor. Tuck looked over at Bryan and saw him fighting to keep his horses calm. He shouted for Bryan to get into the remaining sleigh, and the moment they were both safely seated, Tuck slapped the other pair of Morgans into action.

The pair drawing Grace's cutter were older and slower and hindered by the crowd of spectators, who jumped out of the way as they passed. It didn't take long for Tuck and Bryan to catch up. But then, spooked further by the screams of the onlookers, the horses picked up speed and tore around the corner onto Oak Road.

Tuck held his breath as the sleigh tipped onto one runner, praying that Grace and Susan wouldn't fall out, but the cutter righted itself. "We need to get ahead of it," Tuck yelled to Bryan as he urged the horses on. "When we do, I want you to take the reins. I'm going to reach over and grab onto a halter. Then I need you to slowly bring our horses to a stop. Got that?" Bryan nodded, his eyes wide with fear. "You can do this," Tuck reassured him. "I know you can."

They'd nearly come even with the sleigh and Tuck called

out to Grace. Terrified, she turned to look up at him, but it was as if she didn't recognize him. She and Susan were still crouched on the bed of the sleigh, holding on for dear life.

His strategy worked exactly as he'd planned. Tuck slapped his own horses one more time and they surged ahead. Then he carefully passed the reins to Bryan, stood up and leaned out of the sleigh. He caught the halter of one of the runaway horses with one hand, and just as he'd been told, Bryan started to pull back on their own team. The runaways had no choice but to slow down, too, and gradually both sleighs slid to a stop just a few yards from Grace's driveway.

Bryan cursed vividly, then sent Tuck an apologetic look.

"I agree," Tuck said. He hopped down from the sleigh and came around the front, talking in a soft voice to the skittish pair of Morgans. Then he called to Grace in an even tone. "Gracie, get out of the sleigh. Susie Q, help your mom out of the sleigh. Bryan, you tie off your reins and come down. Take their heads and keep them calm."

He peered around to the side, and the moment Grace and Susan hit solid ground, he let go of the halter. Grace looked a bit dazed but no worse for wear. Susan, on the other hand, seemed exhilarated by the wild ride and stood beside Bryan, chattering about the experience.

"Are you all right?" he asked, taking Grace's arm. Her knees wobbled and he grabbed her around the waist. Tuck had operated on instinct alone to stop the runaway sleigh and he did the same now. He framed Grace's face with his hands and kissed her, long and hard. When he drew back, he pressed his forehead to hers. "You're all right," Tuck murmured against her mouth. "You're all right."

"We could have been killed. What happened?"

"There was a noise," he said. "I don't know what it

was. Maybe fireworks or a car backfiring.'' But as Tuck thought back to the moment the sound split the air, he realized it wasn't a car at all. It had sounded more like a gun. And the flash could have come from the muzzle.

A few seconds later, Alex McAlester ran up, followed by Maureen Cooper and a group of townspeople. ''Are you all right?'' Alex asked. ''I tried to grab them, but I—''

''We're fine,'' Tuck replied, still holding tight to a trembling Grace. ''No harm done.''

''The parade,'' Grace insisted. ''We have to start the parade.''

''Alex, why don't you and Bryan take Maureen back in the other sleigh. Those horses have had a nice run. They should be calm enough now. I'll bring Grace and Susan in this one. We'll use it for Santa. By the time he's ready to go, we should be just fine.''

Alex hopped into the sleigh, then helped Maureen into the rear seat. Bryan jumped up beside Alex. He looked at Tuck and Tuck nodded at him in silent approval. Then Alex slapped the horses softly with the reins and slowly maneuvered them into a wide turn that took them back down Oak Road to Church Street, where they'd started.

''I was so scared,'' Grace said as she stared after them. ''And then you just knew exactly what to do. You—you saved our lives. And—and Bryan, he was so brave.''

''You're all right now.''

Grace nodded, then reached up and gave him a hug. He held her in his embrace for a long time, breathing in the scent of her hair. All of their arguments seemed to fade from his mind. Tuck closed his eyes and enjoyed the feel of her in his arms, wondering if this would be the last time. ''Gracie, is there any reason why someone might want to disrupt the parade?''

"No," Grace said, pulling back. "Why would someone want to do that?"

"That's what I'm asking you. Right about the time the horses bolted, I thought I saw a flash."

"Do you think the horses ran because someone took a picture?"

Tuck shook his head, unwilling to dispel her naive assumption. "No," he said, "that's probably not it." Maybe it would be best to keep this to himself. After all, he wasn't really sure what he saw. Maybe it was a camera. And the sound could have been a car backfiring or some kid playing with fireworks. It might have been a coincidence that they'd happened at the exact same moment.

Though he was reluctant to let her go, he knew they couldn't stay here for the rest of the night. He stepped away from her. "Come on, let's get you back. They can't start the parade without you." Tuck helped her into the sleigh, then climbed in after her.

When they reached the starting area, Tuck pulled to a stop on Church Street. Felix Dorn was there and he grabbed hold of the horses. A moment later, Susan ran up, pushing her way through the crowd. Tears glistened on her cheeks. "They're dead!" she cried, trying to crawl up into the cutter. "Our surprise is dead!"

Tuck felt a stab of concern. Had he been right? Had someone shot a gun?

Grace jumped out of the sleigh and gathered her daughter into her arms. "What's dead, honey?"

"Our surprise. Me and Tuck and Bryan made a little sleigh with the goats. And now they're dead."

Tuck stared across the street to find a crowd gathered around his goats. Then he stepped out of the sleigh and knelt down next to Susan. Huge tears tumbled down her cheeks and her nose was running. If she didn't look so pathetic, he might just laugh. "Honey, they're not dead, they're just sleeping."

She sniffled once and stared at him, wide-eyed. "They're not dead? They look dead."

"No. When those goats hear a loud noise, they just fall right to sleep. All the noise made them fall asleep. Why don't you and Bryan go over and pet them. They'll wake up as soon as you do, I promise."

Susan wiped her nose with her jacket sleeve. "O-okay." She hurried off to find Bryan, and together they began to pet their nine little sleeping reindeer.

"You brought your sleeping goats to the parade?" Grace asked.

"That was our surprise," Tuck said. He took her hand and they followed Susan. The scene looked like a goat pileup on the interstate, legs sticking out in every direction. The VFW band had gathered around the goats and someone had decided to play taps. But then, as suddenly as they'd fallen over, the goats woke, scrambling to their feet, their cardboard antlers hanging crookedly.

Grace began to giggle, and before long Tuck had joined her. He wasn't sure whether it was the sight of the goats or the shouts of surprise from the band or just the stress of the runaway sleigh finally setting in. But they both laughed until tears ran down their faces.

"I guess I'd better get this parade started," Grace said, wiping the tears away. "Before they faint again."

Tuck nodded and then took her hand and walked her to the front of the crowd of participants. "I'll catch up with you after the parade," he said. He brushed a quick kiss on her cheek, and for a moment, their eyes met and held. Then he moved back and watched as she calmly called each group up to the starting point. The floats were parked in order along the side of the street and she gave each driver instructions. At last, with Enos Harrington safely in the first sleigh, the Christmas parade began.

But Tuck didn't stick around to watch the parade pass by. Instead, he walked back down Church Street toward the clump of leafless bushes, determined to find out what had really spooked the horses.

MAUREEN GLANCED OVER her shoulder as she approached the spot on Church Street. Most of the crowd had walked over to Main to watch the start of the parade, but she had a different purpose in mind. She'd heard the sound that had caused the horses to bolt. She'd even seen a white flash pierce the darkness from this very spot. And she'd spent enough time at the shooting range to recognize the sound of a rifle shot.

She bent down and smoothed her gloved hand over the snow, searching for a clue. In the dim light, she saw a footprint and pushed farther into the bushes. There it was, gleaming against the muddy ground. She snatched up the spent cartridge and put it in her pocket, then continued to look for more clues.

Had she still had access to a crime-scene investigation unit, she'd have had them combing the area for forensic evidence. They'd make molds of the footprint and tell her what kind of shoes the shooter was wearing. They'd search for clues to his approach and his escape. They'd pick up every single bit of garbage, every cigarette butt and scrap of paper, hoping it might yield a clue.

What she would do was show the cartridge to Scott Hunter. Scott knew all about Maureen's past and was still investigating the shot fired at Emma Hart last month. The state trooper was aware of Owen Nevil's mission to get Maureen, but Scott didn't know where Nevil was or when he might strike next.

Maureen slowly straightened and looked around nervously. She felt so vulnerable, so completely alone. She'd been able to rationalize the private investigator who had been staying at the inn a couple of months back. And maybe even the incident involving Emma Hart. But this hadn't been an accident. Someone had deliberately spooked the horses, or even worse, had been aiming at her and missed.

"What did you find?"

Hand pressed to her chest, Maureen spun around, her surprised to find Tuck McCabe standing a few feet away. "What?"

"I was wondering what you found. I saw you pick something up from the ground."

"No. I was just picking up my...earring," she said, pointing to the tiny stud in her right ear.

Tuck stared at her for a long moment, then smiled. "Right. And while you were looking for your earring, did you find a spent shell casing?"

"A what?"

"This is where it went off," he said. "I'm glad to know I wasn't the only one who suspected it might be a gun."

"A gun?" Maureen tried to keep her voice calm. "You think someone fired a gun?"

"I do," he said. "You saw the flash the same time I did. An instant before the horses spooked. That's why you're poking around over here."

"It sounded like a car backfiring to me."

"I live on a ranch. I know a little about firearms, especially hunting rifles. Someone shot a rifle. Now, either they were out to spook the horses or the spectators. Or they were aiming at someone. Which do you think it was?"

Indecision warred in Maureen's mind. Tuck McCabe's

suspicions matched her own. But was she prepared to admit that to him?

For such a long time, she'd kept her secret, determined to protect herself and her children at all costs. And now a man she barely knew was demanding answers she couldn't give. "People don't shoot at other people here in Cooper's Corner."

"I don't think he was aiming to hit anyone. If he was, he was an extremely poor shot. I'd guess maybe he had some other motive." Tuck smiled and pointed to her coat pocket. "I'd also be willing to bet you've got a spent shell in there. You want to take that bet?"

"No," Maureen insisted. "I don't have anything in my pocket."

Tuck paused. "I suppose I could take my suspicions to the police."

"No. Don't do that." Reluctantly Maureen reached into her pocket and pulled the shell casing out.

He took it from her fingers and examined it. "No? Can you give me a good reason why not? Some idiot shot into a crowd with a hunting rifle."

Maureen stared at him for a long moment. "I saw it all. I'll talk to our state trooper, give him the evidence and he can investigate. This might be linked to another shooting last month. You don't have to get involved."

"This doesn't have anything to do with you, does it?" Tuck asked, arching his brows suspiciously.

She kept her expression neutral. "Why would anyone want to shoot me?"

He studied her closely. "I don't know. But maybe you can tell me."

"I'll look into this," she said firmly, snatching the casing from his fingers and shoving it back in her pocket. "Besides, you don't want to get tangled up in it."

"Why not?"

"Because you're leaving town."

"You promise you'll go to the authorities about it?" Tuck asked.

"Promise."

Tuck stared at her for a long moment. Either he accepted her promise as the truth, or else he suspected she was keeping a secret that couldn't be told. Whichever it was, he nodded. "I better go. I've got to give Santa a ride down Main Street." He turned and walked away and Maureen breathed a long sigh of relief.

Her secret was still safe, at least from handsome cowboys who lived in Montana. But what about Owen Nevil? Was he here now, watching her from some shadowy spot, staring at her through the scope of a high-powered rifle? She slowly turned and perused the street, her hand clutched around the shell casing in her pocket. Her mind flashed back to that day in court when Carl Nevil, Owen's brother, made his threat of revenge. He'd turned to her and her partner, Dan D'Angelo, sending them both an evil sneer. And then he coldly informed them that they hadn't locked up all the Nevils.

A few weeks later, the informant who sent Carl to trial was killed by a hit-and-run driver. Coincidentally, the accident happened in the week following Owen Nevil's parole from prison. Though her partner had brushed the threat off, it stuck with Maureen. She'd become so paranoid that when she and Clint inherited Twin Oaks from their great uncle Warren, she'd grabbed the chance to leave New York.

Since then, everything had been fine. Dan had sent her postcards from Florida. Frank had kept her updated on Owen Nevil's whereabouts. Until she learned that Nevil had skipped parole, she'd felt safe.

Still, maybe it was just her paranoia. Maybe all these little events had nothing to do with Owen Nevil and were merely imagined threats.

"No," Maureen murmured, staring at the people milling on the street. "He's here. I can feel it."

She grabbed her jacket and pulled it tightly around her, then set off down the street. Randi and Robin were attending the parade with Clint. Right now, all she wanted was to find her girls, take them home and lock them safely inside the house.

THE PARADE HAD ENDED nearly two hours ago. Tuck stood on the front porch of Grace's house, his finger hovering over the doorbell. His truck sat in the circular drive, the horse trailer attached to the hitch, nine goats and four horses inside.

The decision to leave hadn't come easily. After all that had happened at the parade, he'd hoped that Grace would change her mind about his proposal, that she'd realize she couldn't live without him. But she hadn't said anything to him to indicate that her feelings had changed at all. He'd been forced to admit that staying another day would make it even harder to walk away.

How could he leave them? He'd come to think of Grace and her children as his family. But the truth was, Tuck didn't have a family. He was all alone in the world and that's the way he'd stay. Grace had made her feelings clear in the coach house a few mornings ago. Their night together at Twin Oaks was nothing more than great sex. And his proposal, though flattering, was impossible for her to accept.

Hell, he should have known it would all turn out this way. Tucker McCabe wasn't destined to live happily ever after. Life wasn't supposed to be easy for him. And Grace was just too easy to be real. Too easy to love. Too easy to need. Too easy to want.

He gathered his resolve and pressed the doorbell. The door swung open and Grace appeared. She caught sight of his truck and trailer parked in the drive and her smile gradually faded. "You're leaving."

Tuck stood glued to the spot on the porch. "I figured I'd get on the road," he said, an ache growing in his heart with every word that passed his lips. He took a steadying breath. "There's no reason to stay."

"It's Christmas Eve," Grace said. "You can't spend Christmas Eve on the road. I thought you might like to stay and celebrate with us."

He shook his head. "If I stay tonight, Gracie, I may never want to leave. You made your decision and now I've had to make mine. I have a life in Montana and it's about time I got back to it."

Reluctantly, Grace moved aside. "Bryan and Susan are in the library. You'd better say your goodbyes."

With a curt nod, Tuck stepped inside. As he walked through the house, he realized that he'd never see this place again, this house that had become so comfortable for him. He and Grace would be half a country apart, living separate lives. Someday, she might meet a man and marry him and he'd never know. Bryan and Susan would grow up and Tuck wouldn't be there to see it. The ache in his heart grew even more intense.

He found them both in the library, rolls of wrapping paper scattered over the floor. Susan was handing Bryan little pieces of tape when she noticed him standing in the door.

"Tuck!" she cried, scrambling to her feet. She ran to him, launching herself into his arms, and Tuck scooped her up. The little girl reached out and covered his eyes. "Don't look. We're wrapping your present."

"A present?" Tuck asked. "For me?"

"It's Christmas, silly," Susan said with a giggle. "Me and Bryan made you a present. Well, it was mostly Bryan, but I helped."

She took her hands from his eyes and Bryan held out a hastily wrapped package. Tuck smiled. "I'll take this with me and open it tomorrow morning."

Susan's smile disappeared from her face. "You're leaving?"

Tuck gave her a hug and put her down on the floor. "Yep. I've got to take my horses and goats back to Montana."

Bryan looked up at him with the same stricken expression that Susan had on her face. "Did you ask her?"

Reaching out, Tuck placed his hand on Bryan's shoulder. "I did. And she said no. But it's all right. She had some good reasons. And I understand."

"Open the present now," Bryan said.

"You sure?"

Bryan nodded, and with Susan he watched as Tuck carefully removed the brightly colored paper. Inside, Tuck found a photograph of the two children standing on the front porch of their house, holding hands and waving.

"Keegan took it with his dad's digital camera," Bryan explained. "And I printed it out on my computer."

"It's wonderful," Tuck said.

"Bryan made the frame and painted it. And I put the Christmas stickers on it," Susan explained, pointing to a sticker of a Christmas tree.

"I can tell. You did an excellent job. And this will be the perfect thing to remember you both when I'm back in Montana."

Bryan held out his hand. "I'm glad you came to stay with us," he said. "And I'm glad I got to learn more about horses."

For Tuck, that was enough. He knew Bryan wasn't much for expressing himself, but in those words, Tuck knew they'd shared a special bond. "You watch yourself," he said, pulling Bryan into his embrace. "Think before you act and you'll be all right."

Then Tuck bent down and kissed Susan on the cheek. "Bye, Susie Q." He straightened, smoothing his hands along his thighs. "Well, I guess I'd better get going. I've got a lot of miles to cover."

He left them both in the library, standing next to each other, Bryan's arm draped around his sister's shoulders. When she made a move to follow Tuck, Bryan held her back, whispering something into his sister's ear.

Tuck wasn't sure he'd ever done anything harder than walk out on those two children. They'd brought so much to his life in the last two weeks, and he knew he'd had a positive effect on them. He wanted to believe they'd never forget him, but he was realistic enough to know they would.

Grace was still standing at the front door. He stepped up to her, and without saying a word took her face in his hands and kissed her. "I can't believe it's come down to this," Tuck said. "I love you. And I know you love me, Gracie. And we're just letting it go."

"I do love you," Grace said, reaching up to touch his cheek. "But I'm not ready to marry you."

Cursing softly, Tuck turned away. "There's nothing I can say to change your mind?"

He stared down into her eyes, aching to pull her into his arms and kiss her again. But he was afraid that this time, she wouldn't respond and he'd spend the next four days regretting his actions. "Take care," he finally said, leaning over to kiss her cheek.

Turning away from her then, he prepared to walk out the front door "Don't do this to us," he said, his back to Grace. "Don't let me walk away."

"Goodbye, Tuck. Drive safely."

When he reached the truck, he crawled inside and slammed the door. He was almost afraid to look, but when he did, he saw Grace standing on the porch. She waved weakly and forced a smile. Then her smile faded and she turned and walked back inside the house.

As he flipped on the ignition and the pickup rumbled to life, Tuck felt a hollow emptiness settle in around his heart. This was not the way it was supposed to be. He and Grace belonged together. He loved her and she claimed that she loved him. Wasn't love supposed to conquer all?

CHAPTER TWELVE

AN ALBUM OF CHILDREN'S Christmas music filled the house with cheerful noise, but the bright and bouncy tunes did nothing to lift Grace's mood. She and Bryan and Susan had gathered in front of the fireplace to carry on the traditions they'd started their very first Christmas without Dan.

She remembered that time so well. Susan was still an infant and Grace had been an emotional and physical wreck, feeling alone and abandoned. But she'd done her best to make Bryan's Christmas normal, hiding her own anguish behind a tight smile and a rigorous schedule of activities that left no time for tears.

Tonight she felt as if she'd stepped right back to that time, filling their Christmas Eve with inane chatter meant to distract the children from her real feelings. Tuck was gone and she'd never see him again. She'd let him walk out of her life because she'd been too afraid, afraid that by loving him she might repeat the mistakes of the past.

Since Tuck had happened into her life she'd come to one realization. Her failed marriage wasn't her fault. Her only mistake had been to love Dan Penrose in the first place, to trust him with her heart and with her life. But Grace wouldn't make the same mistake twice. If she refused to love, she'd never get hurt.

"Who wants hot cocoa?"

Bryan and Susan looked up from the game they were playing on the coffee table. "None for me," Bryan said softly, his gaze fixed on the string of plastic monkeys in front of him.

"Me, neither," Susan added.

"Come on," Grace said. "We always have hot chocolate with marshmallows before bed. If we don't, then maybe Santa might not come."

Bryan groaned and rolled his eyes. "I'm sure Santa doesn't care what we drink before bed." He dropped the monkeys on the table and leaned back against the sofa.

"Do you think if I write a note tonight for Santa and leave it next to the cookies, it would be too late?" Susan asked.

Grace shrugged. "What do you want to write in your note, honey? I thought you'd already decided what you wanted for Christmas."

"This isn't a regular present. I want to ask him if he can make Tuck come back." Her lower lip trembled and tears swam in her eyes.

The despair in her daughter's face was enough to bring emotion welling up inside Grace. This was exactly what she'd been afraid of. Tuck had been with them only two weeks and Susan had still been devastated by his departure. Heaven only knew how Bryan was feeling. "Honey, Tuck has a home of his own. And people who care about him and—"

"No, he doesn't," Bryan interrupted. "He told me he doesn't have anyone who cares about him."

"That's not true," Grace said.

"It is. One time he was telling me that I should be happy to have a mom who cares about me. And that he didn't have anyone in the world who cared about him."

"I care about him," Susan said.

"So do I," Bryan admitted.

Susan flopped down on the floor and sighed dejectedly.

"I wish he were here. I thought he might be my dad. Why couldn't he be my dad? I never had a dad."

"Not one that you remember," Bryan said, slipping his arm around Susan's shoulders. "I guess he would have made a pretty good dad."

"Come on, you guys, we really don't need a dad, do we?" Grace said, desperate to change the subject. "I mean, we get along pretty well, just the three of us."

"But what about when I get married and have a wife and family," Bryan said. "And then Susan leaves?"

"I'm never going to leave," Susan said steadfastly. "I'm going to live with Mommy for always."

Grace couldn't help but smile. "Honey, someday you'll grow up and leave home."

"You should have a husband, Mom," Bryan insisted. "Otherwise, you'll be all alone. Why did you tell him no?"

Grace blinked in surprise. Bryan couldn't know about Tuck's proposal, could he? Did Susan know, as well? "Tuck lives in Montana. We'd have to move there. You wouldn't want to leave all your friends, would you?" Grace figured that would put a quick end to the conversation, but she was wrong.

"Momtana would be good," Susan said. "Tuck would be there. And the goats. And the horses."

"It's *Montana,* goofy," Bryan corrected.

"And how do *you* feel about Montana?" Grace asked, directing her question to Bryan.

Bryan thought about it for a long moment. "I guess it would be all right, as long as we got to come back in the summer to visit. And Tuck has lots more horses on the ranch. I'd like to learn how to ride. Maybe I could have a horse of my own."

Grace couldn't believe what she was hearing. She looked back and forth between her two children, stunned that the decision she'd agonized over had come so easily to them. She'd known Susan would accept Tuck, but Bryan was another story. "What changed your mind?" she asked.

"I don't know. I guess I need a dad, so I don't mess up. And when I do mess up, Tuck knows what to do. He'd make a pretty good dad."

Grace raked her hands through her hair. This couldn't be happening. Just a few hours ago, she was so certain she was doing the right thing. And now her life had turned upside down again. One of the barriers that stood between them had disappeared. Could she make the others fall just as easily? "I—I'm going to have to think about this," she said. "Tuck's on his way back to Montana and I—"

"We still have our whole Christmas vacation left," Bryan reminded her, scrambling to his feet. He raced out of the room and returned a few moments later with a road atlas. "If we left now, we could spend the rest of our vacation with Tuck at the ranch."

"No!" Susan cried. "We can't leave now. What about Santa?"

Bryan glanced over at Grace, impatient with having to maintain the illusion.

This was happening too quickly. Grace needed time to think. But when she tried to think, strange, crazy ideas invaded her brain. They could leave tonight. And if they drove hard, she'd be with Tuck in three or four days. Suddenly, three or four days seemed like an eternity. She could drive to Boston and buy three tickets on the next flight to—

"Oh, no," Grace said. "We can't go to Montana. I don't even know where Tuck lives."

"His ranch is northwest of Billings," Bryan said as he flipped through the atlas. He found Billings and put his finger on it. "It's a big ranch. I bet a lot of people in town would know how to find Snake Creek."

"We can't leave," Susan insisted.

"No, we won't leave," Grace assured her. She drew a deep breath, unable to believe what she was about to say. "We'll get a good night's sleep and we can leave right after we open presents tomorrow."

But Grace knew she wouldn't get much sleep that night. She was about to risk her heart, to risk her children's happiness, on a whim. She was about to marry a man she'd met two weeks ago. She was about to ignore Maureen's warning, give up her job and her life, and move to a ranch in Montana. Grace Penrose just didn't do things like that!

"That was the old Grace Penrose," she announced, scrambling to her feet. Now that she'd made her decision, Grace knew that she had no other choice. She loved Tucker McCabe, and no matter how hard she tried, that feeling was never going to go away.

"MAKE SURE YOU PACK your toothbrushes," Grace called from the bottom of the stairs. "I forgot to put them in the suitcase, so put them in your backpacks. And bring along some games and books for the car. Montana is a long way away and I don't want you complaining about how boring the drive is."

She waited for an answer, but all she heard were footsteps running back and forth above her head. They'd been up with the dawn, Susan anxious to get to Santa's gifts and Bryan impatient to hit the road. Grace wasn't quite sure how she felt. All night long, she'd drifted between sleep and strange, restless dreams. This was the biggest decision of her life and she hadn't really taken the time to think about it.

Maybe this was what love was supposed to feel like. She'd been so young when she and Dan had started going together. And after all those years, marriage just seemed like the logical step. She couldn't even remember making a conscious decision that he was the one she wanted to spend the rest of her life with.

But she had made that decision now. Tuck was the man she wanted to marry. They'd grow old together. Maybe they'd have another child—or two. Her future was tied to his. But would he be happy to see her? Or would he still be smarting from her rejection of his proposal?

"I guess I won't know until I see him again," she murmured. She shook her head as if to erase all her doubts, then grabbed the suitcases at her feet. "I'm going to start loading the car. I want you both down here in five minutes or I'm leaving you here!"

Susan screamed "no" at the top of her lungs and Bryan shouted that he was almost ready. Satisfied that she'd lit a fire under their feet, Grace hefted up the bags and headed to the front door. When she got outside on the porch, she turned to close the door before heading down the steps. The early-morning sun was low in the sky, causing a glare on the snow. She squinted, then held up her hand until her eyes adjusted.

A moment later, her breath caught in her throat as a shape emerged at the end of the sidewalk. With a soft gasp, Grace dropped the suitcases at the bottom of the steps, her feet frozen in place. Her heart slammed in her chest and she couldn't seem to draw a full breath. "Tuck," she whispered.

His truck and trailer were parked in the driveway and he stood beside the pickup, leaning against the bumper, watching her from beneath the brim of his cowboy hat. She took a step toward him and he straightened and did the same. Slowly, they approached each other, neither saying a word. And when they were standing just a foot apart, Grace still didn't know what to say.

"I'm back," Tuck said, his gaze skimming over her face as if he'd forgotten what she looked like.

Grace wanted to throw herself into his arms and kiss him until she couldn't think straight. But she wasn't sure why Tuck had returned. "You're back. You look tired."

He shook his head. "I drove until midnight, and when I stopped, I realized I was heading in the wrong direction. This is where I wanted to be. So I called the ranch and talked to Ike."

"And what did Ike say?"

"He told me it was time I stopped hiding at Snake Creek and found myself a real life. And he told me if I came back to Snake Creek without you, I was a dad-blamed fool and he'd shoot me on sight. And I told him he was probably right."

"Probably?"

"Well, he was right. So I turned my truck around and headed back here."

Grace smiled. "Funny. I was just getting ready to leave."

"Are you going on a vacation?" Tuck asked, pointing to the bags sitting on the front walk.

"The kids and I were on our way to Montana. We all decided that we wanted to live with you, no matter where that might be. Well, the kids decided that."

"And what about you, Gracie?"

"I knew that all along," she said. "But I wasn't able to see it as clearly as Bryan and Susan."

"Bryan actually wants to leave his friends for Montana?"

"Only if we come back and visit during the summers. I thought I'd keep the house and we could—"

"No," Tuck said.

"No? You want me to sell it?"

He stared up at the facade of the house. "No, I want you to keep the house. We're going to need a place to live during the winter. I figured we could spend summers at the ranch. That's when Ike and Ray need me most."

"You're willing to move here?"

Tuck nodded. "I talked with Alex McAlester a while back and he mentioned he was thinking of taking on a partner. And one of my vet school professors has been trying to get me to teach a course for him at Tufts. I might be able to talk him into a job while I'm getting certified in Massachusetts. It'll be a bit of a drive, but I think it would be worth it."

"And in the summer, we could go to the ranch," Grace said. "I never get much done for the festival when the children are home for the summer, anyway."

"Then I guess it's all settled," Tuck said. "We've reached a compromise that we're both able to live with."

"I guess we have."

"Then there's only one thing to do."

"What's that?"

Tuck smiled and slowly lowered himself to one knee. He reached out and took Grace's hand. "Grace Penrose, I'm going to ask you one more time. Will you marry me?"

A tiny smile curved her lips. "But we've only known each other a few weeks. And I have been married before. And then there's that pesky age difference. I'm not sure I could marry a younger man."

"Forget about all that," Tuck said. "It doesn't matter. I love you. I think I've known since that very first day I met you, when you were slipping and sliding around in the mud at Silas Rawlings's farm. I never thought I'd find a woman I could love, Gracie. And now that I have, I want to make it official. Damn it, Grace, will you marry me?"

"Tuck's back!"

Susan's shriek split the air and Grace turned away from Tuck to watch her daughter race down the front steps. A moment later, Bryan appeared in the front door, carrying his backpack and his jacket. He stopped for a moment, taking in the scene—Grace grasping Tuck's hand, Tuck bent down on one knee. Then he turned and walked back inside the house.

Grace's heart fell. She'd thought Bryan had made a decision about Tuck. But maybe, now that he'd been faced with the reality of the situation, he'd changed his mind. She gnawed at her bottom lip, then turned back to Tuck.

"What's wrong, Tuck?" Susan asked. "Did you lose something in the snow?" Susan grabbed his other arm and tried to pull him to his feet. "We were just coming to see you. I guess it's lucky we didn't leave. Come on, get up. You can come inside and see what Santa brought me."

Tuck reached out and grabbed Susan around the waist, pulling her down to sit on his bent knee. "I have some business to take care of first, sweetie."

"You'll need this."

Bryan appeared at Tuck's side and held out a small velvet-covered box. The burgundy velvet was worn thin and the box was a bit tattered, but Grace recognized it immediately. She looked at Bryan. "Are you sure?"

Her son nodded. "You love him, Mom. And you deserve to be happy."

"And what about you?" Grace asked.

Bryan shrugged. "I'd like Tuck to be my dad. I'm getting older and I think I'm going to need a dad."

"Tuck is going to be our dad?" Susan asked.

Bryan made a face at her. "Duh. What do you think he's doing down on his knee?"

"I thought he lost something."

"No, he's asking our mom to marry him."

Susan looked back and forth between Grace and Bryan. "Oh, Mommy, say yes. Yes, yes, yes!"

Grace laughed. "Well, if you two would let Tuck get a word in edgewise, maybe I could." She held the velvet box out to Tuck. "This is my great-grandmother's ring. She wore it and my grandmother wore it and my mother wore it. My mother gave this to me before she died five years ago. She wanted me to give it to Susan when she got married."

"You can have it for now, Mommy," Susan offered. "I'll borrow it to you."

"So, I guess we're all set," Tuck said. "I've got the ring, I've got the girl. I think I've got permission."

"Go ahead," Bryan said. "Ask her."

"Ask her, ask her," Susan cried, jumping up and down.

"Don't rush me," Tuck teased. He cleared his throat. "Grace Penrose, I love you. And I want to make a family with you and your children. Will you marry me?"

"Yes, Tuck McCabe, I will marry you."

Tuck slipped the ring onto Grace's finger, then kissed her hand. Bryan let out a whoop and Susan a scream as they both tackled Tuck. He teetered on one knee, then tumbled into the snow, dragging Grace along with him until they were all tangled in a heap on the ground.

Tuck reached up and brushed the hair out of Grace's eyes. "Funny how things turn out. I came here to pick up horses and goats, but I also found a family."

"I think we found you," Grace said. "I can't believe I almost let you get away."

"I knew Santa would bring me what I asked for. I knew he'd read my note," Susan said, snuggling up in the crook of Tuck's arm.

Bryan rolled over onto his stomach. "What did you ask for?"

"What I got!" Susan told him. "A daddy. A daddy for Christmas."

THE CHURCH WAS QUIET when Grace and Tuck and the children walked in. The Christmas morning service had ended a few hours before. The scent of beeswax candles and fresh pine hung in the air. Tom Christen walked back and forth through the pews, collecting hymnals and stacking them at each end.

Grace reached out and grabbed Tuck's hand, then gave him a smile. "Are you ready?"

He nodded and they started up the aisle. Bryan and Susan waited at the rear of the church as she and Tuck approached the minister. Tom heard their footsteps and turned. "Grace! Merry Christmas. I'm afraid you're a little late. Service was at eleven, not one."

She sent Tom an apologetic smile. "We're not here for the service. Tom, this is Tucker McCabe."

Tom held out his hand and Tuck shook it. "I've heard of you. You're the cowboy from Wyoming, right?"

"Montana," Tuck said.

"Tuck and I have a special request." Grace slipped her arm through Tuck's and held on tight. "We're leaving for Montana today and we'd like you to marry us."

The minister blinked, his surprise evident in his raised brows and uneasy smile. "Married. I didn't even know you were engaged."

"We weren't," Tuck explained. "But we need to get married before we leave—for the children's sake. And for ours."

"We know it won't be legal since we don't have a license,'' Grace said. "But we'll take care of that later, maybe in Montana. Will you do this for us?"

"I'm supposed to counsel couples before they get married. To make sure they're really ready."

"Believe me, Gracie and I—"

Tom held up his hand to stop Tuck. "I think you two are mature enough to make a decision like this. And it's quite clear to me that you're very much in love, so we can do this right now. Where are your witnesses?"

"If it's all right with you, we'd like Bryan and Susan to be our witnesses."

"Since this is a rather unconventional service, I don't think that would be a problem," Tom said.

Grace turned and motioned to the children and they came running up the aisle. Tom walked over to the pulpit and pulled out a small black book. He flipped through it, then cleared his throat. He looked at Bryan and then Susan. "Are you two ready?"

They nodded excitedly. Tom turned to Tuck and Grace. "And you two are ready?"

"We are," Tuck said with a smile, gazing at Grace.

"Dearly beloved, we are gathered here today to unite Tucker McCabe and Grace Penrose in the bonds of holy matrimony…"

Grace heard every word of the ceremony and answered all the questions, but her thoughts were on what would come after the ceremony, past the kiss and the honeymoon night. She and Tuck and Bryan and Susan would be a family. And maybe someday, she and Tuck would have a baby together and add to their happy family.

Tuck held tight to her hand and slipped her grandmother's ring on her finger. "I, Tucker McCabe, take you Grace Penrose…and Bryan Penrose and Susan Penrose…to be my family."

Grace stared into his eyes as he finished the vows. Then she looked at her two children and saw the joy in their faces. After so many Christmases of making other people happy, she finally had one of her own to cherish. A perfect Christmas.

A Christmas where she received the most wonderful gift of all—her very own Christmas cowboy.

*Welcome to Twin Oaks—the new B and B in
Cooper's Corner.
Some come for pleasure, others for passion—
And one to get things straight…*

COOPER'S CORNER, *a new Harlequin
continuity series,
continues in December 2002 with
DANCING IN THE DARK
by Sandra Marton*

When Wendy Monroe left Cooper's Corner she had
been an Olympic hopeful in skiing…and madly in
love with Seth Castleman. But an accident on the
slopes had shattered her dreams—and her heart. She'd
fled from Seth rather than tell him the painful secret
behind her injuries. Now Wendy has returned home
with just one desire. She wants to be whole again.

Here's a preview!

CHAPTER ONE

WENDY CLUTCHED the banister and looked down the stairs at Seth.

This was the moment she'd feared, the one she'd known was inevitable ever since her father said it was probably going to take longer than he'd expected to get time alone with Dr. Pommier. The longer she stayed in town, the greater the risk Seth would learn she was here. It was one of the reasons she'd come up with excuses yesterday, when her father asked her to go with him while he ran some errands.

"Are you afraid people will recognize you?" he'd said, and then he'd answered the question himself. "I suppose you're concerned they'll ask you questions. We won't tell them a thing until after you've seen Dr. Pommier and he's agreed to do that surgery. Okay?"

What could she have said after that? That she didn't want people to see her limp, or risk bumping into Seth? Either answer made her sound like a coward, so she'd smiled and said, sure, she'd go with him, now that she'd had a little time to get used to being back in Cooper's Corner.

But she was afraid of what she would see in the eyes of the man who'd loved the girl she used to be.

Looking down at him, Wendy knew with relief that she'd had nothing to worry about. What she saw in Seth's face was anger.

"Seth," she said carefully. "You're looking well."

"Hello, Wendy."

"How have you been?" There. There. Wasn't that good? Her voice was steady, her smile surely pleasant.

"Fine." His gaze swept down her body, lingered on her leg, then turned to her face. "And you?"

"Oh, I'm—well, thank you."

"Last I heard you'd been putting in long hours at rehab."

"Yes, that's right. I still do."

"And it's paid off, I see. It's good to see you on your feet again."

"Thank you. Mom?" she said pleasantly. "If we're going to get to that mall—"

"Are you happy, living in France?"

"Very happy, thank you for asking."

"I was surprised to hear you were back."

"Why?" She turned to him again and smiled politely. "This is my home. Why wouldn't I come back?"

"Is this a visit? Or have you come home to stay?"

"Seth, really, it's very nice to see you, but—"

"You didn't answer my question. Why haven't you come home before?"

"Because I didn't want to," she said holding the smile. "Anything else?"

"Wendy," Gina said sharply, "there's no need to—"

"That's okay, Gina. Wendy's right. Where she lives, what she does is none of my business." He stepped back and put a hand on the doorknob. "I probably should have called first."

What had happened to all that calm certainty she'd felt when she first started down the steps and saw him? He was nothing to her now. Then why was the sight of him making her feel as if she was seventeen again and he'd just come to pick her up for their very first date?

"Yes," she said, "you should have."

"Yeah." He cleared his throat. "Well, it's good seeing you again."

"Thank you."

"This is where you're supposed to say it's good seeing me again, too."

"Goodbye, Seth."

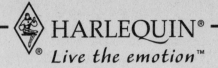

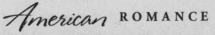
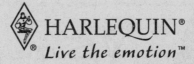

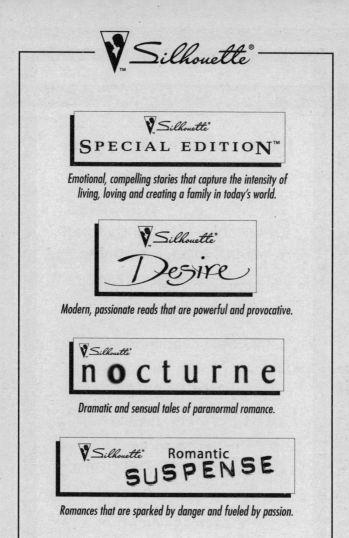

Silhouette®

SPECIAL EDITION™

Emotional, compelling stories that capture the intensity of living, loving and creating a family in today's world.

Silhouette® Desire

Modern, passionate reads that are powerful and provocative.

Silhouette® nocturne

Dramatic and sensual tales of paranormal romance.

Silhouette® Romantic SUSPENSE

Romances that are sparked by danger and fueled by passion.

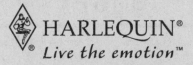

HARLEQUIN®
INTRIGUE®

BREATHTAKING ROMANTIC SUSPENSE

Shared dangers and passions lead to electrifying
romance and heart-stopping suspense!

Every month, you'll meet six new heroes
who are guaranteed to make your spine tingle
and your pulse pound. With them you'll enter
into the exciting world of Harlequin Intrigue—
where your life is on the line
and so is your heart!

THAT'S INTRIGUE—
ROMANTIC SUSPENSE
AT ITS BEST!

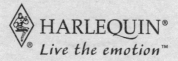

HARLEQUIN®
Live the emotion™

Harlequin® Historical
Historical Romantic Adventure!

*Imagine a time of chivalrous
knights and unconventional ladies,
roguish rakes and impetuous
heiresses, rugged cowboys
and spirited frontierswomen——
these rich and vivid tales will
capture your imagination!*

*Harlequin Historical . . .
they're too good to miss!*

HHDIR06